Hjalmar Hjorth Boyesen

Social Strugglers

A Novel

Hjalmar Hjorth Boyesen

Social Strugglers
A Novel

ISBN/EAN: 9783743367449

Manufactured in Europe, USA, Canada, Australia, Japa

Cover: Foto ©Andreas Hilbeck / pixelio.de

Manufactured and distributed by brebook publishing software (www.brebook.com)

Hjalmar Hjorth Boyesen

Social Strugglers

SOCIAL STRUGGLERS

A NOVEL

BY

HJALMAR HJORTH BOYESEN

NEW YORK
CHARLES SCRIBNER'S SONS
1893

Press of J. J. Little & Co.
Astor Place, New York

TO

WILLIAM DEAN HOWELLS

THIS BOOK IS

AFFECTIONATELY DEDICATED BY

HIS FRIEND

THE AUTHOR

SOCIAL STRUGGLERS

I

THE Bulkleys had originated somewhere in Massachusetts, but they had belonged to those strata of society whose antecedents remain unchronicled. Peleg L. Bulkley prided himself vaguely on having come from the Bay State (I never knew a State which was not a source of pride to those who came from it) ; but he left it to his daughters, who had never been in Massachusetts, to supply the local color and details of ancestral history comporting with their present distinction. To his Western experience, which was of too recent date to furnish material for the myth-making genius, he was not allowed to allude ; though he was at a loss to understand why. It was impossible for him to comprehend the frame of mind to which a merchant tailor's business (and a very big one at that) could appear something to be ashamed of, particularly as he well remembered the pride Mrs. Bulkley once took in the huge plate-glass windows and the big pictorial advertisements in the Sunday papers, showing the rapid rise in the world of the man who bought his clothes of Bulkley, and the accumulation of disasters which overtook him who did not. And what a

source of delight his rhymed and gorgeously illustrated catalogues had been to her and the children!
How they had admired the jingling doggerel about
coats and trousers; and what a work of art that
colored frontispiece had seemed to them, exhibiting
the President and his cabinet beaming with contentment because they had been so fortunate as to
secure suits of Bulkley's manufacture, while the
poor Prince of Wales and a mob of kings looked
disconsolate because they had to put up with the
tailoring of Poole and his consorts.

Peleg was brimming over with anecdotes from
this period of his life, and he had to exercise a severe
self-denial to refrain from lapsing into compromising
reminiscence. He was too honestly American to
sympathize with any effort to conceal his past, when
that past was fully as honorable as that of the
majority of his fellow-citizens. There were, indeed,
moments when his newly acquired gentility affected
him like a strait-jacket which he was aching to
burst; and if it had not been for his three daughters (two of whom shared their mother's social
ambition) he would have had himself interviewed
by *The World* on all the "undesirable" phases of
his career.

There was, of course, his unsuccessful start in the
flour and feed business, in which he failed and compromised with his creditors on thirty cents on the
dollar. Then five years as a "drummer" for a big
Western clothing house, during which he earned in
commissions from five thousand dollars to six thousand dollars a year, besides a gold mine of valuable

experience. Thereupon six years were spent as a partner in the firm, and finally as sole proprietor. In the meanwhile real-estate investments and a lucky mining speculation had made him a millionnaire several times over; and there seemed no longer any good reason why he should continue in the clothing business.

Mrs. Bulkley about this time began to develop alarming propensities. She cut her old friends whom she liked, and submitted to no end of humiliation in her efforts to gain new ones whom she disliked. She had to have a carriage with two liveried automatons on the box; and the Irish housemaid was exchanged for an imposing-looking, side-whiskered English butler, who made them all quake with fear of committing improprieties in his presence. Peleg had always an uneasy feeling while that dignified foreigner was waiting upon them, and could not suppress the conviction that he was laughing at him in his sleeve. He took a sly satisfaction, however, in the consciousness that his wife was fully as uncomfortable as himself, if not more so, because she lacked the sense of humor which enabled him to chuckle at his discomfort.

There was at that time, in the great Western town where the Bulkleys lived, a social clique, which counted many charming and cultivated people and made some pretence to exclusiveness. The aristocracy of pork, though it existed, was not yet recognized; it went to bed regularly at nine o'clock, and slept the dreamless sleep of weariness, untroubled by social ambitions. You might walk up the principal avenue in those days at ten o'clock in the evening, past rows of stately residences, and only discover here and there a stray light in a bed-room window. It never occurred to all the incipient millionnaires, who slumbered in the security of electric burglar alarms, to give the social tone to the city and flaunt their blatant vulgarity in the face of the world as representative of Western civilization. Mrs. Bulkley was well aware that social preferment was not to be attained by cultivating this class of people, and she therefore turned her attention toward a coterie consisting of prosperous professional men, with a sprinkling of merchants and bankers whose thoughts were capable of soaring beyond stocks and real estate. She made cautious overtures to a lady who resided on Pine Street, and whose Wednesday evening musicals were as exclusive as they were (to real connoisseurs) delightful. But she met with a rebuff. Her next move, in which she employed much diplomatic tact, was directed against another leader of the same coterie, who cultivated a lighter tone, gave three or four dances during the winter, and delighted in wit and sparkling frivolity. But here, too, Mrs. Bulkley's overtures were ignored. That wretched tailor shop on State Street rose like a sinister spectre in her path, wherever she turned. The bitter truth was gradually forced upon her, that this sartorial business was an absolute bar to their social advancement. An embezzlement, defalcation, and flight to Canada would have been more readily pardoned than a connection, however remote, with a tailor shop, even though it were a merchant tailor's.

Two years of heroic but unavailing struggles convinced Mrs. Bulkley that the West, properly speaking, had no society; that the town was hopelessly committed to trade, and that pork and refinement could not flourish together. She therefore persuaded Peleg to sell out his business and remove to New York, where his title to consideration as a millionnaire would be more readily recognized. Peleg was, indeed, far from being confident on that point; but he submitted gracefully to his wife's decision, knowing that his other alternative was to submit ungracefully. Women of Mrs. Bulkley's stamp have this advantage over their husbands, that they can make the latter's life a martyrdom until they have their own way; for men, as a rule, disdain the kind of warfare which seems most natural to women, consisting in perpetual, unwearied skirmishing, without decisive battles. At any rate, Peleg, having abundant experience in this chapter, was able to gauge the strength of Mrs. Bulkley's resolution, and having concluded that it was final, he preferred to surrender without preliminary hostilities.

Mrs. Bulkley, at the time of her shaking the Western dust off her feet, was forty-two or forty-three years old, though she would easily have passed for thirty-five. In spite of her humble origin, she looked, superficially at least, a lady. She was one of those remarkable American women who fancy themselves, and frequently are, equal to any position; who assume with marvellous promptness the external varnish of any society in which they are privileged to move; who, if by some miracle they found themselves upon a throne, would not shrink for a moment from the responsibilities of the situation.

I believe I characterize Mrs. Bulkley most completely when I say that she was not silly. She had ambitions which to the profoundly philosophic mind may appear foolish, but which all womankind will agree with her in pronouncing natural, if not wise. She had the strength of character which comes from narrowness of vision and an utter absence of imagination. She saw certain things within her circumscribed horizon with great vividness, and she disbelieved in everything which lay beyond the range of her vision. If she was, perhaps, too clever to be called coarse, there was a certain ruthlessness in her methods which would not have commended itself to a character of finer grain. She carried herself like a general, and exercised the natural despotism of a strong mind. She had a pair of sagacious black eyes which nothing escaped; a slightly Roman nose, and a firmly moulded chin, full of energy and decision. It was a wonder how any man (in spite of her good looks) could have had the courage to marry her with such a nose and chin. But happily men (in their foolish age) marry the women who want to marry them, and exercise only an imaginary freedom of selection. Peleg had no illusions left on that score now; and if he had lost the blessed faculty to laugh at the ills matrimony had brought him, he might have wept over them.

He was at the time of his removal to New York forty-nine years old, and (unlike his wife) he looked his age. Handsome he was not, nor could ever have been. There was something a trifle whimsical in his manner, the result of long matrimonial suppression. A weak desire to please his exacting spouse (though he knew beforehand that nothing he could do would please her) made him always appear at a disadvantage in her presence. His molasses-colored hair was thin on the top and sprinkled with gray; a scant and scrubby beard of the same color adorned his chin; and after the opening of his establishment in Fifth Avenue he received orders from his superior officer (which he hastened to obey) to grow a mustache. The hair, receding from the temples, had left him a dome of a forehead, projecting and curiously gnarled. He was of middle height and inclined to portliness. In dress he was a trifle slouchy, and would have ruined his business if he had transferred it along with his family to New York. Nothing seemed ever to fit him, and whatever he put on appeared equally inappropriate. But, in spite of his uncouthness and utter lack of style, there was something very likable about Peleg Bulkley. The humorous twinkle of his shrewd, bluish-gray eyes took you into his confidence whether you liked it or not, and was utterly demoralizing to any sham dignity. If you wanted to snub him, he appeared not to comprehend it, but took it for granted that you were as good a fellow as he was, when you only came to understand each other. In spite of his subjection to his wife he was amply able to hold his own with men, and his business judgment was said to be unimpeachable. There was "horse sense" in all that he said. A certain contempt for flummery, and a wholesome democratic disrespect in his attitude toward the world in general, stamped him as a true American, and made him nationally interesting even when he was personally unsympathetic. And I am not sure but that his matrimonial submissiveness adds a touch to his character with which it could ill afford to dispense.

IT was exceedingly quiet in the big Fifth Avenue mansion of the Bulkleys, when the decorators had put the finishing touches on walls and ceilings and furniture. Mrs. Bulkley had engaged a well-known artist (who had won his most profitable laurels in decorating the Vanderbilt mansions) and had given him *carte blanche.* A certain amount of mild excitement was derived from watching the progress of his work, and the house seemed almost sepulchrally hushed when he and his assistants were gone. Only an occasional messenger boy, or a man distributing advertisements of soap and perfumery, rang the door-bell; and when shabby-genteel mendicants with romantic biographies called (and they all had romantic biographies) it seemed to the young ladies a grateful interruption. It is a most curious feeling which possesses a person living in the midst of a vast and populous community which takes no notice of him—to which he is a mere undistinguished human atom—an animated agglomeration of dust, labelled for the sake of convenience with a name. The feeling is perhaps proximately one of reckless irresponsibility and the consequent temptation to throw duty, propriety, and all restraints to the winds. To the Bulkley girls, as they drifted wearily up and down the bright length of the avenue, there was something hateful and forbidding in the smiling, well-dressed crowd, which roused a dim hostility within them. They were so lonely—so drearily and horribly lonely—in the midst of these prosperous idlers who passed them by with the blank stare of indifference. How often they deplored their mother's ambition, which had brought them to this sorry pass, and how they longed for the cordial, informal, and congenial West! They went to the theatres, of course (those perennial resorts of the vast throng of prosperous New Yorkers who are unrecognized by society), and they made a business of exploring the churches with a view to joining the one from which they might derive the greatest social advantage. They had originally been Baptists, but had gradually drifted away from that denomination, as it ceased to be socially congenial. But it was no easy thing to decide the question of their new allegiance, especially as a mistake might prove fatal to all their aspirations. The summer came while they were yet surveying the field, though Mrs. Bulkley had then gotten so far as to decide, preliminarily, that they were to be Episcopalians. She would as cheerfully have become a Mahometan, if she had believed that it was for her advantage. The third daughter, Peggy, who was the wit of the family, was the only one who rebelled against this cold-blooded scheming; and when her mother demanded her reason for declining to join the church, she declared that it was too much like signing a contract to be good, and she preferred to leave it optional. That was, however, only her way of saying that she objected to her mother's motives.

She was a privileged person, this same Peggy, though every member of the family (except her father) made a point of disapproving of her. She had been a good deal of a tomboy when she was a child; and long skirts, though they interfered somewhat with her freedom of movement, had failed to curb her adventurous spirit. She said whatever came into her head, and from sheer perversity delighted in trampling upon the conventions which Mrs. Bulkley, with anxious care, was endeavoring to observe. She hated the social ambition which was imposing such unnecessary restraint upon them; picked up undesirable acquaintances and refused to drop them; flaunted her Western independence in the face of people whom it was important to conciliate. If she had not been so original and amusing, her mother and sisters would never have tolerated her conduct; and, as it was, they barely tolerated it. What made it doubly hard for Mrs. Bulkley to put up with this obstreperous daughter's disrespect was the fact that she felt what serious censure was hidden behind the merry mask. And then, again, Peleg (though he said nothing openly) encouraged her by his approval, and laughed at her sallies of wit with an almost challenging appreciation. It was as if his cowed spirit lifted its head tentatively in this exaggerated mirth, finding a grateful outlet for its rebellion.

To complete Peggy's portrait, let me add that she was a dark-eyed, slim brunette and of good height; but she carried herself in a sort of loose-jointed, hap-hazard way, common to Western girls in her station of life. To put it mildly, she had no style, and despised it, perhaps because she felt that it was unattainable. Her face, without being beautiful, was extremely pleasing, and her large, mirthful eyes lighted up her features with an animation which was not a bad substitute for beauty. No single feature was remarkable for regularity, refinement, or, in fact, for anything; but the *tout ensemble*, nevertheless, made an impression of freshness, alert intelligence, and good sense. It was a face which you would scarcely have encountered outside of the United States, because it illustrated a personality which was purely American.

The two other daughters were less pronounced characters, though every American girl is, in my opinion, a more pronounced character than, pre-matrimonially, you are apt to give her credit for. Sally, the eldest, was of the type known as golden blonde. She was placid, acquisitive, and a trifle indolent. Beautiful she was, both as to color and form, disdainful, and supremely selfish. She was always more or less uneasy about her health, read health papers, and had a mania for trying patent medicines. Faith healers, magnetic doctors, and other quacks were constantly curing her of diseases which she never had; and it was, indeed, a marvel, considering the experiments of which she was made the subject, that she managed to look as fresh and rosy as she did. Besides her mania for doctoring herself as well as others, Miss Sally had another marked idiosyncrasy. She liked to hoard things, to contemplate her possessions, to expand with an agreeable sense of opulence. This was an instance of atavism in her case, for her paternal grandfather (and many thrifty but obscure New England ancestors before him) had had this passion for saving, and had wasted their lives in futile economies. She could never quite grasp the idea of her father's wealth, because five or six millions presented only a dazzling blank to her fancy, and still less could she comprehend that her own function was to assist him in reducing, not in increasing, his hoard. Her mother, however, who knew this little peculiarity of her daughter, discounted it in advance, and supplied a hundred channels of expenditure for every one Miss Sally stopped up. She engaged riding masters, dancing masters, fencing masters, and what not, for all the three sisters, with a view to their physical improvement, and the acquisition of that secure and erect carriage which is supposed to be indicative of birth and inherited culture. She even herself took riding lessons for the purpose of reducing her weight, but she had the good sense to engage the ring for herself alone when she went through her apoplectic performances.

It was not to be denied that the three Misses Bulkley did present a better appearance after their first winter in New York than at the time of their departure from their native city. Barring a certain vague *gaucherie* which is sufficiently common to make exceptions noticeable, and a slight want of freedom and grace of movement, they were indeed remarkably attractive.   Dignity in a woman of defective breeding always becomes repellent stiffness, just as her cordiality is apt to be too emphatic, effusive, ebullient.   Those indefinable touches of high breeding, which seem a quality of blood rather than an external acquisition, and form an atmosphere of exquisite simplicity and ease about their favored possessors, the Bulkley sisters had not yet acquired.   But they were pretty enough to make these subtle deficiencies pass unnoticed.   To any one who knew their parents, it would always remain a matter of wonder where they got their faces from, as in the case of nine American girls out of ten the same reflection is apt to obtrude itself.   Nowhere else in the world is nature so breathlessly and impatiently aspiring, taking so long a step in the refinement of the race type in a single generation.   Miss Sally's striking beauty had on more than one occasion attracted attention, and overtures had been made to her from various quarters.   But Mrs. Bulkley, knowing how much depended upon their first launch in society, made careful inquiries before responding to advances, and finding, in every instance, that the gentlemen who desired admission to their house had, strictly speaking, no social status, she firmly but politely declined their acquaintance. When some of them, counting on Miss Sally's romantic susceptibility, endeavored to reach her through epistolary appeals to her sentiments, they had no better luck; for Miss Sally's sentiments were too well regulated to lead her into an indiscretion.

The second daughter, Maud, who had also more
than ordinary good looks, was the intellectual member of the family. She read Browning, raved about
Shelley, and recited "Give me the dagger" in
blood-curdling tones. She took lessons in elocution
from a well-known actress, and would at one time
have gone on the stage if her mother had not pre-
vented her. She was generous to a fault and easily
moved. Once, when she was twelve years old, she
came home barefooted, having presented her shoes
and stockings to a beggar girl who had aroused her
compassion. She was constantly restrained from
acting on such impulses by her more prudent sister,
who declared that, if it were not for her interfer-
ence, Maud would some day come home entirely
disrobed.

There was to Maud a kind of emotional luxury
in being able to relieve distress. For the same
reason that she preferred tragedy to comedy, and
wept copiously (though not without a lugubrious
zest) at fictitious misery, she revelled in every
opportunity for romantic action, and dreaded
nothing so much as the humdrum prose of life.
They had a standing joke in the family about her
providing herself with half a dozen handkerchiefs
when she went to the theatre ; and Peggy, who was
not above playing an occasional prank, always presented her with one or two dozen handkerchiefs
on her birthday, accompanied by an appropriate
epistle.

Maud dreamed of a literary *salon*—something in
the style of the Hôtel Rambouillet—and would

have liked to invite authors and artists to the house. But here she was again met by Mrs. Bulkley's inexorable veto. Her idea of attracting fashion, by giving literary evenings and cultivating brilliant conversation, was pronounced too absurd for consideration.

The Germans have an adjective, *schwärmerisch*, for which we have no equivalent in English because we have not the quality which the word represents. *Schwärmerisch*, imperfectly paraphrased, indicates the dreamily sentimental effusiveness, the fantastic exuberance of feeling, the romantic self-contemplation and luxurious melancholy, to which Teutonic maidens are liable, before their homeless sentiment has found a legitimate object upon which to expend itself. Maud Bulkley exhibited, in a paler and feebler form, this Teutonic tendency. But like all American girls (whom I have known) she was too essentially rational to be really *schwärmerisch*. A cool, sobering criticism and practical sense suggested always the ridiculous phase of everything that savored of sentiment, and restrained her from ever yielding to her romantic impulses. Though she dreamed and rebelled, and wrote stumbling verses overflowing with nameless yearnings, she remained in her innermost self sane and rational, imagining herself all the while as passionate as a Byronic heroine. In her callow years she gloried in the possession of a long list of romantic qualities which she was far from possessing, and expended a good deal of unappreciated affection upon men whom she did not know --particularly leading actors. Her sister Peggy

twitted her constantly on her unrequited attach-
ments, and asked her jokingly at breakfast whom
she was in love with to-day. It is barely possible,
however, that in this semi-humorous characteriza-
tion I do her injustice; for Maud was at heart a
noble and generous girl, whose sentimental exuberance was merely an incident of youth, and the mark
of a rich nature. She was what is called an aspiring girl, had generous enthusiasms, and was apt to
forget herself in her interest for others. The tears
came readily into her eyes when she heard or read of
an heroic deed or an instance of noble self-sacrifice.
She had a natural affinity for all that was fine ; but
was withal a trifle chaotic, untutored, dimly grop-
ing, because she had never been guided or directed
by any one wiser than herself.

Maud, though resembling her sister Sally, lacked
the latter's rich coloring and stately dignity. She
was tall, straight-backed, and had that general build
which between thirty and forty develops into a
pleasant *embonpoint*. Her ashy-blonde hair formed
an agreeable contrast to her sister's golden-blonde
—agreeable, not to Maud, but to the unprejudiced
beholder. For (to be frank) Maud was not very
fond of Sally and was not apt to appreciate her fine
points as heartily as the latter expected. If Peggy
had not kept the peace between them by diplomatic inventions calculated to produce good feeling, they would have found their relationship more
than ordinarily burdensome. Sally, having always
been told that she was a beauty, demanded admiration as her right, and would have borne an imputa-

tion against her character with greater equanimity than even the suggestion of a criticism of her physical perfections. Peggy, who made no pretensions in that line, gave without stint the praise which her sister's vanity required, but in her heart she liked Maud much better. For Maud was good-natured, generous, and easy to get along with. A trifle quick-tempered she was, perhaps, but her anger never lasted long, and she readily forgave those whom she had offended. She did not sulk for days and spoil the family breakfast, luncheon, and dinner by her moody silence and cold unresponsiveness, as Sally frequently did when the world seemed out of gear to her, and the course of creation failed to satisfy her.

This is a very uninteresting household, you will say, without the least possibility of romantic developments. Granted. But it is the kind of household you are likely to meet with any day among the new millionnaires who have come to New York to spend their Western millions. Such as they are, you will have to put up with them; for they are the *dramatis personæ* of the following veracious narrative.

To a man of Mr. Bulkley's wealth the question must have presented itself a hundred times how his fortune would be likely to affect the fates of the three girls who were to inherit it. What tortured him more than anything else was the thought that unworthy men, who loved their prospective millions, might easily impose upon them, and then after marriage, by hook or by crook, get their money away from them. His first plan for the prevention of this was to make a will, leaving the portion of each daughter in trust, and giving her only the right to dispose of the annual income. But the virtual control of the property would, in that case, have to be given to the trustees; and he might be running quite as great a risk with them as with the fortune-hunters. After much speculation he finally hit upon a project which satisfied him completely. He gave to each of his daughters one hundred thousand dollars outright during his lifetime, and imposed upon each the duty of investing, controlling and managing it. He afforded them freely the benefit of his advice, and lost no opportunity to inculcate sound financial maxims. That high interest means increased risk they knew as well as they knew their A B C. What he hoped to do was to give them, without their suspecting it, a fair business education, and initiate them into the meaning of simple financial transactions, so that they might be able to protect themselves and not give their signatures blindly, without a clear understanding of the consequences. He also limited them, during his own lifetime, to the income of this one hundred thousand dollars, so as to have them learn by experience the value of money and the necessity of careful management. In this way he expected to leave them well equipped for the difficult position of female millionnaires.

He got a great deal of quiet amusement, too, from watching the manner in which each daughter conducted her financial affairs. Sally studied the real-estate article in the morning papers with as absorbed an interest as any man, and (after a few salutary mistakes) showed a sagacity and shrewdness which put her father entirely at his ease regarding her future. As he expressed it in his homely way: "The man who wants to get the better of her would have to get up very early in the morning." By auction purchase and sale of real estate, improved and unimproved, she managed to get an income of eight thousand to ten thousand dollars out of her capital. Peggy, though she made many more mistakes and lacked natural gift, proved very teachable, and by means of her good sense got a tolerable notion of the elements of finance, though she never penetrated into its deeper mysteries. After having lost six thousand dollars of her capital in an electric-light company (in which she had had a firm faith) and two thousand dollars more in a land improvement scheme, she put all her remaining money into some first-class gas stock and unimpeachable railway bonds, and contented herself with cutting her coupons and cashing them at the bank.

Maud was the only one of Mr. Bulkley's daughters who was absolutely devoid of business sense. She would have lost her entire capital in less than a year, if her father had not interposed and saved her from further blundering. She could not fix her mind upon figures, and her thoughts always wandered when he tried to explain to her wherein her mistakes consisted. She was so delightfully irrational in such matters, and asked questions that betrayed such depth of ignorance, that Mr. Bulkley came near tearing his scant locks from his head in his despair at making her comprehend. She had a thousand uses for money, and was an expert at spending; but even the simple process of depositing a sum in a bank, and drawing checks against it until the sum was exhausted, presented difficulties to her mind. No amount of persuasion or argument could induce her to add up the stubs in her check book, and every month or so she would wax indignant at the receipt of the following epistle:

" MADAM: Your account appears to be overdrawn to the extent of $——. Please send your book for examination."

Maud knew positively that she could not have spent that amount of money, and her check book showed conclusively that it was the bank officials who were at fault and not she. But after an amiable and deferential interview, during which she said none of the sharp things she had intended to say, she invariably returned home in a humble frame of mind. Once it turned out that she had credited herself twice with the same check of six hundred dollars; having put it down in her book when she received and intended to deposit it, and once more when she actually did deposit it. Another time she had made out checks in the bank on loose blanks and failed to record them, etc. At the end of two or three years of this sort of experiences Mr. Bulkley gave up the hope of making a financier of Maud.

The annual nightmare of having to decide where to spend the summer, which makes half the winter a burden to every New York paterfamilias not having a country place of his own, began to assert its oppressive influence in the Bulkley household about the middle of January. They discussed Newport, of course, and despatched Peleg on two futile expeditions to that capital of American snobdom. But he came back utterly discouraged, not because of the prices demanded for the villas (for he was both able and willing to pay anything in reason or beyond it), but because of a certain alien air about the place which affected him like a snub or a rebuff, before he had yet opened his mouth.

"The whole place seemed to be turning up its nose at me," he said to Mrs. Bulkley, after his return; "all the houses I looked at seemed to be shrugging their shoulders at me in a sort of cussed French way; and the real-estate agents, guessing from my get-up what an undesirable coon I was, asked me prices that would have made your hair stand on end, like the fretful porcupine's."

"But, Peleg, we must expect that," his astute spouse replied; "we must make up our minds to stand snubs until we are in a position to return them. Every dog has his day, they say; and we shall have ours. You may be sure I shall have a pretty considerable score to settle when my day comes."

Peleg had some difficulty in doing justice to this argument ; for as the ability to distribute snubs had no attraction whatever to his cheerful soul, he could anticipate no compensation for present suffering in so barren a privilege. Though he had never been particularly conscious of his dignity, it did try him sorely to enjoy so slight a consideration in the community where he was compelled to live. He did not dare confess it, but it was nevertheless a fact, that he would have given half his fortune to take the limited express back to the West and resume his former place among the merchant princes of the city he had abandoned. But that is one of the disadvantages of being married, that you may have to substitute your wife's ambition for your own, and cultivate with a wry face tastes for which you have not the least liking.

Happily Mrs. Bulkley became convinced, not by anything her husband said, but by the reading of the society articles in the Sunday papers, that it would, in the end, prove more advantageous to postpone the Newport campaign for a couple of years. Men of great wealth were so numerous there that even a millionnaire might be easily overlooked or

purposely ignored.   A small and exclusive community, where the people would necessarily come
into closer contact, would serve her purpose better ;
for one friend, or even a mere acquaintance, among
the socially elect could be utilized in a hundred
ways, and by substantial benefits might be made to
serve his own ends in furthering hers.   To the task
of finding such a place the whole family now bent
their energies ; but, strange to say, they made no
headway, until a fortunate accident decided the
question for them.

Maud, in vague search, as usual, of her anony-
mous hero, was attending the Saturday matinée at
Daly's, which she rarely missed.   Peggy was pre-
tending to chaperon her, insisting that unless she
took Maud's unguarded heart in her keeping she
would be sure to lose it on the way.   The elder
sister was so well accustomed to this sort of banter
that she minded it very little, and was sometimes
even tempted to join in ridiculing her own susceptibility.   It was a rainy afternoon in April, and both
sisters were provided with silk umbrellas, with silver
handles of very elaborate workmanship.   The play
was well under way, when two young men, of quiet
and gentlemanly appearance, dropped into the two
vacant seats next to them.   Peggy gave Maud a
little nudge, which the latter interpreted as a joke
at her expense, and returned with resentful energy.
For the sight and proximity of these young men
(particularly the nearer one) had communicated a
slight flutter to her heart and a pleasant little
undercurrent of excitement.   She watched, appar-

ently, the play, and laughed when the rest laughed; but she could not have told what she was laughing at. A sort of impersonal consciousness of the youth at her side, whom she dared not look at for fear of appearing immodest, imparted a dim exhilaration to her whole being, and took such possession of her faculties as to deprive the words and gestures of the actors of all meaning. It was, of course, very ridiculous, and she was herself well aware of it. Nay, it occurred to her that there was something almost vulgar in having so inflammable a heart. But then, on the other hand, her neighbor on the right was an extremely impressive phenomenon. There was an air of quiet reserve about him which seemed to her highly aristocratic; and his features wore an expression of severe neutrality, with a little touch of disdain. He was not strikingly handsome; but, as men go, rather up to the average of good looks. What made him impressive to Maud was not, however, any pretension he might have to beauty, but his *noli-me-tangere* air, his aloofness, his silent notification to the world in general that he would rather not be troubled with its acquaintance. In the city whence she came, everybody was hail-fellow-well-met; everybody slapped everybody else on the back, and a certain democratic communicativeness pervaded all social strata. Everybody's autobiography was at everybody else's disposal, at the slightest hint; and a sort of hap-hazard, loose-jawed, vulgar loquacity spread from the board of trade into every drawing-room. She perceived now, all of a sudden, how dignified life might be; and, with the

suddenness which characterized all her mental processes, she determined henceforth to cultivate silence
and a dignified aloofness of demeanor.

It was amazing how expressive the clothes even
of a man could be, Maud reflected ; and she began
furtively to take note of her neighbor's attire, with
a view to persuading her father to sport a similar
style of costume. The gnarled cane with the enormous handle, the light checked trousers, the patent
leather boots, etc., would surely improve Mr. Bulkley's appearance, even if he dispensed with the
monocle, which she knew no power on earth could
induce him to adopt.

When the drop curtain was rung down at the end
of the second act, Maud was startled by a hearty
laugh, and she saw her dignified neighbor nudge his
companion, as if to rebuke his mirth. She had a
good mind to do the same to her sister Peggy, who
was also laughing until the tears ran down her
cheeks; but just at that moment she caught a sort
of humorous side-glimpse of herself, and had to
smile at her own absurdity. At the same time a
pang lodged in her heart at the thought that she
had not been born to the higher refinements of life,
but had to admire them half-enviously, as something
beyond and above her.

The two young men engaged during the *entr'-
acte* in a desultory conversation which she could
not avoid overhearing. She had now a good chance
to observe the further one, who was obviously
(though in an unobtrusive and inoffensive way)
returning the compliment. There was something

forceful and positive in his bearing, with a percepti-
ble undercurrent of geniality; and the glance which
strayed toward Maud's face and past it seemed to
betray a kindly interest in her and in the whole
audience. His hair was brown, and his mustache •
uncompromisingly red. His clear blue eyes constituted a most agreeable commentary to a personality
which Maud felt sure could not be anything but
charming. She could imagine without effort the
style of banter he would be sure to employ in his
intercourse with women; and she could fancy herself disapproving of it (as implying a disrespect for
her intellect), and yet, in her heart of hearts, liking
it. It was very odd, too, that chance should have
furnished his strong and expressive face with so
complete a foil as was afforded by his severely
proper and dignified neighbor. And yet Maud
was, for a while, in doubt as to which of the two
she admired the more. For in point of style the
nearer one was undeniably superior, and style was
just then a matter of vast importance to Maud.

"Look here, Marston," she heard the genial one
remark, "what are you going to do with your place
down at Atterbury, if you go to Europe?"

"Shut it up, I fancy."

"But that would be a pity. Why don't you rent
it to some respectable party? You can get three
thousand dollars, at the very least, in rent for three
months; and that is not to be despised."

"If you want it at that price, you can have it."

"I—a poor man who works for his bread—where
am I to get the three thousand dollars?"

"Look here, Phil, I am getting tired of your pretence of poverty. You know you can afford to do whatever you like."

Phil grew suddenly grave, and, raising his opera-glass to his eyes, feigned interest in some lady in the gallery.

"You know your governor would give you anything you asked him for," Marston continued.

"Perhaps; but perhaps I don't choose to ask him," retorted Phil, almost savagely.

"But for a fellow of your education and prospects, Phil, don't you think it is a trifle queer to be in trade—down-town?" his friend persevered tranquilly.

"Queer? Well, that is just as you take it. I, for my part, should find it queerer to do nothing."

Maud was anything but pleased when the rise of the curtain put an end to this conversation, though she was fully aware of the impropriety of listening. She dreamed through the last act of the play, smiled feebly at this and that joke which occasionally penetrated the film that wrapped her senses, and was mildly shocked at Peggy's mirth. At the close of the performance she rose half mechanically, and, with a dazed expression, waited to let the two gentlemen pass in front of her. While she was standing thus, having pushed back her seat, a man behind her calmly reached over and took her umbrella. She did not notice it, but Peggy, with prompt decision, grabbed the thief by the wrist, and said: "Let go that umbrella."

The man smiled at her with placid insolence, and moved on as rapidly as the throng would permit.

"Why, Maud, that man took your umbrella," exclaimed Peggy, loud enough to be heard by all, while she pointed at the man, who was pushing vigorously toward the door.

She perceived at once that she had been guilty of a breach of etiquette in not quietly submitting to the loss of her sister's thirty-dollar umbrella. She saw that even Maud was deprecating her agitation. But just as she was biting her lips and resigning herself to the inevitable, she became aware of a slight commotion in front of her, and caught a glimpse of the thief's face distorted with pain. A tall young man with a red mustache had seized his arm with an iron grip, just as he was trying to slip by, and Peggy heard him say, in a quiet tone of command:

"Give me the lady's umbrella."

The thief, without a word of protest, surrendered his booty, and was allowed to disappear in the crowd. As the two sisters found themselves in the lobby, where the little silken-robed Celestial sits distributing programmes, the tall gentleman—the young man who had been addressed by his companion as Phil—lifted his hat to Maud, and said:

"Permit me to return to you your umbrella."

"I am greatly obliged to you, sir," she replied, with a blush, which she feared was excessively countrified.

"O, Maud," whispered Peggy, teasingly, when the two young gentlemen were beyond earshot, "let me feel your pulse."

"If you don't stop, Peggy," Maud averred hysterically, "I shall never, never forgive you."

IV

IT is strange what ridiculous things people will
do, knowing them to be ridiculous, and suspecting,
too, that they will appear ridiculous to every one.
But the most singular of all is that these absurd
things, which deceive no one, yet may do something
toward a person's social advancement. When, for
instance, Mrs. Bulkley adopted a coat-of-arms consisting of a lion *couchant* in a field of blue, and the
motto *Semper Fidelis*, she scarcely expected any one
to believe that she had any legitimate right to these
heraldic distinctions. But she did not hesitate, on
that account, to have them painted on her carriage
door and her china, and to have them engraved on
her writing paper and envelopes. Likewise she
ordered for her husband several hundred cards bearing the name Mr. P. Leamington Bulkley, and spent
a week trying vainly to induce him to use them.
It was of no avail that he held up to her the ter-
rors of the law, and insisted that to change one's
name required a legislative enactment. Nothing
could persuade her, she averred, that he had not the
right to change that disgusting middle name, Lem-
uel, into Leamington, if he was so inclined, without notifying the whole country of it. It was bad
enough that P stood for Peleg ; but, as long as there
was no help for it, she would consent to let it stand.

The world—and particularly that part of it which calls itself New York society—is apt to take a person, as well as a family, at its own estimate; and a family which makes no claims to unusual consideration will never receive it. A false claim is, for such purposes, far better than none. For there is a tacit agreement in American society (based, perhaps, on a common sense of insecurity) not to subject pretences of this sort to a too curious scrutiny. At all events, Mrs. P. Leamington Bulkley, with a lion *couchant* emblazoned on her carriage and her stationery, stood a far better chance of arriving at the goal of her desires, than Mrs. Peleg L. Bulkley, with her unpalatable past unemblazoned with mendacious heraldry.

Maud developed, after the encounter at Daly's, a sudden interest in the seaside resort named Atterbury, and made with her mother a visit to the southern coast of Long Island. They were both a trifle awed by the august names attached to several of the cottagers, some well known to them from American history, and others from the society columns of the newspapers. They perceived instantly that if they could get a foothold here it would be a most auspicious opening of their social campaign. But though there were at least a dozen cottages unrented, and the month of May close at hand, they experienced unforeseen difficulties in coming to terms with the agents. These gentlemen exhibited a hesitation and reserve in dealing with them, not at all characteristic of their profession, and refused to commit themselves to any agreement without

first communicating with the owners. Mrs. Bulkley, at Maud's suggestion, made a discreet offer of
three thousand dollars for a villa of palatial dimen-
sions belonging to J. Marston Fancher, Esq., and
grew so irritated at the agent's failure to take her
up, that she came near giving him a piece of her
mind. She would just as lief have, offered four
thousand dollars, or even five thousand dollars, but
was afraid of advertising her undesirability by ex-
ceeding the market rates.

Having derived the impression, while dealing
with the agents, that it was a great favor to be
allowed to rent a villa in Atterbury at any price,
she was not a little surprised at receiving a letter,
two weeks later, offering her the Fancher cottage
at a rent of three thousand five hundred dollars.
Though she was aware that the price was a preposterous one, she yielded to Maud's entreaties and
made Peleg sign the lease without delay. Thus one
point was gained ; and during the first week in June
the whole Bulkley household, including Peleg, three
daughters, six servants, and eight horses, were transferred to Long Island. They were attended by a
long procession of tradespeople in buggies, market
wagons, and sulkies from the depot to the Fancher
cottage. Butchers, bakers, grocers, and milkmen,
who lay in wait for every newcomer, seized the opportunity as Mr. and Mrs. Bulkley dismounted from
the carriage to solicit their patronage and thrust
their business cards into their hands. Peleg, who
had a sneaking sympathy with their enterprising
importunity, would have stopped and discussed the

question with them in a friendly way, if a severe
" Mr. Bulkley " from his better half had not recalled
him to the proprieties of the occasion.

Atterbury consists of seventy or eighty cottages
—colonial, Queen Anne, and nondescript—some
clustering about a small lake, and others scattered at
varying intervals along the sandy dunes which form
a bulwark against the waves of the Atlantic. The
roar of the surf always fills the air as a dim undertone; and the white spray rises at high tide above
the brown dunes, and after each storm puts a briny
coating on the walls and windows of the more adventurous villas. There is something individual and
peculiar about this little seaside nest, which it shares
with no other place on the American continent;
and it is a fortunate thing that so few people (comparatively speaking) have discovered its charm. I
may add that it is the endeavor of every cottager
at Atterbury, as far as possible, to prevent the discovery from becoming general. He prides himself
on the delicacy of sense which enables him to enjoy
what would escape a less finely organized being,
and he recognizes a subtle freemasonry among those
who have once been admitted within the sacred precincts. If it rains daily for three weeks in Atterbury (which, to be sure, is a rare occurrence) it is
held to be base treachery to call attention to the
fact, unless it were to comment upon the peculiar
healthfulness and beneficence of the Atterbury rain.
For everything in Atterbury, from the people to the
sand and the beach grass, has some peculiar charm
or virtue which discloses itself only to the initiated.

And until you begin to discover this, and to show yourself duly impressed by it, you are a rank outsider. No mere financial consideration will induce a cottager to part with a foot of ground to you ; and the polite toleration with which you are treated, if you are undesirable, will reduce you to a state of humility or of irritation which will affect your health and make you long for more congenial company.

This by way of friendly satire. For the fact is, the cottager is right in all his claims concerning Atterbury, and the outsider is wrong. There is not a more well-bred community to be found on this side of the Atlantic, nor a more delightful and salubrious summer climate, nor a wider and more glorious horizon. But at the time the Bulkleys invaded the place, there was one thing lacking. Atterbury had no Episcopal church. The Methodists and Baptists had their meeting-houses in the old village (built with that genius for ugliness which characterizes the ecclesiastical architecture of these denominations). But the old village was something by itself, and its inhabitants had nothing to do with the cottage community, except to supply its material needs and prey upon it to the full extent of their opportunity. The need of a church, in the proper sense of the term, had long been felt; and the plan of building one had been long and abundantly discussed. It was during the third week of the sojourn of the Bulkleys in Atterbury, and before a single soul, except petitioners for their trade, had called upon them, that an agent (who got a commission of five per cent.) was started on the round of the cottages to solicit subscriptions for " St. Paul-on-the-Dunes." Having received no explicit instructions to omit anybody, he introduced himself to Mrs. Bulkley with that peculiarly oily, commercial affability which is supposed to be irresistible to customers. There was a tincture of patronage, too, in his manner, as that of a benevolent native explaining the mysteries of the place to a stranger. He had not talked long before the thought flashed through Mrs. Bulkley's mind that here was her opportunity. She asked the agent to wait on the piazza while she went to find her husband.

Peleg was dozing over the New York *World*, in an easy chair in the library, and woke up with a start when his spouse addressed him.

" Mr. Bulkley," she said (she no longer called him Peleg), " I want you to put your name down for one thousand dollars on that list."

" A thousand dollars? " repeated Peleg, wonderingly, as he took the paper and, rubbing his sleepy eyes, tried to adjust his intellect to its contemplation.

" St. Paul-on-the-Dunes," he murmured. " What the devil do I care about St. Paul-on-the-Dunes ? "

" But I care, Mr. Bulkley ! "

This was uttered with an ominous emphasis which made Peleg prick up his ears, like a horse who scents danger. But he felt a trifle cantankerous, and his sense of the absurdity of subscribing one thousand dollars to a church in a strange place gave him courage to rebel.

" Since when? " he asked with that veiled challenge which she always found so irritating.

" Oh, well, I expected that," she ejaculated, dropping into a chair with an air of resignation. " I suppose I shall have to din it into your skull for the fiftieth time. But the agent is waiting out on the piazza."

" Well, let him wait. He can afford to wait a month for one thousand dollars. He won't make such a commission from anybody else's subscriptions around this pond. Look at that nabob Barrington, he has put himself down for two hundred dollars, and Van Horst for five hundred dollars, and Bailey for one hundred and fifty dollars. What the deuce is the sense of my building a church for these high and mighty cusses who turn up their noses both at you and me, and the girls too ? "

" Well, Mr. Bulkley," the lady replied with unexpected gentleness, " why should they take notice of us? They don't know us. And likely as not they don't want to know us. Now, we must make them want to know us; and a thousand dollar subscription for the church will make enough talk to bring some at least to our side. They have got to recognize us socially or they have got to decline the money. But if they accept the money, they can't ignore us any more."

" But, Gussie, do you think they are such fools as not to see your game ? "

" Not a bit. They'll take it as a bid ; but it is so big a bid that I reckon they'll think twice before declining. In order to rise in society we have got to make ourselves useful to those who have social influence. This subscription will give them a hint of what we can and will do, if we are properly treated."

"But is the game worth the candle, Gussie?"

"Not to you, perhaps, but to me and the girls it is worth everything. It is only a question whether you are willing to invest one thousand dollars to give your daughters a chance of rising in the world, and marrying gentlemen of position instead of drummers."

"Don't you be hard on the drummers, Mrs. Bulkley," sighed Peleg, with a reminiscent smile which was full of sadness.

"Then you'll subscribe?"

Mr. Bulkley, rising cumbrously from the depth of the easy chair, heaved another sigh, and fumbling about on the desk for a pen, attached with the utmost deliberation a gnarled and decrepit-looking signature opposite to the figure one thousand dollars.

"Well, it is your investment, mother, not mine," he observed, in a stertorous voice and with a lugubrious mien, as he handed her the paper.

V

Mr. Marston Fancher did not only not go to
Europe as he had intended, but he came very near
going to Canada. An adverse fate had, so to speak,
played football with his dignified person during
the last weeks, and it came near breaking him up
altogether. Mr. Fancher had been induced by a
financial magnate, with whom he occasionally dined,
to engage in a mining speculation which turned out
disastrously. The courts were invoked, and sundry civil suits were commenced against Marston
Fancher, in which much came to light that reflected
unfavorably upon his intelligence, though not upon
his integrity. And yet, though his actions and his
motives seemed as clear as the daylight, he had a
sense of nervous insecurity which he was unable to
shake off. He felt like a fly caught in a horrible,
sticky spider's web, and there were moments when
to be beyond the reach of lawyers and summonses
appeared the height of earthly felicity. Then the
newspapers had gotten hold of his case and served
it up with sensational headings in daily instalments,
until Fancher seemed to himself a marked man,
eternally disgraced. In the clubs to which he belonged he had to endure the torture of knowing that
he was talked about, though the conversation always
ceased when he entered. The society weeklies, in

which he had always figured as a conspicuous character, simply revelled in his misfortune, and worked it up in spicy paragraphs abounding in malicious innuendo. It was while these trials beset him that Fancher (though well knowing that the Atterbury cottagers would not soon forgive him) rented his villa, "Thorn Hedge," to the Bulkleys. He needed the three thousand five hundred dollars, and, as Peleg had no objection to paying the entire rent in advance, it proved simply a godsend to the embarrassed financier. It saved him from the necessity of selling at an enormous sacrifice a piece of valuable real estate (in the upper part of Fifth Avenue), which, pending the upward movement of the population, was held in trust for his mother and his sisters.

It was about the middle of July before his affairs were so far arranged as to allow him to take a vacation, and he then resolved to rent for the remainder of the season a tiny old-fashioned cottage at Atterbury named "Nestledown." Though he was conscious of having given offence to his fellow sojourners by the sea, he chose to brave their displeasure rather than to seek fresh fields and pastures new. His mother and two sisters he had shipped off to Europe early in May, and of 'all his horses he had only kept two. With his magnificence thus clipped and curtailed Marston Fancher reappeared upon the scene of his former triumphs. To help him bear the unsuspected ills to which an existence thus reduced and limited is subject, he had persuaded his friend Philip Warburton to be his guest as long as his vacation lasted. Warburton's personality exerted a kind of fascination over him which he had difficulty in accounting for. They had known each other since they were small boys, and their acquaintance had commenced auspiciously by Philip's thrashing his friend. It was the wear and tear of life, and a community of experiences rather than of interests, which, more than anything else, had made them fond of each other; for they were as unlike as possible, and, both by their pursuits and positions, were drawn apart rather than united. Marston, to be sure, had, strictly speaking, no occupation. He was a man of leisure, a club man and capitalist, who had inherited a good name and safe investments. His family were Knickerbockers of the most exclusive tendencies, and they were related to Livingstons, Stuyvesants, Schuylers, and Van Rensselaers, and, in fact, to no end of Dutch colonial magnates. They were not extravagantly rich, by any means, and affected a certain aristocratic disdain for those who were. They were under the impression that Second Avenue, in the neighborhood from Twelfth to Twentieth Street, in which region they possessed a commodious but unpretentious domicile, was still the fashionable quarter of New York; and they pretended to look down on Fifth Avenue as belonging to a later era, the home of snobdom and the *nouveaux riches*.

Being reared in such an atmosphere, and naturally in accord with the aspirations of the society in which his lot was cast, Marston Fancher was, in a measure, debarred from becoming a remarkable man. His ideal in life was propriety; and, as an unfriendly critic had once remarked, he was so damnably and obtrusively proper that you felt like kicking him. But that there was something more to him than his rigid and starchy exterior seemed to promise was indicated by his long-sustained intimacy with Philip Warburton. For Philip was not a man who could be patted on the back, and far less patronized. Whatever that something was which he professed to see in Fancher, it was not sufficiently obvious to any one else to modify the general estimate of his character. Habit, probably, accounted a good deal for their intimacy (for they had lived in adjoining rooms at college and been constantly in each other's society), and an exchange of mutual services of an unobtrusive sort had strengthened the half-accidental relation. Philip laughingly declared that he found Marston restful, and he liked his damnable propriety, too, as he liked to contemplate anything perfect of its kind, even though it were to himself unattainable. That kind of eccentric friendships between men of utterly antagonistic characteristics is, after all, not so rare that it needs any deep psychological explanation. It is not only in women that men are likely to be attracted by their opposites. As far as Philip was concerned, it was indeed difficult for any one to refrain from liking him. There was an aggressive and breezy independence about him which broke like a north wind into Marston's carefully adjusted and well-ordered world and turned the furniture topsy-turvy. He ridiculed the latter's precise habits and respect for Knickerbocker tradition in a way that Fancher would have tolerated from no one else. And the amusing part of it was that Marston consented to overlook Philip's occasional outbursts of savage humor, because he had gotten it into his head that his friend was a most remarkable man—in fact, a man of genius, to whom necessarily more latitude ought to be granted than to ordinary mortals. It was of no use that Philip protested against this view, and proclaimed himself a simple-minded and mediocre bungler. There were certain facts in his career, Marston maintained, which had very much the look of the kind of things that are related in the biographies of remarkable men. In the first place, Philip's father, who was a Scotchman, had started in life as a carpenter and had worked himself up by industry, frugality, and perseverance, until he was now a contractor on a large scale and a man of some property. There was something harsh and rugged about him, which, after all, went well with his uncompromising integrity and contempt for shams. For he was Scotch to the backbone, red-faced, blue-eyed, bristling with scornful criticism which his hard rolling r's made still more derisive; but in spite of his masterful spirit, which brooked no opposition, he was a good, stanch, warm-hearted, virile man, who commanded not only the respect but the admiration of all who had occasion to test the mettle of his manhood.

You would have fancied, of course, that no one held him in higher esteem than his only son. But unhappily Philip was too much a chip of the old block to get along peaceably with his father. The old man was subject to bad moods, in which he was apt to say cutting things which rankled in his son's heart and could not be forgotten. He took great pride in Philip's cleverness and varied accomplishments; but, although at heart he believed him to be as fine a specimen of a young man as ever breathed, he could not forbear scolding him and complaining of him and making him bear the brunt of his ill temper. While Philip went to college, the old gentleman told him, whenever he was at home for a few days, that he never had had such chances, and that if he had been so abundantly blessed as his son, he would have amounted to a good deal more in the world than he now did. Never did he let the young man suspect what satisfaction he took in his progress and universal popularity; and far less did he afford him a glimpse of the deep affection he cherished for him. While, as a matter of fact, he gloried in being able to afford Philip everything in the way of friends, leisure, and learning which had been denied to his own harsh and barren youth, he could not refrain from nagging the boy for availing himself of these very advantages which he had purposely thrown in his way. One day, a few months after Philip's graduation, when the old man had called him a spendthrift and an idler, a rather unpleasant scene ensued. It was the hundredth time, at the very least, that he was expatiating upon the degeneracy of modern youth, and hinting what he himself might have become if he had been born with a silver spoon in his mouth.

Philip sat listening in dogged silence to the harsh reproaches, which seemed doubly gruff and wounding with the bristling asperities of that rasping Scotch accent. Suddenly he got up with a very white face, and in a quiet and perfectly respectful manner remarked:

" Well, father, since that is your opinion of me, I don't want to stay with you any more. If you can't afford the money which I spend, I'll pay you back what I owe you. And I beg of you that you will kindly not give me a shilling until the day I ask you for it. Good-by."

He held out his hand to the old man, who was, however, so overcome with amazement that he forgot to grasp it. He consoled himself, as he heard Philip slowly mount the stairs, with the reflection that the boy was bluffing him, and that, even if he left the house for a couple of days, he would soon come to terms, when he found out what it meant to make his own living. He even thought that it might prove a good discipline, and should not therefore be discouraged. He accordingly made no effort to interfere with his son's purposes, when, that very evening, he sent an expressman for his trunk and himself departed a little before midnight. The next he heard of him was that he had taken some inferior position in a wholesale drug house down-town, and had hired a room in a respectable boarding-house in Sixteenth Street. For six months the old man walked about with a dull heartache, hoping daily for Philip's return. He was so unutterably miserable that he could scarcely drag himself out of bed in the morning, or interest himself in anything but the question of Philip's condition and whereabouts. One day, in order to ease his aching conscience, he went to the tailor whom Philip employed, and after a preliminary chat asked, as if casually: " By the way, does my son owe you anything? "

The tailor, after having examined his ledger, declared that the young man owed him seventy-two dollars.

" Well," said Mr. Warburton, pulling out his check book and making out a check for seventy-two dollars, " here it is, but don't tell him that I paid it."

It did not require much ingenuity on Philip's part, however, to discover who had settled his tailor bill, and, with a resolution born of the moment, he went straight to the sartorial artist whom his father patronized—a canny and old-fashioned Caledonian, who went in for wear rather than for style, and whose garments, intended chiefly to grow in, had been among the severest afflictions of his boyhood. After having mildly chaffed the gnarled and tousled little man (who was so bent that he looked almost humpbacked), and listened to his reproaches for having gone in search of strange sartorial gods, he finally managed to state his errand.

" How much does my father owe you now, Sandy? " he asked with an air of mischief. " I have a particular reason for wishing to know, which I will tell you about later."

Sandy, who carried his ledger in his head, was coaxed to divulge the amount of the debt, which proved to be one hundred and ten dollars.

"I want to pay it for him, Sandy," the young man remarked, with a sly glance which flattered the old tailor. "I know you will oblige me by accepting it."

Sandy, to whom money never came amiss, needed no persuasions to take the check; but when, in the course of a few days, old Mr. Warburton came to settle up his account (for he had a horror of bills) and had to be informed of the transaction, he gave the tailor such an overhauling that the latter felt as if he had been thrashed, when his irascible customer had done with him. Mr. Warburton's first impulse was to interpret Philip's action as a premeditated affront ; but as he walked away, bristling with a sense of outrage, his thoughts gradually took a milder turn, and the humorous aspect of the case began to appeal to him. It was tit for tat, after all. He could not help chuckling at the joke, even though it was at his own expense. The manly sense of independence which prompted the retaliatory act seemed the more admirable the more he contemplated it, and by the next day he was so much mollified that he determined to go and see Philip. He found him in the warehouse down in Worth Street, in his shirt sleeves, with brown overalls, and a big apron covering his entire front. The perspiration was dripping from his brow, and his fingers were stained with malodorous chemicals. He had been taking a hand, apparently, in rolling in some barrels which were being hoisted up by pulleys from the street below. Now he picked up a book from the head of a barrel and began to mark off the items which another clerk called out in a high, monotonous voice. The old gentleman learned that there had been a strike and that the firm were short of workmen; therefore, every one had to turn in and do his best. He was not himself a man who was afraid of work, even the roughest; but somehow it cut him up more than he had expected to see Philip, who was utterly unaccustomed to toil, in the coarse attire of a workingman, stooping over boxes and barrels, and scratching and blistering his soft skin. As his presence had not been observed, Mr. Warburton did not trust himself to speak to his son that day. He knew he would break down if he attempted it. He would postpone the interview until next week or next month. He made up his mind now that he owed Philip an apology for having called him a good-for-nothing spendthrift and idler. For a man of his pride and reserve it was no easy thing to make such an admission. He concluded not to repeat his visit to the warehouse until he was ready to make the *amende honorable.* But unhappily, before he had time to carry out this intention, an incident occurred which revived his angry feeling. An enterprising newspaper reporter had got hold of Philip's history and published it, with sensational headings and sundry romantic embellishments, in the Sunday edition of one of the great dailies. From a photographer he had procured the picture of a handsome young man

which might or might not be Philip, and this was
printed at the head of a column of the most nau-
seating stuff that ever appealed to a sentimental
girl's fancy. The story was entitled "A Drug
Clerk's Romance." The father, it is needless to
say, was painted in the most unflattering colors.
He was represented as the tyrannical parent of
melodrama, and the son's heroism was duly ex-
tolled and illustrated with crude cuts. Philip spent
a week in a futile search for the author of this
mawkish romance; but as the editor of the newspaper refused to give his name, except in court,
Philip never succeeded in identifying him. Unluck-
ily the old gentleman, who was cruelly hurt by the
publication, did not know the ways of modern jour-
nalism, and therefore held his son, in some way,
accountable for the facts which the story contained, though he acquitted him of responsibility
for the fiction. Accordingly he banished the
thought of reconciliation from his mind, and became daily more incrusted in his harsh and solitary
misery.

This was yet the state of affairs during the summer when Philip went to visit Marston Fancher at
Atterbury. He had then been three years and a
half in the wholesale drug business, had been
repeatedly promoted, and was earning what for a
man in his position was a good salary. But his
father had as yet taken no step toward a reconciliation, nor had Philip received the least inkling of the
state of his feelings toward him. He was firmly
convinced that, as his father had wronged him, it

was his place to make the first friendly overture;
and, much as he loved and admired the old man,
he could not compromise his own honest pride
and manly dignity by professing to justify his
conduct.

4

VI

THE great question which agitated Atterbury in the month of July of that memorable summer was whether the Bulkleys should or should not be elected to membership in the Beach Club. The Beach Club was a joint-stock company ; and although the stock was assessable and paid no dividends, it was eagerly bought by the property holders of Atterbury, chiefly in order to prevent undesirable parties from getting hold of it. The real founder of the club and its principal shareholder was Marston Fancher, and he had taken care to dispose of the remaining shares to people whose social standing was unexceptionable. Unhappily, however, he had during his recent financial troubles been obliged to pledge the entire amount of his own stock as collateral for a short loan, which he was unable to repay when it fell due. The sacred and inalienable stock of the Beach Club was therefore sold, and, as it happened (perhaps not without malice afterthought), fell into the hands of P. Leamington Bulkley. It gave Peleg a more genuine satisfaction than he had experienced since he left his beloved West, when one evening he came home from the city with these stock certificates in his pocket and spread them out on the library table before the astonished vision of his spouse.

"Now, Gussie," he cried in that high, cracked voice which with him always indicated excitement, "by jimmie-crack-corn, now we'll squeeze those blanked high nobs. Here's the stuff, Gussie, that will bring 'em to terms. We have been here now for five weeks, and have thrown out one thousand dollars bait in the shape of a subscription to their St. Paul-in-the-Beach-Grass, but not a durned one of 'em has as much as nibbled on our hook. But here I have engineered a neat little corner on them, and I reckon they will soon be crawling on their bellies to get out of the hole I have put them into."

Mrs. Bulkley listened with a puzzled and disapproving frown to this gleeful harangue, until suddenly something dawned upon her ; and, with eyes in which a resentful spark glittered, she begged Mr. Bulkley to repeat his statement and explain his plan. The girls, who scented something unusual in the air, were attracted to the library by the high-pitched exhilaration of their father's voice, and dropped into the comfortable cushioned wicker chairs that were scattered about the room. "I tell you," Peleg was exclaiming, "I hold the whole blanked lot of 'em here in the hollow of my hand."

"How so, father?" Peggy demanded innocently. She knew how sore he felt at their having been ignored so long by the social leaders, and she sympathized keenly with his resentment.

"Look-a-here, girls," he ejaculated gayly, slapping the bunch of stock certificates against the palm of his hand, "here is the lime that will fetch the bird, and don't you forget it. This very night I shall write to that numskull committee of governors, and inform them, very politely of course, that I have bought a controlling interest in the Beach Club; and that I have concluded to pull down the Casino and build half a dozen cheap cottages on the land for rent to people in moderate circumstances, who have hitherto been debarred by the high rents from enjoying the salubrious climate and social privileges of Atterbury. There is nothing those confounded high-flyers hate worse than people in moderate circumstances. They run from them like pestilence. By jimmie-crack-corn, shouldn't I enjoy planting six liquor-selling Irish aldermen right in the midst of their beautiful and exclusive snobdom! Or, perhaps, a seaside home for destitute children— say from Five Points Mission or Chatham Street? Now, girls, what do you say? I will be hanged if I don't think that that is a pretty neat scheme. I thought it all out as I was coming down in the cars. The governors will then smell a rat, of course, and if they don't elect me a member of their confounded exclusive top-lofty society I'll engage to eat every one of them."

The plan was now discussed from various points of view, and both Mrs. Bulkley and Sally were inclined to think that it was a good one. Maud and Peggy, however, were of opinion that the thinly veiled threat might have exactly the opposite effect of what was intended. These men were both rich and high-spirited, and, rather than be dictated to by an outsider, they were capable of pulling up their stakes and moving elsewhere.

" Why not rather try this plan ? " Maud proposed. " You write to the governors, saying that you have accidentally come into possession of a controlling interest in the club, but that you know how unwilling they are to have it pass into the hands of people who hold it only for profit, or something in that style. Then, why wouldn't it do to say that you put the stock at their disposal at the exact amount that it has cost you ? "

" But what the deuce would be the object of that ? " queried Peleg, indignantly.

" Why, this, of course. You would make them feel ashamed of themselves, and if they accept your offer they would be in honor bound to elect you."

" Yes, and you may be sure all the things that you might do, if they didn't elect you, would occur to them without your telling them," Peggy remarked in a tone of vivacious assent.

Peleg had to be labored with for a full hour before he could see the beauty of this plan ; but when finally he was won over, the exquisite irony of the situation added to his zest in writing the letter to the governors. It was a cautiously worded document, in the composition of which the whole family assisted ; and though the reluctant scribe cried out in shrill protest against the courteous phrases that were dictated to him, he was overruled by so unanimous a vote that he had nothing to do but to acquiesce with as good a grace as he could muster. The fateful missive was duly despatched to the chairman of the committee of governors, and in three days came the reply, accepting Mr.

Bulkley's generous offer, informing him of his election to the club, and apologizing for inevitable delay, owing to the pressure of business, etc., etc.

To the unsophisticated Peleg the battle was now won and the fruits of the victory seemed secure. But when Mrs. Bulkley and her two elder girls attended the next Wednesday afternoon reception at the Beach Club they had a sorry time of. it. Conscious though they were of being, as to dress at least, completely *comme il faut*, they received no cordial reception. Mrs. Van Horst, the hostess for the occasion, shook hands with them rather frigidly, remarking interrogatively, " Mrs. Bulkley, I believe?" but did not volunteer to introduce them to anybody; and, judging by appearances, nobody seemed anxious for their acquaintance. They sauntered about the grounds with an acute sense of discomfort, which they sedulously strove to disguise by a sham animation and labored vivacity among themselves. They betrayed the liveliest interest in the tennis-players, and knocked the ball back with their sunshades when it bounded over the lines. But there was something horribly dismal in this elaborate fooling, and their hearts were like lead within them. It is wonderful what ingenious tortures women can invent for each other; but I doubt if there is any that, for exquisite cruelty, is comparable to the pointed and conspicuous snubbing in which a whole assembly unites in order to humiliate some poor intruder. Mrs. Bulkley had supposed that, after Peleg had so magnanimously thrown away all his trump cards, as he expressed it, there would be some disposition to recognize the club's indebtedness to him for having refrained from using his power to anybody's detriment. She began now to regret having yielded to Maud's quixotic folly, instead of frankly indorsing Peleg's vindictive scheme. It was obvious that the girls suffered as much as she did under those supercilious sidelong glances which the fine ladies occasionally deigned to bestow upon their toilets; but still harder to endure was a certain vague, unseeing stare which looked through them or over them as if they were so much vapor or thin air.

"Mother," Maud murmured in a heart-broken whisper, between two high-pitched laughs, "I can't stand this any longer. Let us go home."

"Not for the world, child," Mrs. Bulkley retorted; "we've got to brazen it out."

"It would never do to go home now," Sally observed placidly; "it would be like giving up. We have got to stick it out, though I don't like it any better than you do."

"Peggy was wise in refusing to go," Maud faltered, with a desperate effort to preserve her composure; "she guessed what was in store for us, and she simply made up her mind that the game wasn't worth the candle."

The lawn in front of the Casino, where the ladies were sitting, presented at that moment a very pretty picture. The tennis courts, which were surrounded by high fences of wire netting, were occupied by old and young people in various styles of picturesque undress. The married men, with their shirt sleeves rolled up to their elbows, and bright jockey caps on their heads, stopped every now and then to mop the perspiration from their brows; but fell to, after each pause, with a zeal which betrayed that their object was health rather than amusement. Some of them, who were getting too stout, belabored the elastic ball five to six hours a day for the purpose of reducing their flesh; and those who were dyspeptic leaped and frolicked conscientiously, with a view to improving their digestion. Bareheaded college boys in white flannel, with sunburned arms and necks, played with a lazy security and skill against merry young damsels, who emitted an occasional shrill yell of excitement when an exceptional shot was made, or the ball bounded into the face of some spectator. All over the close-clipped, velvety lawn, which was as intensely green and soft as that of any English country seat, people lounged in familiar groups on benches and chairs, or on the grass; and the sunshine, tempered by a salt breeze, poured down upon them; and the surf, which beat with a perpetual boom against the dunes, sang in their ears. It was the bitterness of bitterness to those two Western girls to see the free and easy demeanor of the young lads and maidens, indicating cousinship or an acquaintance dating back to knickerbockers and pinafores. The abbreviated Christian names that darted hither and thither through the sunshine, accompanied by exclamations of remonstrance and surprise, had a still finer sting; and there came a moment when Maud fancied that all this familiar by-play was gotten up for their benefit, or was, at least, a trifle emphasized by the fact of their presence. There seemed to her, in her misery, a note of consciousness in the gay laughter of the girls; and in all the delicious fooling which goes so well with youth, she imagined she saw a direct purpose to wound them. And yet she was not exactly angry; or, at least, not half so angry as she was envious. There was an air of refinement about these young people which seemed almost to justify their exclusiveness. Maud was not quite sure but that she, too, if she had been born in this tempered zone of golden ease and luxury, might have been a little jealous of her privileges, and looked askance upon aspirants for admission.

She had about exhausted her histrionic talent, shamming a dozen airs of careless gayety and unconsciousness of criticism, when she saw two gentlemen, mounted on handsome horses, come trotting up the winding road to the Casino. She gave her sister's arm a pinch which nearly made the latter cry out, and felt the color flare into her face with the most embarrassing effect. For scarcely a glance was required to identify these interesting horsemen. They were the two friends whom she had admired so much in Daly's Theatre, one of whom had restored to her the stolen umbrella. She watched them furtively as they dismounted and turned over their horses to the liveried groom who came forward to receive them. The one whom she knew as Philip was the taller of the two, and carried himself with a certain easy fling which was very attractive. The other was Mr. Fancher, their landlord. He walked with a certain rigid erectness, as if his joints were not sufficiently lubricated. Maud voted him stunning, however, and noted with ungrudging admiration the air of extreme propriety and stylishness which radiated from his person like a halo. As to face and manner, however, Philip was the more incisive personality. His fine blue eyes had a frank and luminous gaze which lit up his features, particularly when he smiled, and gave them a look of rare distinction. He was broad-chested, and gave the impression of great muscular strength.

The two young men made a little sensation as they strolled out upon the lawn; and the ladies, at whose chairs they paused to discuss the game or the weather, received them with an animation which was a tribute to their importance. They made the round of the company, and finally settled down at the feet of a young married woman whom no masculine creature could pass by without self-denial. This lady, whose name was Mrs. Castleton, had a fascination to all young men—and to old ones, too, for that matter—which aroused no jealousy, because it was so universally recognized. She was one of those rare women whose sweetness of character shone from her face, and whose ready and intelligent sympathy stimulated all that was fine in a man, and made every one feel at his best in her presence. And the wonder of it was that she was no less delightful to her own sex than she was to her male admirers. She was so free from all small arts and petty manœuvres, and was so incapable of suspecting any meanness in others, that the mean

became temporarily noble when she talked with
them; and every one seemed to become, for the
moment at least, what she believed him to be.
Fancher had been enrolled among her worshippers
since the days when he was a junior in college; and
he had many a time remarked to himself, in the strict-
est privacy, of course, that it was his deuced bad luck
which had postponed their acquaintance until she
was no longer within his reach. Later he became
considerably humbler, and concluded that he was
altogether too stupid a man to win the love or even
the toleration of so brilliant a woman. Tolerate
him she did, to be sure, in her infinite kindness,
simply because she was too generous to snub anybody. A bit of a snob though he was, he never did
her the injustice to suppose that his family distinction had a hair's weight of influence in her estimate
of him.

It may be expedient, perhaps, to add that Mrs.
Castleton was blonde—blue-eyed and fair-skinned.
She was of good height and had a fine figure, with
a hint in it of pleasant *embonpoint* in years to come.
A certain dazzling clearness, which was made up of
subtler ingredients than fair flesh tints, seemed to
characterize her both physically and morally. There
was something warm and radiant in her glance, nay,
in her whole being. What impressed one in her
conversation was a largeness of view which inclined
to charitable judgments, and saw ameliorating
circumstances where others saw none. What she
hated above all was the hard, petty, fault-finding
narrowness which plumes itself on imagined superi-

ority, and stalks along in empty-headed scorn of all that makes life worthy and noble. Her smile, one of her worshippers declared, was the best argument he knew for the immortality of the soul; for he fancied that God never could have the heart to let anything perish that was so inexpressively lovely. Her children surely thought so—for she was the happy mother of three—and no one could ever be said to have known Mrs. Castleton until he had seen her in the company of her small son and daughters. Fancher had frequently had this privilege; and if it hadn't been for her knack of checking audacious compliments, he would have told her in sufficiently extravagant language the impression she made upon him. But there was again the distressing fact, as it appeared to Marston, that she was happily married, and that her husband was a fine, virile, and prosperous man whom everybody liked, and who, in the secure sense of his possession, could afford to extend a good-humored indulgence to the poor fellows who had been less fortunate than he. He made them, in fact, welcome in his house, offered them excellent cigars, treated them as good friends, and never honored any one by regarding him as a possible rival.

It was at the feet of this charming woman that Fancher and Warburton seated themselves, after having paid their respects to the dowagers, and exchanged the usual chaffy remarks with the young girls who watched the games. Warburton had made Mrs. Castleton's acquaintance on a trans-Atlantic steamboat and shared his friend's admiration of her; and Mrs. Castleton, to whom a streak of originality in a man was a refreshing phenomenon, was rather inclined to distinguish Philip by her special liking.

" Look here, Mrs. Castleton," this enviable favorite of fortune remarked, bent apparently upon abusing his privilege, " I had deluded myself with the idea that you were somewhat superior to the petty standards that govern women in their intercourse with each other."

" Well," exclaimed Mrs. Castleton, vivaciously, " *à propos de quoi?* "

" I have been watching for the last half hour," Philip continued, with a vague undertone of indignation in his voice, " those three miserable women whom nobody speaks to, and who are exerting themselves so pathetically to make believe that they are having a good time. I have seen one of them before, but I don't remember where."

" Why, they are the family which have taken Thorn Hedge," Marston explained casually ; " the father is from the West, and is named P. Leamington Bulkley. I presume the daughters are named something in the same line."

" But isn't that the girl whose umbrella was stolen at Daly's some weeks ago? Don't you remember the tremendous way she blushed as I handed it back to her? "

" Yes, you are right ; it is the very same."

Marston briefly related the incident to Mrs. Castleton, Philip putting in here and there some embellishing touches.

"And because of this thrilling adventure you want me to call upon her; is that it, Mr. Warburton?" Mrs. Castleton queried, with a mischievous glance at Philip.

"No, not exactly that," the latter replied, with unexpected seriousness; "but it seems to me a needless cruelty to invite these ladies to a club reception, and then pointedly ignore them. I can imagine how they feel, poor things! It always makes me mad to see a woman put in that position. They seem to me very nice and lady-like girls; and the mother—well, what do you think of the mother, Mrs. Castleton?"

"I should judge her to be a good, sensible woman," the lady replied, "and something of a general."

"But you don't think she is a lady according to the Atterbury standard?"

"I am not prepared to say that. All I can say is that it would scarcely do for me to introduce them, when Mrs. Van Horst, who is the hostess for the afternoon, has neglected to do so."

"But if I ask you—mind you, I am well aware I am treading on dangerous ground—what I mean to say is, that if, out of my boundless admiration for you, knowing how good a heart and how bright a mind you have, I venture to beg you to make the acquaintance of those ladies, will you snub me as I deserve, or will you make allowance for my masculine crudity and forgive me?"

"Since it is you, Mr. Warburton, I'll do the latter."

" Look here, Phil," Marston put in rather cautiously; " this is a more complicated affair than you may be aware of."

And turning to Mrs. Castleton he related the incident of Bulkley's purchase of his stock in the club, and the disposition he had made of it. He spoke hesitatingly and with embarrassment, fearing to reveal the confidential information which he had obtained as a member of the board of governors.

" But that was very handsomely done, don't you think so ? " Mrs. Castleton queried, when he had finished.

" Yes, especially when you consider what he might have done."

" And considering the way his family have been treated since they came here," the lady remarked thoughtfully.

She sat with her bright face bathed in a warm golden glow as the sunshine filtered through her yellow parasol, and the wind played with a little loose curl above her ear, which had escaped from its confinement. Her daughter, a charming little six-year-old child, came up and whispered something in her ear and clung caressingly about her, as if reluctant to leave. Mrs. Castleton smoothed the child's hair, bestowed a few maternal touches upon her somewhat rumpled attire, told her not to play too roughly, and kissed her cheek as she ran away. It seemed as if her thoughts had suddenly clarified during her occupation with the child, and with her frank eyes fixed upon Fancher she presently continued, as if no interruption had intervened :

"I think perhaps it can be managed. You are their landlord, you know, and it would be only nice of you to introduce yourself to them. I'll take a stroll with you on the lawn; and you may introduce me, as on the spur of the moment."

She arose and took Marston's arm, while Philip sauntered along at a leisurely pace on her other side. They stopped twice on the way to exchange winged platitudes with this one and that one on the subject of the game; and finally, as they drifted, apparently by chance, toward the three lonely ladies, Fancher stepped forward, leaving Mrs. Castleton in Philip's charge, raised his hat to Mrs. Bulkley, and made his little speech.

"Will you permit me to introduce myself to you, Mrs. Bulkley," he began with elaborate courtesy; "I am Mr. Fancher, and have the honor to be your landlord. Unhappily, my mother and sisters are in Europe, otherwise they would have taken pleasure in calling upon you, before this."

"You are very kind, I am sure," Mrs. Bulkley replied, a trifle awed by his appearance and the ponderous propriety of his manner. She had never in her life been addressed with a politeness so finished and deferential; and the novelty of the experience made her, perhaps, for an instant lose her bearings and appear a little awkward. "It is a very nice place you have, Mr. Fancher," she added, anxious to retrieve herself; "such a lovely view of the ocean on moonlight nights. The only thing I don't like about it is those big hedges about the house; for all the bugs in creation seem to collect in them, and make a dash for the lamps the moment you open the windows."

She became aware before she had gone far in this speech that she had struck a wrong tack, but stop she couldn't, and therefore talked on from sheer desperation. Maud, who stood with burning ears and a wildly palpitating heart, listening to the conversation, would have given her mother a nudge, if she had not been afraid of being detected in the act by some of the hundred eyes that were watching them. For this was an intensely dramatic moment; and there was not a person on the piazza of the Casino or on the wide green lawn who was not aware that Fancher had taken the bull by the horns and was braving the wrath of Mrs. Van Horst and the Ladies' Reception Committee. Maud, to be sure, had only the dimmest notion of the complications of the little drama, in which she was presently to take a part, but she had a general idea that a battle of some sort was being fought, and that the issue was trembling in the balance. Sally, who was placid and a trifle obtuse, was scarcely conscious of anything except that her mother was neglecting the opportunity to introduce her; and she managed by ocular telegraphy to send her a message, reminding her of the omission. This was, however, a superfluous precaution; for Mrs. Bulkley was only waiting for the proper moment to effect the introduction; but, somehow, felt a vague *gêne* which made every moment seem equally inappropriate.

" My daughter Miss Bulkley, Mr. Fancher," she

muttered finally, with awkward abruptness; " my daughter Miss Maud, Mr. Fancher."

Fancher again lifted his hat, and executed his admirably severe bow to the two young ladies.

" I believe I have had the pleasure of seeing you before," he began, addressing himself to Maud, whose treacherous blush again threatened to disgrace her ; " if I am not mistaken you are the young lady to whom my friend Mr. Warburton restored a stolen umbrella at Daly's Theatre."

" Oh, yes, to be sure," Maud exclaimed, with hypocritical surprise, as if the incident had long since escaped her mind ; " I was so stunned by the unexpectedness of the thing that I believe I didn't even thank him."

" Then I will afford you the opportunity now," Fancher remarked, turning to Philip and Mrs. Castleton. " Mrs. Castleton, permit me to introduce to you Miss Maud Bulkley. Mr. Warburton—Miss Bulkley."

The other introductions, including Mrs. Bulkley and Miss Sally, were accomplished without the least embarrassment ; and the whole affair was invested with a happy air of fortuity, as if it were entirely due to the prompting of the moment. With half a dozen conventional phrases, permeated with sweet kindliness, Mrs. Castleton put the three ladies at their ease, and in the course of five minutes all their awkwardness and misery evaporated like mists before the sun. There was something in the atmosphere surrounding Mrs. Castleton which made those privileged to breathe it move and speak with a happy freedom. She was so far above that uneasy vanity of small souls which is termed "showing off " that she seemed, on the contrary, only bent upon affording every opportunity to the person with whom she talked of shining at her expense. Never in her life had Maud come in contact with any one who had so completely fascinated her; she could not remove her eyes from Mrs. Castleton's face, and even the robust and genial Warburton was in part eclipsed by the radiant personality of his companion. The way Mrs. Castleton carried herself, the way she held her head, the gentle and exquisite intonations of her voice, the cadence of her laugh, all seemed to Maud's generous enthusiasm stamped with a natural distinction which marked a higher order of creature than any she had hitherto encountered. This was the *grande dame* indeed, who was impressive without effort, distinguished without hauteur, and beautiful without vanity.

Nothing of any consequence was said by any one during that memorable walk over the green lawn of the Casino. But the sky seemed high and serenely radiant above the heads of the two young girls, and the sod soft as velvet beneath their feet. They went into the Casino and drank tea; exchanged civilities with several persons who came up and were introduced; praised the Atterbury climate (which was a sure and easy way to popularity), and manifested a cautious interest, being fearful lest they appear intrusive, in the church on the Dunes, the Village Improvement Society and other Atterbury institutions. At half-past five o'clock their carriage arrived, with due pomp and clatter and rattle of silver harness. It was an extremely handsome and dignified landau, highly *comme il faut* in all its appointments, which moved with a certain stately cumbrousness, as if it belonged to people of consequence. On its dark-green lacquered panels, which looked almost black, was displayed a small coat-of-arms in red and gilt ; and the beautiful, spirited bays which stood prancing before it exhibited in half a dozen places on their harness the same heraldic design in silver.

Having been assisted into this gorgeous vehicle by Fancher and Warburton, Mrs. Bulkley and her daughters drove out through the great wrought-iron gate and swung out upon the highway with becoming *éclat*, and leaned back among their cushions in the happy consciousness of having at last made their entrance into society.

VII

In the course of the next two weeks carriages of all descriptions began to find their way up the wide road, lined with hawthorn, which led up to Thorn Hedge. It was beautiful to see with what good grace they surrendered, all these great ladies, when once a surrender had become the part of prudence, and with what dignified ease they ignored all past unpleasantness. They were cordial, but not too cordial; they never lost, in their readiness to let bygones be bygones, a certain fine reserve, which conveyed the faintest kind of hint, perhaps, that they were not unconscious of the favor they were bestowing. Peleg had to be kept out of the way, of course, during these visits; though Peggy, who stoutly refused to be a party to his concealment, vainly strove to persuade him to invade the drawing-room.

"No, daughter," he would say, with a half-whimsical distress in his face, "I am just as much obliged. But I ain't creditable, don't you see, and your ma would be awfully cut up."

"But it's shameful, father," Peggy would exclaim, generously identifying herself with her abused parent, "to pretend to be other than we are. If we are discreditable, from these people's point of view, why not stay where we belong, then, and associate with people to whom it is natural to think and behave as we do?"

"Ask your ma about that, Peggy," he would reply, fearful of encouraging her disloyal opinions. "I never had much bringin' up of any kind, you know, and I ain't much of an expert on the ways of fine society. I never set myself up as bein' much to brag of in that line. I am a sort of how-do-you-do kind of fellow—that's what I am," he added, with an uneasy laugh, thrusting his hands into his pockets and taking a stroll through the room.

Before the month of August was at an end all Atterbury had called upon the Bulkleys with the exception of Mrs. Van Horst; and it soon became obvious that her failure to find her way to Thorn Hedge was not accidental. It was surmised by many that she had taken offence at Mrs. Castleton's making the acquaintance of the Bulkleys at the Casino without her introduction. The denizens of Atterbury were much too civilized to quarrel— because they knew what an infinite variety of misery can flow from a little social feud of that sort—and Mrs. Van Horst, though she may have harbored a slight resentment against Mrs. Castleton, abated not one whit of her cordiality toward that popular lady when they met on the beach or at afternoon teas. But of the Bulkleys she never spoke; and if any one mentioned them in her presence, she affected an affable indifference, or inquired about them as if she had not been aware of their existence until this moment.

It was curious, on the other hand, what an amount

of interest Mrs. Bulkley and her daughters displayed in Mrs. Van Horst, as the weeks passed without any sign of an overture. She was the one drop of gall in their cup of triumph, and she was in danger of spoiling the whole cup. It seemed odd to them that Mrs. Van Horst, who according to all accounts was of a kindly disposition, and moreover conspicuous in church matters, should wish to inflict a humiliation upon them; and they exhausted themselves in conjectures as to who could have slandered them or by malicious truth-telling prejudiced her against them. They finally built up an ingenious theory, and fixed the responsibility upon a lady in a Western city who was by marriage remotely connected with the Van Horsts, and they promised themselves the satisfaction of some day repaying their debt to her with compound interest. This whole Van Horst business, and the endless, futile, and exasperating discussions which it occasioned, nearly drove Peleg to distraction, and made him take to his heels at the very mention of that dreaded name. He had a very simple and sensible explanation of the affair; but it was for that very reason scouted by his " women folk," who could not content themselves with anything " savoring so of the merchant tailor business," as Mrs. Bulkley was wont to say when she wished to squelch her spouse and make him realize his deficiencies.

Now, the fact was that Peleg was very nearly right. Mrs. Van Horst was not in correspondence with her cousin in the West, and had made no inquiries of her concerning the Bulkleys, nor had her Western cousin (as the ladies surmised) maliciously volunteered information. Mrs. Van Horst, though her disposition was, generally speaking, benevolent, was a lady of severely circumscribed sympathies. She knew very little about the world outside of her own little, favored set, and had an idea that all true refinement and gentility which the city contained were to be found among those who had access to her drawing-room. She had been brought up in a touchingly conceited and exclusive little circle of Knickerbockers, in which the air was luxuriously tempered (all dangerous nineteenth-century draughts being carefully guarded against) and a dignified and self-satisfied stupidity prevailed.

Mrs. Van Horst was, indeed, so great a lady that she could have afforded to know anybody she chose; for the fact that she chose to know a person would have been a sufficient social passport even to exclusive circles. She was entirely above the petty and degrading necessities of those who have to select their acquaintances with diplomatic caution, with a view to furthering their own ambitions. Mrs. Van Horst was so magnificently secure in her own position that she could have been as eccentric as she liked in regard to her social preferences. But the fact was, she was both too conservative and too cautious to make approaches to any one whose antecedents she did not know for at least two generations. She took up artists, singers, and musicians occasionally in a condescending way and made them fashionable in her set, but that implied, of course, no recognition of social equality. She had a notion that very terrible things were constantly happening beyond the precincts of her own delightful coterie, and she was extremely anxious to protect her family from contaminating contact with the vulgarities which she believed to be rife round about her. All the people whom she did not know she desired, on general principles, not to know, and shrank from their overtures as a hothouse-reared sensitive mimosa shrinks from the contact of rude fingers. " Those dreadful people " was her favorite term for the social leaders whose doings she read about in the newspapers, but who could not by any stretch of fancy be identified with the old and dignified New York to which the Van Horsts belonged. It was not so much pride, then, as a kind of vague timidity and inbred conservatism which made her ignore the Bulkleys; and when to this was added a little personal pique at the way Mrs. Castleton had made their acquaintance and introduced them at the club reception, what was at first a mere hazy disinclination to make advances became a settled determination to repel advances.

In the olden time, when humanity had more red corpuscles in its blood than now, such smouldering ill will as existed between the Van Horsts and the Bulkleys would have blazed up in an open feud which would have furnished the author of this veracious narrative with fresh and thrilling incidents. But Peleg, unhappily, was not the sort of man who went about spoiling for a fight, being, as his wife asserted, imbued with a pusillanimous commercial spirit ; and old Mr. Van Horst, who was a great *gourmet*, confined his heroic feats to the dinner-table.

The fact, then, was that people were so distressingly well behaved in Atterbury that nothing of a sensational character happened, and if the horses had been as civilized as their masters nothing of the least consequence would ever have occurred. But, like most rich people, these prosperous dwellers by the sea had a weakness for fast horses, and the Bulkleys had not sojourned long in their neighborhood before they too became infected with the same passion. Maud would give her father no peace until he had commissioned her former riding master to buy her as handsome a mount as he could find in New York or environs, the price, however, not to exceed six hundred dollars; and when, shortly afterward, the professor of equestrianism arrived with a superb black mare of Kentucky breed, the girl's joy knew no bounds. She was in the saddle early and late, exploring the labyrinthine wooded roads about the village, and gave her groom no end of trouble by her reckless riding. The mare, which was named Sultana, was an extremely intelligent beast, but displayed her intelligence in adapting her behavior to the strength and horsemanship of her rider. When the groom or the riding master mounted her, she was gentle and docile as a lamb; but when Maud was on her back, she cut up preposterously, refused to go beyond the gate, and sometimes flung herself about perversely and insisted upon going home whenever the roads parted. Then they had a struggle of five or ten minutes, until the groom was compelled to dismount and lead her for a couple of hundred yards, and perhaps, at Maud's suggestion, give her a cut of the whip at parting. Then Sultana would take to her heels and dash along the road at a breakneck pace, and never slack up until it suited her own convenience. Fortunately she had an easy and beautiful gait, and her dainty feet beat a light three-quarter measure upon the road-bed, which made it a question of nerve rather than horsemanship to keep in the saddle. And Maud, though her heart was in her throat, managed to retain sufficient presence of mind not to lose her grip on the reins.

Now, it was a peculiarity of Atterbury that a new horse (if he was in the least remarkable) attracted a good deal more attention and aroused a good deal more interest than a new human arrival. Sultana did not fail to come in for her share of notoriety, and Maud, incidentally, as Sultana's rider. Fancher, who prided himself on a knowledge of horseflesh which he was far from possessing (he was invariably cheated in his purchases), pronounced the emphatic opinion that that Western girl cut a devilish good figure on horseback; and young Van Horst, who rarely got his eyes sufficiently open to see anything, made the profound observation that her costume came from London. These two facts jointly considered filtered through the community and made a favorable impression. They had, however, nothing to do with the felicity which Maud enjoyed when, one afternoon, she was joined by Philip Warburton, who rode one of Fancher's horses, and, quite *sans cérémonie*, fell into conversation with her and constituted himself her cavalier. He wore a brown riding jacket, saddle-twist trousers of the same color, and a small soft hat. There was something delightfully sunburnt, robust, and manly in his general make-up, which did not fail to impress the inflammable Maud.

"It is against my principles, Miss Bulkley," he said, as he rode up behind her, " to allow a charming young lady on horseback to waste her sweetness on the desert air. As I am just pining for a good companion, won't you accept me for your escort? "

There was a merry twinkle in his eyes as he spoke, and in his manner a certain easy masculine superiority which had not the least resemblance to conceit. The conceited man, though he may be funny, is never humorous; and Philip was too large-hearted a man to be conceited. His was a quietly humorous acceptance of life, with infinite compassion and intelligent sympathy for all forms of human folly, sin, and misery. He laughed readily, but there was something sympathetic in his laughter, something that put an end to restraint and made confidence easy. Maud, who had been told that he rarely condescended to converse with young girls, felt flattered at his offer and managed to murmur something by way of acceptance.

"That's a stunning mare you have got," he observed, after a while.

" Yes," she answered, as if half-addressing Sultana, and patting her on the neck. "She is a dear, bad, naughty beauty, that is what she is, but her temper is capricious. One day she is as gentle and well behaved as a lamb; and the next she leads me a dance over highways and hedges, leaps fences and ditches, and cuts up terribly. Then we generally get home, both of us bathed in perspiration and aching in every joint."

"You ought to thank your stars that you get home at all," Warburton chuckled, as he viewed Sultana's points with the eyes of a connoisseur. They continued to talk horse as they trotted along easily over the smooth road, and at the end of fifteen minutes they were beginning to feel acquainted. Philip mentally pronounced Maud a wholesome girl, and extremely good-looking. The close-fitting riding habit set off her handsome figure, and her freshly glowing face and rich hair above it made a good picture. She showed, moreover, a great appreciation of everything he said; and what man is proof against that insidious flattery? It was not flattery, however, on Maud's part, but the sincerest tribute of admiration. For the very reason that she liked Philip so well, she was disposed to find his remarks cleverer than perhaps they were ; and he, naturally, finding such a sympathetic response, such resonance in her soul for whatever he said, felt tuned up and stimulated to a degree of brilliancy above his everyday level. There came a pause finally, during which they rode hard through a bit of oak forest where the branches hung so low that they had to dodge and stoop in order to keep from being knocked out of the saddle. But that proved a pleasant diversion, too, as, in fact, everything that happened heightened their good humor and their pleasure in each other's society. They were both so steeped in a sense of well-being that they could scarcely conceive of anything being so disagreeable as not to afford a fresh exhilaration.

"How do you like Atterbury, Mr. Warburton?" Maud asked (for with Philip any commonplace might suffice to start an interesting conversation). They were now out of the woods, riding at a moderate pace over a brown moor, with the wind singing in their ears, and the Sound shining like a huge burnished shield on the northern horizon.

"Oh, I like it too well for my own good," he answered thoughtfully. "I am ashamed of liking it so well."

"Ashamed? Why should you be ashamed?"

"Well, it is not easy to explain. I have seen enough of the sterner side of life, Miss Bulkley, to have a sneaking sense of guilt when I am too comfortable. If you could strike the average of human well-being, or rather ill-being, it would fall vastly below the condition of pampered ease and luxury in which we are here wallowing. Pardon the crude phrase; but nothing else will express it. People have here entered into conspiracy to be agreeable, and to ignore all that is not agreeable."

"And you don't like that?" Maud queried with the liveliest wonder. "I only wish people would enter into that sort of conspiracy against me. But where I came from——"

She was going to say that people had entered into a conspiracy to be disagreeable; but, remembering that she was not to refer to that period of her existence, she stopped short, and, giving the mare a sly dig with her heel, had all she could do for five minutes in quieting her.

" You were saying that you didn't like to have people too agreeable," she observed, anxious to resume the conversation, as she finally persuaded Sultana to stop her senseless pirouetting.

" Excuse me. I must have expressed myself very obscurely," Philip rejoined, laughing. " The fact is, I am perpetually struggling with myself, accusing myself of being too fond of the things which I ought to dislike ; of feeling strongly drawn to people whom I ought to disapprove of."

" But why ought you to disapprove of them, pray ? "

" Well, I shall get into deep waters if I tell you that, Miss Bulkley. Don't you think that mare of yours is an unsafe animal for a lady to ride ? "

" No, I thank you. I am not going to let you off like that. Get into your deep waters, sir, and to the best of my ability I'll try to follow you."

" Won't you excuse me, please ? "

" No, no, no," she cried with mock fierceness. " That's the sort of thing I never forgive a man— giving me a glimpse of a delightful topic, and then shirking it on the plea that it is too deep for the feminine intellect."

" I beg your pardon, I didn't say that."

" Well, you meant it, which amounts to the same thing. You were about to give me the reason why

you did not disapprove of Atterbury as you ought
to. Now, wasn't that right?"

" Yes, perfectly, for——"

" For one so shallow. Very well; don't apolo-
gize."

Philip rested an amused glance upon her for a
moment, then gave an abrupt little laugh and exclaimed :

" Upon my word, I never was so abused in all my
life."

" Well, you see there is no escape," cried Maud,
gayly. She was really so eager for his opinions that
she was scarcely conscious of being a trifle inconsid-
erate in her urging.

" Well, nonsense apart," Philip resumed, after a
pause, while a sudden seriousness settled upon his
face, " I frankly confess that I am something of a
√red. I think the world is out of gear, and I can
perfectly well conceive of a civilization far better
than ours, without yet proposing any radical amend-
ment to human nature. It isn't fashionable to hold
such views, I know, and my only dread in expressing them is that my listener shall believe that I hold
them for their picturesqueness—as a striking and
interesting drawing-room effect—which, after all,
does not influence my conduct. That is the reason
I usually keep these things to myself—at least until
the time comes to do something more than talk."

There was to Maud something so wholly unexpected in this ebullition that she scarcely knew what
to say. She had never philosophized concerning
life and its problems; nay, she had never suspected

that to a person who had money enough, and the access to good society, it could present any problems whatever. She knew that some terribly disreputable, shaggy, and wild-faced foreigners came here from Europe and proposed to turn our admirable civilization upside down; but that a gentleman of Warburton's culture and social standing could sympathize with such criminals had never occurred to her as a remote possibility. He detected at a glance that some such idea was passing through her mind; and, smiling half-compassionately, he said :

"There, you see what you have brought down upon yourself by your insistence."

She made no immediate reply, but rode on for some minutes with a thoughtful frown upon her brow. A swarm of mosquitoes (for they were now on the north side of the island, which the mosquitoes are permitted to frequent) were dancing about the heads of the horses, and she tried ineffectually to chase them away with her whip. To the lovers of these brown, windy moors, with the vast blue heavens above and the great ocean spread out on both sides, there is a subtile exhilaration in every breath, and a richness of delight in the contrasting tones of forest, sea, and sky. It was all washed in with a broad, free hand, boldly effective, and yet full of exquisite gradations and semi-tones that ran the whole gamut of color, without a single jar or break. Philip, who was extremely impressionable, never tired of contemplating these splendid stretches of wind-swept air and sea, or of listening to the strange noises of the gale, now like the blare of distant

6

bugles, now like the clattering hoof-beats of aerial chargers, as they frisked and gambolled through space in glorious freedom.

Maud, who (like most women) regarded all things as of minor consequence in comparison with herself, was half-disposed to resent his silence, until she met his eyes, and was struck by their look of deep contentment.   Then she, somehow, forgot that she had meant to be offended, and her old admiration for him reasserted itself, and swept all petty feelings out of sight.

" I should regard it as a great favor, Mr. Warburton," she said quite humbly, " if you would tell me why you think society is so very bad. "

She had struggled so hard to get where she was (though she was well aware that it was not far), that it made her uneasy to hear him disparage the great institution that represented to her the summary of all that is desirable upon earth.   He had, perhaps, a dim notion of what that little note of regret in her voice meant, and he resolved to refrain from shocking her further.   " Have you ever heard of a London experiment known as Toynbee Hall ? " he asked, as she thought with the intention of shirking her question.

" Yes: it's a place in the slums, where young men of good family go to live ; isn't that it ? "

" Yes ; and, do you know, that is to me the most beautiful modern instance of a real desire to help the poor and helpless—to lift the world to a higher level.   It is what I should like to do myself—and what I shall hope some day to do."

" Live in the slums ? "

" Yes."

Maud's astonishment knew no bounds. It appeared that her companion's ambition was diametrically opposed to her own. She aspired to enter the most exclusive society—was, in fact, already at its threshold, peeping through the gates ajar ; while he, who was securely and as she fancied comfortably inside, longed to get out and settle in the slums.

Philip, watching her tell-tale face, which had not yet acquired the mask of well-bred neutrality prescribed by fashion, felt the need of further explanation, and continued pleasantly :

" Did it never strike you that we are here to fight, not to dawdle away our time in pleasant frivolities and interchange of vapid civilities? Here in Atterbury you would be justified in believing that the world is a charming place, where no serious problems exist, where everybody is moderately good, prosperous, and happy ; where fine manners, uprightness in conduct, and admirable restraint of all coarser impulses and desires are not the exception, but the rule. A silent agreement seems to exist to render all the harsh and difficult things of life as smooth and graceful as possible. People live here in a tepid, carefully moderated, hothouse atmosphere, charged with delicious odors, like the young prince in ' Rasselas,' in that secluded valley of Abyssinia, whence all cares and sorrows and pangs and miseries had been scrupulously barred out. And in the end, like the prince, they will begin to hunger for the wholesome stimulus of care, and, as Browning says, ' welcome each rebuff that turns earth's smoothness rough.' A man, to be alive, must be in touch with life ; and here people are too well bred to mention anything which is stern or unpleasant. It jars upon their refined tastes. Scarcely an echo reaches them of the great discordant, tumultuous life, with its passions and cries of distress. Mere good breeding is a poor ideal, after all, for a man to strive for (though incidentally a most admirable one); and that is the standard by which every one is here mercilessly judged. They make their well-bred little speeches, pay their well-bred little compliments, fiddle their well-bred little tunes, while Rome is burning."

"Then you really think it a misfortune to be rich?" she ejaculated, leaning forward and patting the mare's glossy neck.

"Yes, if wealth entails the loss of human sympathies, as in nine cases out of ten it seems to do, I regard it as a misfortune. If it means, as in this country it seems to mean, the loss of vital contact with humanity, the contraction of one's mental and spiritual horizon, a callous insensibility to social wrongs and individual sorrows, a brutal induration in creature comforts and mere animal well-being, the loss of that divine discontent and noble aspiration which alone makes us human—if it means this or any part of it, it is the greatest calamity which can befall a man. And it is because Christ foresaw that these were the natural effects of great wealth, and the security and ease which it engenders, that he declared that it was easier for a camel to pass through the eye of a needle than for a rich man to enter the kingdom of heaven."

" But I have been told that the needle was one of the gates of Jerusalem."

Philip burst into a harsh, sarcastic laugh. "Yes," he said grimly, " that is a fair specimen of the way they pervert even God's word for the comfort of the millionnaire. I presume before long we shall hear that the place where Dives was perspiring so pitifully and crying out to Lazarus was a Turkish bath in Jerusalem, and Abraham's bosom was the name of the frigidarium."

He paused, rather vexed with himself for having again been carried away by his zeal, and glanced half-curiously at Maud to see whether he had not, after all, wasted his eloquence. He could not instantly determine what her attitude was, for there was something exclamatory in her expression, but whether of dissent or approval was not quite clear.

" Pardon me if I have bored you," he said a little ruefully ; " I know this is not a topic which usually interests ladies."

There was no surer way of arousing Maud's attention than by making an imputation against her sex. She was armed *cap-a-pie* with pugnacity where the mental or moral equipment of womankind was concerned.

" I should say it was just the topic to interest women," she flashed ; " and the surest way to interest women in it is—is——"

"To insist that it doesn't concern them," he fin-
nished, laughing.

"Now that is horrid! That is the first remark I
have heard from you which is not worthy of you,"
she exclaimed, with a pout which was delightfully
feminine.

"Well, I was bound to give you a glimpse of my
cloven hoof sooner or later," he retorted lightly;
"and the fact is (do not bristle, please), I have not
so profound a respect for womankind generically and
collectively as I perhaps ought to have. I have an
unbounded admiration for two or three individual
women whom I have the felicity to know, whom I
regard as the noblest results of the human evolu-
tion, so far. But the young girl is to me chiefly a
pictorial object, and, as such, charming; but I can
never fancy myself tied to one for life without a
horrible suspicion lurking in the background that
some day I might want to get rid of her."

"Get rid of her? Why, pray, any more than she
might want to get rid of you?" Maud queried a
little dubiously. She was not quite sure whether
Warburton was fooling, in which case the seriousness of his face was highly misleading.

"I should, of course, accord her the right to re-
taliate," he answered, fixing upon her his quiet eyes,
in which there was a gleam of mischief, "though I
can scarcely imagine how that woman could be
constituted who should be possessed of such a savage impulse toward me. My grievance against the
young American girl is that there is no seriousness
in her—that she is perpetually chaffing—that she

is a pampered and spoiled plaything, who is tre-
mendously impressed with the respect and what not
that is due to her, but has only the vaguest possible
conception that she owes the world anything in
return, or has any duties or obligations toward anybody except her own sweet, wayward, adorable, and
perverse self."

" But in spite of that tremendous indictment,"
Maud replied argumentatively, " the American girl
seems to be greatly in demand all the world over at
present, and particularly in England."

" Yes, because the English aristocrat demands,
above all things, to be amused, and the American
girl is altogether the most amusing specimen of her
gender that has so far been produced.   She is, moreover, vastly cleverer than the English girl, and vastly
prettier, which no man who is not blind as a bat
would think of denying."

He glanced at Maud with an audacious light in his
eyes, as if to verify the allusion; and she betrayed
again the deficiency of her early training by a slight
embarrassment, instead of taking him laughingly to
task as a society damsel would have done.   But to
his masculine sense this little *gaucherie* was by no
means displeasing.   It seemed rather a tribute to
his importance, and had the effect of an uninten-
tional flattery.   A vague tenderness for her, or,
perhaps, a mere kindliness, insinuated itself into his
mind.   As they rode along at a leisurely pace over
a bit of brownish-green salt marsh, where the road
was filled in on an understratum of logs, he began
to note with a lively interest certain lovely " points "

about her which had hitherto failed to impress him.
First, the outline of her head was extremely good,
and her voice had a very sweet cadence. She was
as far removed as possible from the smart and forward Western girl of fiction who glories in outraging
the proprieties. He had been in the habit of divid-
ing women into two classes; viz., the vain, petty,
frivolous kind, who can never quite get away from
their preoccupation with their own selves, and the
generous, large-minded kind, with whom discussion
is possible, because they are capable of soaring above
millinery and personalities, and of viewing the world
from other than the personal angle. Philip was much
relieved at being able to include Maud definitely in
the latter class; and from the moment he had settled that, his idea of her gained a refreshing distinctness, and his fancy added a number of pretty touches
which belonged to the character he had given her.

At this point, Sultana, for some reason, objected
to the turn the conversation had taken, and, as the
road forked, made up her mind to go home. She
shook her head with a very human disgust, when a
sharp pull at the curb rein interfered with her purpose ; but with true feminine persistence stuck to
her point, refusing to take the right road as long as
there remained the remotest chance of her being
allowed to take the wrong one. Maud displayed
both good-temper and good horsemanship by the
way she managed her ; but becoming at last exas-
perated at the mare's perversity, she asked Philip to
give her a cut of his whip across the haunches.

"If you'll excuse me, I'd rather not do it," he

replied. " It is bad policy for any one to strike a horse except its rider."

" Very well ; then I'll do the best I can myself," Maud observed, with a flushed air of resolution ; and with all the force of her arm she brought down her whiplash upon Sultana's tender flanks.

"That will teach you manners," she would have said if she had had a chance to finish ; but Sultana, who resented this way of being taught manners, made a bound into the air which came dangerously near unseating her rider, and then repeated her old experiment of running at a desperate speed as long as her wind and her resentment lasted. To Philip, it looked very much as if the mare were running away, and he spurred up his own horse to overtake her. But, ignominious though it was to be left behind, he had to reconcile himself to his fate and watch with his heart in his throat the constantly diminishing figure of his companion, as she darted away through sunshine and shadow, and yet contrived somehow to keep in the saddle. At a turn of the road, where it leads down to the Glenarvon beach, he lost sight of her ; and it was five minutes, at least, before she rejoiced his heart by appearing, sound and whole, seated in the saddle, patting the dripping mare and speaking soothingly to her. The white beach glittered in the sunshine, and the dimpled surface of the Sound was so dazzlingly bright that it made the eyes ache to look upon it.

" It was a great pity you let her run away," Philip began at random, as with a sigh of relief he satisfied himself that Maud was unharmed.

"Run away? Why, not at all. She didn t run away," Maud retorted, with a kind of brazen brightness.

"Then I'd like to know what she did?" Philip ejaculated, with an incredulous laugh.

"Why, we just had a little spin; that was all."

She appealed to him with a guileless sweetness which made it seem brutal to disagree.

"All right! It doesn't matter to me what you call it," he observed, with perhaps the faintest touch of vexation; "but, please, don't do it again."

It seemed heartless of her to treat thus his evident anxiety, for which, from her point of view, there appeared to have been no cause; and he could not help feeling a trifle foolish at having needlessly wrought himself into such a state of agitation. He was far from suspecting that she had been, nay, was yet, in a state of inward tremulousness (which her looks utterly belied), and that the least bit of sympathy would have completely unnerved her. Her bright and beautiful mendacity was simply a defensive armor which covered a wildly palpitating heart.

Philip, a trifle disillusionized, but anxious to be helpful, dismounted and tied his horse to the door of one of the bath-houses, whereupon he unbuckled his saddle, and with his saddlecloth rubbed the foam from Sultana's neck, flanks, and hind-quarters. Maud protested feebly at first, but knowing well that on a windy day like this the precaution was necessary, she thanked him briefly. The thoroughly efficient manner in which he performed the humble task, and without the least parade of false dignity, impressed her most agreeably. Sultana seemed to appreciate his attentions, and gave a low, friendly neighing when he had finished. Then he swung himself into the saddle again, and struggling through the deep sand, in which the horses sank down to the fetlocks, they reached the road and started homeward. Their relation had somehow assumed an entirely different complexion since this stupid incident, and they lapsed easily into commonplaces, speaking to each other, as it were, through an invisible wall. And all this time a doubt was tormenting him whether he had, after all, classed her aright.

VIII

THE ride with Philip left an undertone of agitation in Maud's mind which her studiously placid exterior was far from betraying, and the only one who was sharp-sighted enough to discover symptoms of perturbation in her was Peggy. The elder sister, who had always freely confessed to the younger all the vagaries of her wayward heart, and knew what interpretation to put upon her sympathetic and good-natured banter, felt, this time, no impulse to be confidential. They had always got a good deal of " fun " out of life together, and nothing ever happened, whether grave or gay, from which they did not extract considerable amusement. Peggy, who had a turn for comedy and a great fund of shrewd common sense, burlesqued the absurdities of their visitors; and Maud, whose risibles were easily moved, laughed until her sides ached at Peggy's inimitable mimicry. If they were sometimes merciless in detecting and exposing ludicrous traits, there was no malice in their satire, but rather a mere bubbling over of youthful spirits. Peggy was endowed with such a keen sense of humor that she could no more have repressed her tendency to satirize than she could have suspended her breathing. It is, however, not improbable that a sort of outlawed feeling which they had in Atterbury—a sense of being merely tolerated by the exclusive society at whose gates they had so long been knocking—gave zest to their habit of caricature, and made everything fair game that fell into the clutches of their freebooting fancy. No one would have suspected, from the extreme propriety of demeanor which these damsels observed in the parlor (though Peggy, to be sure, was even there subject to occasional lapses), the mad pranks which they played upon each other, or the uproarious fun in which they were capable of indulging. Sally, of course, never participated in any of these undignified performances, and often reproved her sisters, declaring that she was ashamed of them, and threatening dire disclosures. But as she never carried out these threats, and, moreover, was too much occupied with her own health to do anything that might cause worry or annoyance, Maud and Peggy were only drawn into a closer companionship by her august disapproval.

It was no wonder, therefore, that Peggy, in the present case, resented Maud's reticence. Having never had any serious *affaire de cœur* of her own, and believing herself incapable of any sort of tender sentiment toward the male sex, she regarded her sister's behavior as enigmatical if not impertinent and intentionally provoking. She felt a right of proprietorship in Maud's secrets, established by long and undisputed tenure; and she could not comprehend what perverse spirit had possessed the usually communicative and amiable girl, who, by the redundance of her sentimental experience, had hitherto absolved Peggy from the necessity of having any of her own. She tried to tease her, insinuating that Mr. Warburton had proposed to her, or that she had proposed to Mr. Warburton and been refused. She invented outrageous fictions with a charming air of bravado, and exhausted herself in teasing innuendoes intended to surprise or provoke her sister into confession. But Maud, though she was not on her guard against such surprises, was so absorbed in her own emotions as to appear callous. She would scarcely have been moved by an accusation of murder. Her condition was, even to herself, so enigmatical that she made no attempt to account for it. Why had this man invaded her life in this ruthless fashion; and what strange quality was there in his looks, his speech, and his manner which set her heart in such tremulous commotion? She had known handsomer men—perhaps even men who had impressed her as being cleverer—but she had, in her limited experience, never before met a man who paid her the compliment of revealing his real self to her by conversing with her as he would with an intellectual equal. The perpetual chaffing which passes for conversation between men and women had never been congenial to her, but she had never known until now that anything better existed.

It was during the last week of July. Philip's vacation (as Maud well knew) was nearing its end. She grew extremely restless, and the thought seemed unendurable to her that he should actually be going away without making an attempt to see her. The humiliating inference (from which there seemed no escape) that he had made a deeper impression upon her than she upon him haunted her with a torturing persistence. The only way she could soothe this feverish activity of thought was by physical exercise. She had a dim idea that she could run away from the tormenting suggestions that drove her blood to her cheeks, and made her heart beat at an alarming tempo.

The beach, with its perpetually changing vistas of sea and sky, drew her at such times with a strong attraction ; and she walked mile upon mile over the white stretches of sand (in which her small, high-heeled shoes made the absurdest tracks) without having the least notion of the distance she had traversed. The fresh wind, which tumbled with such glorious freedom and wanton abandon over the wide expanse of grayish-blue water, presented an obstacle to be overcome, and she set her head against it and fought with it until she half forgot her distress in the zeal of her pugnacity. It was on one of these promenades along the beach that she stumbled upon a small hut, scarcely big enough for a man to stand upright in, surrounded by clothes lines from which depended a variety of linen habiliments of male and female persuasion. A high-keyed, wind-tossed voice, with a note of indescribably wild gayety, seemed to rise from somewhere in the beach grass ; and the words, constantly repeated, which Maud presently distinguished were these :

> "Oh, you bet,
> I'm a pet,
> And my name is Olivette !"

There was a mellow rotundity—a sort of muffled flute note—in the quality of the voice, which was distinctly agreeable; and Maud paused curiously, looking up and down the dune to discover the singer. But there was no human being in sight. A bare, wind-swept solitude, inhabited only by seagulls and sandpipers, stretched before her up and down the beach. Except for the smoke which every now and then rose from the chimney, she would have judged that the hut had been abandoned.

It lay snugly sheltered in a hollow of the dune; and the sand, which blew in a continual drizzle over the roof, had half buried it on the windward side. The host of fluttering garments, inflated by the breeze into a semblance of human anatomy, further obliterated it from view, affording only now and then a glimpse of a battered cabin door (which had obviously been taken from a wreck) and the white-washed, mud-plastered chimney. The monotonous strain :

> " Oh, you bet,
> I'm a pet,
> And my name is Olivette ! "

was now coming nearer and seemed to proceed from some one hidden among the flapping garments. Suddenly a great gust of wind came rushing up the dune and turned the whole mimic anatomy upside down. Then the song stopped and Maud found herself face to face with a comely young mulatto woman who stood grinning at her with friendly familiarity. The girl, truth to tell, was so startled at the sight of her that she had to catch her breath.

"How-de-do, miss?" said the mulatto woman, stretching out her plump brown hand. "You doan' know me, but I know you, Miss Bulkley, you bet yer life. I do yer washin', I do. My husban' he's a white man, miss; no white trash neither, but a gemman, a real white gemman. He b'long to de bontons—he do, Miss Bulkley. My husban' he make no big show heah, but he b'long to de bontons all de same. You know him, miss; he's de gemman whut ketches de fish and lobsters as I sell to yer maw."

Maud remembered distinctly a rather good-looking man of twenty-five or thirty, with a weakish face and a remnant of gentlemanly bearing, who was in the habit of lounging in the neighborhood, and was usually followed by a boy carrying a basket of fish.

"Oh, yes," she said, "I remember him; he is a foreigner, I think."

"Jesso. He b'long to de nobility, mam; no end ob high nobs—kings and chukes and things—in his fambly. He's a lawd, miss, dat's whut he is—Lawd Edward Percy Malcolm McGregor Middleford. But he don't kyeer ter say nuthin' about it—an' so he call hisself only Mistah McGregor. His paw—he's a chuke, his paw is—he send him to Sou' Ca'lina and give him a big plantation. He's a eddicated gemman, Mistah McGregor is. But he got ter drinkin' an' gamblin'; an' he kep' a race-track on his place. An' dat's whut finished him. Dey swindled him out ob his eyes—dat's whut dey did—dem white folks did. An' he, like a goose—he didn't suspicion whut kind o' friends he was a-keepin'."

" Ah, indeed," Maud answered vaguely, having made a pretence of listening. " Would you allow me to sit down a minute and rest ?   I find I am quite tired."

" Bress yer heart, honey, whar's my manners!   I was jest gwine ter offer you a chayah, but I ain't got no sense when I am flustered.   I knowed you was a bonton befo' I sawed you.   I tole Mistah McGregor so.   Mistah McGregor, he's my husban', ye know. He's eddicated, he is.   He's got heaps an' heaps ob larnin'.   He got inter trouble wid his paw, in de ole kentry."

" How could you know I was a bonton, as you say, before you saw me ?" Maud asked, smiling.

" By yer und'clo's, miss, I knowed it fo' sho'."

" By my underclothes ?"

" Yas.   Dem sham ladies, dey's allers mighty fine an' 'spensive on de outside, miss, jes' like a rooster, but und'neath dey's all cheap cott'n an' sham.   But yo's not dat way, miss."

She made no sign to bring her visitor the promised chair (as Maud soon discovered, because she had none), but talked on with a joyous and guileless glibness, never waiting for an answer, and bursting every now and then into the peculiarly stertorous negro laugh, whenever anything amusing occurred to her.   Maud saw nothing particularly funny in the reminiscences that provoked her mirth; nay, was inclined to find some of them very sad.   She referred quite incidentally to her husband's drunkenness (which she seemed to regard as a disease that in nowise ought to lessen any one's esteem for him), and she declared in the most cheerful way that they could not keep any crockery or furniture, because he always smashed it when he got drunk. She returned again and again to the statement that he was a bonton (she pronounced the word exactly as it is spelled, with no attempt at French nasals), and with a childish glee gloried in his undoubted gentility.

"But don't you sometimes get very lonely here?" Maud asked, in order to show her sympathy. "I don't suppose you find many of your own people here to associate with?"

The "bonton's" wife, instead of answering, rose abruptly, shook her apron, and, assuming a defiant attitude, stared at Maud with a face full of indignation and disgust.

"People? Hum! I doan' 'sociate wid niggahs, mam," she burst out, with scornful emphasis. "I doan' like pore folks—I doan' like 'em! Mistah McGregor, mam, he wouldn't let me run about with niggahs. No, mam, he wouldn't. I wouldn't disgrace him, mam, he bein' a bonton; and his paw— he's a chuke, and he'd git awful mad ef he heared I was a-runnin' wid niggahs."

She continued pouring out a stream of indignant protestation for fully five minutes, and Maud, fancying that she had by her unfortunate remark cut herself off from further confidence, rose from the ground, where she had been sitting, and moved up the slope of the dune. She had hardly taken three steps, however, when her hostess caught up with her, and with a face beaming with good-nature urged her again to be seated.

" Why, bress yer heart, honey," she began, in her most cajoling tones, "doan' you go! Doan' you git mad, honey! I doan' mean nuthin' at all; I's jes' got a almighty 'tankerous tongue, and it jes' gits the 'vantage o' me and runs on onbeknownst to me, a-sayin' things as'll git me inter de pentenchury fo' sho' befo' I die. Doan' you mind me, Miss Maud; I ain't no great shakes. My maw—she was a slave, my maw was—she had her tongue burned mighty nigh clean off fer tellin' a lie. Dat's what my maw did."

She now went on slandering herself and adducing a multitude of circumstances that were to her discredit, with the same fluent and joyous glibness with which she had recently bragged of her husband's grandeur. Maud, feeling vaguely sorry for her, and having no genius for rebuffing any one, however burdensome, asked her in a random way where her husband was.

" My husban'? Mistah McGregor, you mean? Why, he jes' runned down to Mistah Fancher fer ter git some terbaccy and things. Mistah Wa'burton—Mistah Fancher's friend—yo' know him, miss, doan' you?" (Here Mrs. McGregor gave Maud an excruciatingly sly wink, as if to hint that her acquaintance with Mr. Warburton was of a peculiarly tender sort.) "Wal, now, he tuck a monst'ous shine ter my husban'—to Mistah McGregor, dat is—he's jes' monst'ous fond o' him, miss."

" Do you mean to say," Maud inquired, with suddenly awakened interest, " that your husband associates with Mr. Warburton? "

" Ya-as, dat's jes' whut I say. Mistah Wa'burton, he have natchel good feelin's, he have. He's a gemman from de crown ob his head ter de sole ob his feet—dat's whut Mistah Wa'burton is, mam. He ain't no pore ign'nt creeter, like dem stingy willagers dat ain't wuff deir wittels. He know a gemman when he see one, Mistah Wa'burton do, mam, and dat's why he's so monst'ous fond of Mistah McGregor."

Maud took this statement with a large grain of salt, but for all that it furnished food for speculation. She could scarcely believe that Philip had sought to attract the drunken Mr. McGregor for the charm of his society, and she swiftly divined that he must have taken him in hand in the hope of reforming him. The new view of his character which this suggested opened vistas beyond, where no end of conjectural perfections might dwell. So eager was she for everything connected with Philip that she had no sooner secured it than she longed to be alone, so that she might weigh it, contemplate it from all sides, rejoice in it, as a miser does in a newly acquired gold piece. She took leave somewhat abruptly of her garrulous hostess, and, setting her forehead once more against the wind, walked along the top of the dune toward a little inlet of Cockroach Bay, where the Atterbury Yacht Club have put up a temporary boat shed and intend in time to build a sumptuous clubhouse. There were two catboats lying at the pier, one with flapping sails, but the place seemed otherwise deserted. The wind was increasing in strength every minute, and strained her fluttering skirts over her limbs with such force that she had to stand still, being unable to move an inch. It seemed, on the whole, preferable to take a short cut home along the Tinker's Lane and the empty lots, and with this purpose she ran down the dune and struck the path that led up to the boat shed. Being by that time quite out of breath, she seated herself on a pile of boards that lay on the sheltered side of the boat-house, and became presently aware that some one was talking inside, and that the voice belonged unmistakably to the man who was rarely absent from her thoughts.

"It isn't the question of the money, McGregor," Maud heard him say. "I would just as soon make you a present of that boat. But I want to educate you to a sense of financial responsibility. You will never learn to hold your head up and feel like an honorable man until you have learned to be ashamed of receiving what you have not earned. When you can give me proof that you have kept sober for three months, without a single relapse, I'll get you employment in the city, and I'll do all I can to put you on your legs again. But don't try to deceive me, McGregor. If you lie to me again, I swear I'll throw you off and never stir to pick you up, if you lay in the gutter at my feet."

"But that nigger girl," a whimpering voice objected; "how can I ever get into the company of gentlemen again, as long as I am married to a nigger, don't you know?"

"Shame on you, McGregor, shame on you!" the first voice exclaimed, with indignant scorn.

"Where would you have been to-day if she hadn't taken pity on you?"

"Dead, probably. But what a fool I was, all the same, to marry her. But tell me now, old fellow, is a ceremony performed by a nigger preacher legally binding where one of the parties is white?"

There was a silence of fully half a minute, followed by a bang, as if something had been hurled against the wall.

"Good God! What a contemptible cur you are!" cried Warburton's voice, in a loud explosion of wrath. "Have you, then, no sense of decency, man, not to speak of honor and gratitude? What has that poor misguided creature been doing since she picked you up ill with the yellow fever in New Orleans, but to nurse you, and support you by taking in washing, and putting up with your laziness, ill-temper, and abuse, without a murmur?"

"Yes, I know it. I don't pretend that my conduct is anything to brag of. But then she hasn't been accustomed to anything better. I don't say that—that I'm a particularly grand match, don't you know; but, then, you know—I—I'm a gentleman born, surely—and—and—if you should succeed in putting me on my pegs again, don't you know—I'm not chaffing, old chap, I mean every word of it—won't it be rather—what shall I say—embarrassing to be dragging along a coffee-colored wife in one's train? Wouldn't it be decidedly prejudicial to my social success? For a gentleman of my name and position, don't you fancy, could do a deuced lot better than that in this country—that is, if it's half true what I've been told of the predilection of American heiresses for titled Englishmen."

There was another pause, longer than the first, at the end of which Warburton apparently got up and approached the door. For McGregor, in the tone of one who sees himself deserted, called after him, in a plaintive whimper :

" Now, I say, Mr. Warburton, you won't go back on a fellow like that, will you ? Hold on there—now, I say, you don't know how deuced bad you make me feel. I didn't mean, of course, don't you see—I didn't mean that I wanted to throw her off. I'll do just as you say, Mr. Warburton, only don't go back on a fellow, just when he is trying his best to—to reform, don't you know, and get the better of old habits."

The answer to this outburst came in a tone of calm and not unkindly dismissal. " McGregor," were the words which Maud heard, " you'll be sure to go to the devil, and I don't see but that the shortest road which you would be likely to choose for yourself is preferable to any roundabout road by which I might take you. I never quite measured your baseness and worthlessness until to-day ; and, sorry as I feel for you, I have no choice but to give you up."

" Then you take back your word ? You won't give me the chance ? " inquired McGregor, with a dogged surliness.

" Yes, I'll stand by my promise, though I have no idea that you'll keep yours."

"We shall see. And how about the boat?"

"Oh, I make you a present of it. As long as I thought you worth saving I insisted upon payment, for your own sake, not for mine; but now it doesn't matter."

Maud started up with a guilty blush, as the conversation here abruptly ended, and absent-mindedly hurried down the path toward the beach. She had been too intensely interested to realize that she had been playing the eavesdropper, and now her only desire was to escape undetected. But she had not walked far before she became aware that some one was following her; and, glancing back over her shoulder, she saw Philip's tall figure looming up against the horizon. He was striding along with a rapid, swinging gait, and was now scarcely twenty feet behind her.

"Well," he cried, lifting his hat and smiling pleasantly, "if you want to race with me, I think the odds are against you."

She paused in the middle of the path, and returning his greeting waited for him to come up.

"I appear to be in luck," he said, extending his hand and enclosing hers in its friendly grasp. "I was just debating with myself whether I ought not to pay you a farewell visit this afternoon, and here you kindly solve the question for me."

"If it is a question of 'ought,' Mr. Warburton," Maud replied, with a touch of resentment, "then I am glad if I have taken the decision out of your hands."

He stared at her with dawning surprise; then,

with a frank laugh, and eyes that rested on her with evident pleasure, he replied:

"That was pretty bad, I admit. You'll pardon me, won't you? But I am unaccountable to-day, Miss Maud. I've had no end of unpleasant things to think of—least among which is not the thought of leaving you."

It was the first direct allusion he had made to his liking for her, which had hitherto been purely inferential; and instantly that uncontrollable blush, which had caused her such mortification, swept in a crimson wave over her countenance.

" I am afraid you wouldn't be sorry to leave me, if you knew what I've just been doing," she rejoined, with nervous hilarity. " You know, I have been eavesdropping. I sat down on that pile of boards, and all of a sudden I heard you talk inside to that Mr. McGregor; and it never occurred to me what a contemptible thing I was doing, until I had heard the whole story. It was so thrillingly interesting, that, like the wedding guest, ' I could not choose but hear.' My conscience, if I have any, kept as still as a mouse—didn't make a sound—until there was nothing more to hear. And then I grew so ashamed of myself that I had to run. Now, what do you think of that ? "

She talked with the shrill fluency of an excited canary bird, feeling all the while the strained note in her words, and hurrying on with a desperate determination to overcome it. There is a disadvantage in being in that transitional stage in which Maud was, halfway between the *naïve* and unthink-

ing spontaneity of the rustic and the utter sophisti-
cation of the woman of the world. She had neither
quite the charming coyness of the blushing peasant
maid, on the discovery of love's momentous secret,
nor yet the superb self-possession of the social cam-
paigner, to whom the secret is primarily of commercial or strategic value. But to Philip, who loved
the remnant of unspoiled nature in her, her ready
blush seemed an indication of a simple and affectionate heart; and her obvious embarrassment at
the remotest allusion to sentiment made her doubly
adorable.

" It was an accident which you could not help,"
he said, resting upon her a glance full of admiring tenderness; " and, moreover, nothing was said
which I have any objection to your knowing. That
McGregor is a worthless scamp, and I think this
time I am done with him."

" Didn't he say that he was a titled English-
man ? " Maud inquired, with the zest of her sex for
the romantic.

" Yes ; he is the third son of the Earl of P——,
and is really the Honorable Edward Percy Malcolm
McGregor Middleford."

" But what brought him so low? His wife, I
believe, takes in washing, or goes out to wash by the
day."

" He's a drunken brute, and his family shipped
him over here to get rid of him. He made a scandal in London, some years ago, by cheating at cards,
and he was expelled from the turf for repudiating his
bets. I was a fool to suppose that a decent man

could be made out of such material; but it isn't the first time I have made that mistake, and probably it will not be the last."

They had now reached the end of the pier, where the two catboats lay; and Warburton, with an abrupt change from the tone, half of disgust, half of regret, with which he had related McGregor's history, turned to Maud, and with a challenging light in his eyes exclaimed:

"What do you say, Miss Maud? Have you the courage to intrust your precious life to my seamanship? I've hired this boat for the season, and, as I go back to the city to-morrow, I've got to return it to its owner, who lives at Morton's Cove. McGregor was to have done it for me; but he would be sure to go to the bottom in such a gale as this."

He pulled in the boat, jumped into it, and taking hold of the sheet, which was writhing and coiling in the bottom like a snake, he cried against the wind:

"I was only joking, Miss Maud. This isn't weather for women to be out in. But you'll forgive me, won't you, for not offering you my escort? If you'll permit me, I'll call upon you to-night."

"Then you don't want me!" Maud shouted back, somewhat piqued. There was a latent rebellion in her heart which made her always yearn to do what she was dared to do.

"Want you? Of course, I want you. But you'll get a trifle wet. And, honestly, I'd advise you to stay at home. It's blowing up pretty lively."

He had scarcely finished the last remark before the girl made a leap from the pier, and he had

just time to catch her in his arms when the boat
gave a lurch and came within an ace of upsetting.
It shipped a little water on the leeward side, but
not enough to call for any bailing. Philip seized
the tiller and swung the boom about; the flapping
sail snapped and banged like the cracking of pistol
shots, then suddenly bulged out. and the boat flew
with splendid speed down the inlet and out into the
open bay. Maud was sitting on the forward thwart
with a half-anxious smile about her lips, as if she
was not sure whether she ought to be delighted or
frightened. She kept her eyes steadily on Philip's
face, which was calm, almost stern. He was apparently unconscious of her presence; for his eyes
watched with a strained look the water, the sail, and
the horizon, and she fancied she detected a vague
uneasiness in their expression.

" You don't think there's any danger, do you, Mr.
Warburton?" she asked, with a little nervous laugh
which did not sound at all merry.

" No—not yet," he answered laconically.

At that moment the boat careened heavily, and
a shower of salt spray dashed over the bow and
drenched her. She gave a little shriek, and was
on the point of flinging herself over to leeward.

" Steady there!" Philip commanded, in a voice
which made her jump. She had never in her life
been addressed in such a tone by any gentleman.

" Heads down!" he called out presently, and
scarcely had she time to duck her head before the
boom swept away over her with a flap and a whin-
ing creak; the boat gave a lurch and careened to

starboard, while the spray again dashed into her face. She did not realize as yet that there might be danger, simply because her astonishment at Warburton's manner absorbed her to the exclusion of everything else. The sternness, if not pointed indifference, of his address dealt her self-esteem a poignant wound; and she scarcely knew that she was drenched to the skin, because her indignation at his lack of courtesy kept her warm. It must be borne in mind that she was a landlubber, born and bred, and had never been in a sailboat except in a light breeze on Lake Michigan.

"You must be wet," he observed, after a while, rummaging with one hand in a lock-up under his seat; "here is a blanket which may keep you from catching cold."

He spoke in a much gentler tone now, and there was a very kindly light in his eyes as he tossed her the blanket.

"I don't think I shall need it," she replied perversely, as it fell in her lap; "I am not at all cold."

"But you will be presently. Better put in on. Or, if you prefer oilclothes, they are at your service."

He thrust his disengaged arm once more into the mysterious locker and flung out a sou'wester and a complete suit of yellow oilclothes. He seemed to avoid looking at her as he did so, but scanned the horizon with the same strained, frowning glance. She looked herself in the same direction and saw a broad, black track spreading over the water and sweeping toward them.

"Oh, what is it?" she screamed, with a thrill of panic.

"A squall," he replied. "Look out! Don't let the oilclothes go overboard!"

The boat was now scudding along at an arrowy speed, with a surging gurgle of the water about the bow, and seething and foaming eddies in its wake. There was a glorious sense of exhilaration in this furious motion; and the waves, as they hurled themselves against the bow with a tremendous splash and then whirled away with a hissing swish, imparted an anticipatory tension to the nerves, which yielded, as soon as the shock was over, to a pleased sense of relief. Maud, where she sat, felt every thud, and every now and then, as they shot up into the wind, received a fresh shower-bath.

"Better put on the oilclothes," Philip urged, with a sort of impersonal kindness.

"But I shall look so perfectly ridiculous."

"Never mind that. I was going to say that I won't look at you; but, on second thought, I know I should succumb to the temptation."

There was a gravity in his manner, as he uttered these apparently frivolous words, which seemed to invest them with a portentous meaning. Rather to escape from a vague embarrassment than because she felt the need of them, she began to busy herself with the oilclothes, and in a spirit of adventure pulled on the yellow coat and buttoned the enormous horn buttons across her breast.

"The hat, too," he cried admiringly; "it'll be very becoming."

She picked up the sou'wester, fixed it coquettishly on her head, wrong side foremost, and tied it under her chin.

"Bravo!" he shouted. "What a lovely sailor! I assure you, you look bewitching."

The wind, though blowing a stiff gale, had kept pretty steady so far, and the threatened squall had taken a turn southward, so that they were able to steer clear of it. But they now approached a long, sandy headland, at the end of which stands the Cockroach lighthouse. Here the tide is apt to run with great vehemence, and there are, moreover, shoals that have a deceptive, blackish-green look, as if there were fathoms of water. There was a menacing dark-cerulean tone in the air to the north and west, and, though the sun shone in fitful and uncertain gleams, the sky was full of ominous signs which it was well for Maud that she did not understand. Her companion's gallantry and the undisguised admiration in his glance had chased away her ill-humor and tuned her into a mood of exalted well-being. She was eager to continue the conversation in the same vein, and her absurd nautical costume gave her a delightful sense of irresponsibility and adventurous bravado. But as she was leaning forward, waiting for Philip's next remark, she was struck with a curious change in his face. There came a set and fiercely determined look about his mouth, and his eyes again scanned the horizon with a grave and strained intentness. There was nothing in his expression that directly indicated anxiety; but she fancied that it was only by the tremendous strength of his will that he kept his muscles in such sedulous placidity. Following the direction of his eyes, she saw the northern sky suddenly darkening, and black, slanting lines, as of an approaching storm, sweeping down upon them.

"Do you know how to reef a sail?" cried Warburton, in ringing tones that rose above the wind.

"No."

"Then come here quick, and hold the tiller."

Rudely awakened from her revery she rose, and, in response to his command, tumbled aft, grabbing him by the shoulder to keep from falling.

"Hold this, too, and as steady as you can," he said more quietly, handing her the sheet and putting her disengaged hand on the tiller; "and don't you budge."

Jumping up, he began with marvellous despatch to reef the sail, but had only secured three reef points when some heavy raindrops dashed into his face, and with splendid uproar of lashed waters and foam-crested waves, the squall bore down upon them. He stood his ground for another minute and tied another reef-point; then, as a tremendous whitecap broke over the bow and made the inside bottom float, he grabbed sheet and tiller again, and sent the boat flying up into the wind.

"Can you bail?" he asked Maud, with a breathless composure, flinging her a tin basin which he hauled out from the locker under the seat.

"I'll try," she answered bravely.

She stooped down, trying to scoop up the water;

8

but the floating bottom slipped under her feet, and
made it impossible to bail.

" Never mind," he said ; " perhaps we shall make
it yet ! "

She seated herself, with a queer sense of helpless-
ness, on the forward thwart, while the rain poured
down upon her in torrents and drummed on her
sou'wester and oilcoat with a gusty hum, as on a
tin roof. All the fear which had taken possession
of her, when the danger was yet remote, had left
her ; and she sat pale and calm, with the water
streaming down her face, gazing at Warburton,
who, with his teeth set and a frowning vigilance,
watched the sea and the sky, and steered the boat
with steady eye to every whim of the wind. He
seemed to Maud the very embodiment of manly
vigor and beauty, as he sat there, so calm and
secure, while his own life and hers were trembling
in the balance. He looked so strong and lithe and
masculine, with his fine, serious face, robust frame,
and the loose-fitting nautical shirt and trousers enveloping his sinewy limbs. There was something
conspicuous and naturally eminent about him which
impressed his most trifling word and act with the
stamp of his personality. She vaguely marvelled
at herself, as she sat thus absorbed in Philip ; for
she had never dreamed that she could feel so light
and free in the presence of a danger which, however, she could not bring herself to realize. For
Philip inspired her with a confidence which rose
superior to winds and waves in stormy commotion.
There was something stern and masterful in his

glance which would make it a luxury to obey him. With most men it seemed a perfectly farcical proposition when, in the marriage service, you were requested to obey them. The stronger personality, regardless of sex, was bound to subordinate the weaker, and no promises could avail. But Philip could justly demand obedience ; for, wedded to any womanly woman, he would necessarily be the dominant partner.

"Heads down!" came the command again, and this time with a rousing clarion note which put all reveries to flight. With a creaking groan which sounded half like a shriek the boom flew away over her stooping form, and the shortened sail, as the wind caught it, made the boat bound away over the surging sea, plunging its nose into the next billow, so that the spray spurted high over the gunwale and lashed her crouching back.

At that moment a scraping sound was heard under the keel, and the boat's motion was retarded.

"Pull out the reefs!" yelled Philip, rising in his seat and straining with all his might to reach the nearest reef-point, which he pulled out. His example rather than his words made her comprehend what she was to do; and in the next instant the sail flew to the top of the mast, the boat was fairly lifted out of the water, and it scudded along like an animated thing in a cloud of flying spray. For two minutes she sat blind and stunned, clinging to the thwart, hearing only the "swish, swish" of the spray and the beating of the rain on her back. Then, as by a miracle, all was changed, and when her vision cleared she saw the headland far astern and smooth water round about her.

" Please take the tiller," said Philip, very quietly; " she is drawing too much water."

Lifting up the inside bottom, he seized the basin and began to bail. Though she possessed no nautical knowledge even of a rudimentary sort, she was dimly aware that if it had not been for his quick resolution and skill they would both have been lost. She fancied herself being carried out into the Atlantic by the resistless tide, and she saw the sharks coming toward her through the transparent water, and with a hideous greed tearing her to pieces. Somehow she felt as if she had known Philip for years. She could not imagine a time when she had not known him, and she found it difficult to realize what her life could have been without him. This stirring experience had established a bond between them which nothing could break.

The rain had now almost ceased, and the sun broke through the cloud-rack and shone with a tearful brightness upon the brown, sloping shores of Cockroach Bay. The long stretches of blooming heather gleamed and twinkled with myriad raindrops, and a large, splendid rainbow spanned the horizon from north to south.

Having finished bailing, Philip took his seat at her side, relieved her of the tiller, and with a deft tack ran the boat into Morton's Cove, where the owner presently came to receive it. Then he hurried Maud up to the Cockroach inn, which is a highly æsthetical Queen Anne edifice, surrounded by half a dozen more or less pretentious cottages of similar style. Here they found that the guests had been watching them excitedly through telescopes and opera-glasses, and offered odds on their chances of reaching shore. Maud was taken in charge by half a dozen ladies, supplied with clothes enough to dress a regiment of Amazons, and smothered in kindness. She could not help feeling a trifle heroic, of course, but she exerted herself honestly to give Philip the credit for whatever heroism there had been displayed. The ladies, however, would not listen to any other version of the story than their own; and they persisted, in spite of her deprecations, in attributing to her a gallantry, resolution, and cool audacity which cast Philip entirely into the shade. Maud was, at length, so bewildered at their conflicting accounts of what they had seen that even her own recollection became confused and she found it difficult to distinguish between fact and fiction. She was glad when Philip informed her that he had secured a horse and buckboard, which were now waiting at the door. So she took leave of the hospitable ladies (of whose garments she had made an equitable selection, so as to offend none), and, mounting the buckboard, she drove off in the gayest of spirits, and reached Thorn Hedge in time for dinner.

IX

PHILIP made his farewell visit upon Mrs. Castleton that same night, and found her at the piano, counting one, two, three—four, five, six, for the benefit of her fourteen-year-old daughter Mildred. The girl, who loathed practising, was delighted at his arrival. She kissed her mother with a girlish effusion which was but an expression of her sense of relief from the odious task, and she came near kissing Philip, too, but caught herself just in time to remember that perhaps it wouldn't be proper. Her mother patted her cheek and laughed at her affectionate *gaucherie ;* and Philip caught her in his arms as she was about to escape, and after a mock quarrel and a little romp stole a kiss on her cheek as he released her. She ran out of the room, blushing like a peony, but proud, happy, and bashful, with all the violent feelings of fourteen in joyous commotion.

Mrs. Castleton's parlor consisted of a huge chimney and fireplace made of rough granite, around which a number of low, cushioned rattan chairs of a variety of shapes were scattered. The room was finished in light and dark ash, exhibiting the tints and texture of the wood ; and a broad, magnificent staircase, easy of ascent, led with indolent windings to the second floor. There was something spacious and hospitable about the room which impressed you as an audible welcome. A certain rich and home-like cosiness invited you to linger and made it difficult to depart. Books in choice bindings were to be seen on tables and chairs, and there was an indefinable air of refinement and good taste about everything which the house contained. The hostess, who was the presiding genius of this lovely home, had a native grace and dignity in her bearing which put every one at his ease in her presence. She appeared always to Philip as an illustration of how enormous a woman's opportunities are in our American life, if she has the wit and the gift to avail herself of them. This whole household revolved visibly about Mrs. Castleton, and was animated by her genial contentment and governed by her wise, firm, and affectionate spirit. How could these children, born of such a mother, guided and fashioned by her loving supervision, fail to become noble men and women, and in turn the centres of similar homes, radiating blessings upon all those who in future shall spring from them, or come within the sphere of their beneficent influence? How infinitely wide and ramified is, therefore, the influence of one good and high-minded woman, who takes a lofty view of her calling! And how much poorer would, in turn, our land be for the loss of one such life, or its failure to seize and make the most of the golden opportunities which God has put in its way!

Reflections of this character always invaded

Philip's mind whenever he entered Mrs. Castleton's house.

"I see you have something on your mind, Mr. Warburton," the lady observed, as soon as the child had ascended the stairs.

"You know I am going back to the city to-morrow," Philip replied; "and you surely would not expect me to be hilarious with the chance of not seeing you for three months."

"Ah, that is very nice, but not strictly true. You have something else you want to confide to me. Your face is so transparent that it is useless for you to try to wear a mask."

"Why shatter my armor of self-esteem in this ruthless manner, Mrs. Castleton?" the young man exclaimed, with his good-humored laugh. "However, it is only to your subtile insight I appear transparent. Ordinarily, I fancy I can be as successfully hypocritical as any woman."

A few minutes of this preliminary banter, which was like a light prelude to a grave theme, sufficed to bring their minds into tune before the note of confidence was struck. It was a peculiarity of Mrs. Castleton that she could jest without being frivolous; for a certain rich undertone of individuality gave resonance and color to her lightest remark, and, moreover, the lovely amplitude of her person, both physical and mental, which paused on this side of redundance, was like a beautiful accompaniment which nobly interprets the text, imparting to it a genial glow and afflatus.

"And then you are going to return to your

malodorous chemicals and ledgers," Mrs. Castleton was saying. " I should think the transition would be cruelly abrupt after your month of delightful idling here in Atterbury."

" Oh, yes, I shall not find it pleasant. But then I am so made that martyrdom has a certain attraction to me. An unpleasant task is a wholesome, bitter tonic which my disguised Scotch-Presbyterian self requires to keep up its self-respect. There is a hereditary strain in me which has a subtile relish for the disagreeable. If the sun were shining warmly on one side of the house, and a sharp north wind were blowing on the other, I verily believe that this foul-weather strain in me would make me prefer to sit down in the blast."

" But if you are such a foul-weather Jack," Mrs. Castleton remarked, with mischief in her eyes, " you ought not to take young ladies with you when you go sailing."

"Ah, then you've heard," said Philip, straightening himself up in his chair, and gazing at his hostess with a sort of anticipatory excitement.

" I won't say ' A little bird sang it to me,' for a whole chorus of little birds have been singing nothing else to me, since you returned about six o'clock."

" They must have been female birds."

" Well, some of them were ; but one of them was my neighbor the doctor, who watched you from his piazza through his telescope, and got all the life-saving crew ready to put to sea, and his resuscitating apparatus spread out on the beach."

"I hope you are joking."

"No, my dear sir, I am not joking. You have supplied a long-felt want—a first-class, thrilling sensation; and at the next meeting of the Village Improvement Society, I shall have Mr. Castleton move a vote of thanks to you."

Philip listened with a thoughtful mien to this recital, contemplating all the while the heel of his boot with a lively interest.

"What do you think of her, anyway, Mrs. Castleton?" he asked, lifting his head abruptly and fixing upon his interlocutor a gravely questioning glance.

Mrs. Castleton divined at once how much he had at stake in that question.

"I like her very much," she answered, with simple sincerity; "she has the material in her for a lovely wife and mother."

He was in no haste to reply to this verdict, but sat pondering it, and finding it marvellously satisfactory.

"I am aware that question was not quite fair, Mrs. Castleton," he observed after awhile. "You couldn't help yourself. You knew I was not disinterested."

"Perhaps I did. But if I had not liked the young lady I shouldn't have said so, even at the risk of displeasing you."

Philip again sat silent for a minute or two, nursing his leg, and looking thoughtfully at the wide stretch of tumbling waves which was visible in the dusk through the windows. Mrs. Castleton gave some directions to a maid who entered with a large ornamental lamp, which was placed upon a tall tripod of wrought brass. The shades were drawn, and a fire of driftwood was lighted upon the hearth.

" Tell me what you like about her," demanded Philip, when the maid had vanished behind a *portière.*

" Well," Mrs. Castleton answered with that charming air of candor which made her good opinion a support to the self-respect of every man who possessed it, " I like, first of all, her daring to be herself. I divide people into two classes (with many subdivisions); those who are themselves, and those who are constantly trying to appear what they are not."

" You mean those who talk for effect—who try to show off ? "

" Yes ; and you, being an obtuse masculine creature, can have no idea what a torture that is in a woman's life. Eight women out of every ten you meet are possessed by an uneasy demon who impels them to make jacks of themselves by draping themselves in all sorts of imaginary grandeurs, and talking with a view to impressing you with their social or intellectual or ancestral magnificence. If they succeeded I could pardon them. Their glib and fluent mendacity often arouses my admiration. But the fact is, very few of them are clever enough to carry such a part. They invariably strike a false note in the very opening sentence ; and then the illusion is gone, and it is you who have to play the *rôle* of the admiring and gullible dupe who believes every fairy tale that is told to him."

"I am glad," Philip remarked, with an amused smile in his eyes, "that you don't class Miss Bulkley in that order. I fancy that's what makes her so lovely in my eyes—that she is fundamentally true and free from the quirks and contortions of an uneasy vanity."

"Then I presume you are ready to accept my congratulations," said Mrs. Castleton, cordially.

"No; I was afraid you would jump at that conclusion. The fact is, the infatuation is all on my side. I have no special grounds for believing that Miss Bulkley reciprocates my interest. And with your permission, Mrs. Castleton, that's the reason why I am impelled to impose upon you by my confidence."

She leaned her head on one side as he spoke, and listened with that radiant interest which women usually display in secrets of the heart.

"You make me extremely curious," she said.

"But I shrink from going any farther. I am afraid you will repudiate me and all my works when you hear what I am going to ask you."

"I hope you are not going to ask me to sound Miss Bulkley's heart with reference to its feelings for you."

"No, not as bad as that. I'll undertake that sounding myself, when the proper time comes."

"And pray, then, what am I expected to do?"

"What I want you to do, Mrs. Castleton," Philip began, laughing off a vague embarrassment, "is to keep an eye on Miss Maud; radiate a little of your rare sweetness upon her; and, above all, notify me

if you find anyone hunting, with the remotest
chance of success, upon my pre-empted preserves."

" That is a very delicate task you intrust to me,
Mr. Warburton," his hostess replied, with eyes full
of benign sympathy (for she divined what depth of
feeling was hidden under his jocose words).

" Just because it is a delicate task, I came to you,
Mrs. Castleton ; and I see already in your eyes that
you are not going to refuse me."

" How could I refuse you, Mr. Warburton? No ;
I'll be frank with you. It will afford me the sincerest pleasure if I can be of service to you. I feel
honored by your confidence, and should have felt
a trifle jealous if you had bestowed it upon anybody
but me."

A thrill of satisfaction rippled through Philip's
frame as he listened to this cordial assurance. She
was stanch and true, as always. She was a friend
who never failed. Woman though she was, she
endured every test, and in the decisive moment surpassed all expectations. Why are there so few of
these rich and radiant souls in the world? Why
have the many whom nature has often nobly
equipped been spoiled by some fatal flaw, like a
loose or untuned string in a piano, which produces
a dissonance in every other chord you strike?

There was something so inexpressibly harmonious
and peaceful within the sphere of her presence, that
Philip could have sat for hours in silence, luxuriat-
ing in a certain delightful feeling of home which
always stole over him in this house. The driftwood
logs crackling on the hearth, the great lamp with its

luminous circle of light, the open piano with Diabelli's duets, which the dear little rebellious girl had been practising; the gleam of the fire upon the polished brass of the fire irons; the books, the pictures, the dolls asleep in the sofa corner—all appealed to a dormant marital and paternal sense in Philip, and awakened dim yearnings in his heart. Having taken in the scene and revelled in it, he got up somewhat reluctantly, and bade Mrs. Castleton good-night.

"By the way," she said, as he was fumbling in a corner for his walking stick, "would it be indiscreet to ask if you have any particular cause for anxiety? Am I to direct my Argus gaze in any special direction, or only be generally circumspect and vigilant?"

Philip grew suddenly thoughtful.

"You know," he burst out, with a comical scowl, "girls are so awfully uncertain—sort of incalculable and frisky—in matters of this kind. I am tortured by the vision of some wholly unsuspected person— some young Lochinvar out of the wild West—popping up serenely and carrying her off, *sans cérémonie*, while I have been making a fool of myself, wasting no end of tender sentiment on somebody else's sweetheart."

"Then it is this young Lochinvar from the West you want me to look out for?"

"Yes, precisely. There's no one else I am afraid of for the present."

"Very well; if such a character turns up in the course of the summer, I'll give you timely warning."

"Thanks; you are very good. If I ever get to

be President of the United States, I'll make Castle-ton grand vizier, or minister plenipotentiary and envoy extraordinary to Borrioboola-Gha, or anything else he may like."

" Thanks ; nothing would suit him better."

They shook hands for the second time, and Philip plunged into the windy night, with Mrs. Castleton's voice ringing in his ears.

X

FOUR or five weeks after Philip's departure, Maud was aroused from her late matutinal slumbers by the consciousness that some one was staring at her. With a dim notion that Peggy or her mother had invaded her room in search of something, she opened her eyes lazily, and was not a little startled at the sight of the yellow face of Mrs. McGregor, gazing at her with the most undisguised admiration. She showed, no doubt, how shocked she was by the extreme coolness with which she returned Mrs. McGregor's greeting; but that cheerful matron, in no wise disconcerted, seated herself at the foot of the bed, and, in a soothing and cajoling voice, in which there was an undertone of jollity, remarked :

" Doan' yo' fret, honey ! Yo' know Phœbe, bress yer deah heart—Phœbe McGregor? I ain't gwine ter hurt yer, honey—doan' yo' pucker up yer beau'-ful face at me like dat, now. I's been in ladies' rooms befo'—fine, beau'ful ladies in Souf Ca'lina."

" But what do you want, Mrs. McGregor? " asked Maud impatiently, raising herself on her elbow. " You surely didn't come to my room at eight o'clock in the morning only to pay me compliments."

Mrs. McGregor, instead of committing herself to a direct answer, let her liquid dark eyes rest admiringly upon the young girl, whose form was vaguely outlined under the thin covering, and with a little gurgling negro laugh she exclaimed :

"Yo' look mighty sweet lyin' dar now, Miss Maud! Mighty sweet you do look—and dat is Phœbe McGregor is a-tellin' yo' so."

"But, Mrs. McGregor," cried Maud, now really vexed, "what right have you to come unannounced into my room before I am up in the morning? Who showed you the way, I should like to know, and what is it you want?"

The mulatto woman, not in the least disconcerted by her wrath, remained sitting, smiling with a kind of insinuating confidence. She had the abject adoration of her race for luxurious surroundings, and she simply revelled in the dainty elegance of this room—the rich toilet articles of ivory, cut glass, and silver; the vague perfume which pervaded the atmosphere; the fine texture and precious quality of the garments which lay scattered on chairs and lounges; and the complex wants, so far above her own rude frugality, indicated by all this gorgeous confusion.

"My husban', now, Miss Maud," she began leisurely, "Mistah McGregor, dat is—he's mighty stuck-up; he doan' run no man's errands, Mistah McGregor doan'. He's a bonton, Mistah McGregor is, an' dat is why he doan' want ter do no work—'cept he goes a-scootin' off, when the weather is fine, an' ketch some fish."

"But why did you ever marry such a good-for-nothing?" Maud queried, entertained, in spite of herself, by her guest's garrulity.

" Me ? Why did Mistah McGregor marry me ? "

Whether she really misunderstood, or considered the question, as it was put, as too preposterous to answer (Mr. McGregor being a bonton), Maud did not trouble herself to determine.

" Yes," she observed lazily, " why did Mr. McGregor marry you ? "

" Wal now, Miss Maud," the mulatto woman replied, with a half-sheepish expression and an amused gurgle in her throat, " it wa'n't for my beauty, fo' sho'; I reckon it was for my damn killin' ways."

Shocked though she was at the rudeness of this reply, Maud could scarcely help laughing ; and Mrs. McGregor, encouraged by this inferential approval, went on with a long and highly embellished autobiography, nine-tenths of which was obviously fiction. The real tragic part of her experience, in which she had displayed a heroic disregard of danger in her devotion to Mr. McGregor, she did not even remotely allude to ; and Maud concluded that she was probably ashamed of it, or perhaps not aware that it was at all laudable. Her Mr. McGregor was not the poor, drunken wretch whose life she had saved when he was dying of the yellow fever, but a luxurious, aristocratic idler, who most probably did not work because he was too high-born and magnificent, and not used to the plebeian ways of meaner mortals. And it was this quality in Mr. McGregor which gave an aristocratic tinge even to his misbehavior.

The occasion for her visit was presently divulged in a haphazard, incidental way, at the end of half an hour's conversation. Mr. Fancher, it appeared, was going to give a fox hunt, followed by a hunting breakfast, and in order to give Mr. McGregor a job he had intrusted to him the distribution of the invitations, and imprudently paid him five dollars in advance for this service. But Mr. McGregor, being altogether too great a gentleman to act the part of a messenger, had given the invitations to his wife, commanding her to see that they were delivered to the proper addresses. But unhappily Mrs. McGregor could not read : and this was the cause of her intricate and circuitous behavior. She did not dare to come straight to the point and ask Miss Maud first to pick out her own invitation, and then to tell her which to deliver at the six or eight neighboring villas. She fancied, in her simplicity, that a good deal of flattering cajolery ought to precede such a request, and she congratulated herself on her shrewdness when Maud, with a half-shamefaced eagerness, began to rummage through the invitations, arranging them in the topographical order of the villas, and liberally imparting her instructions and warnings against mistakes.

Mrs. McGregor finally took her leave, with profuse expressions of gratitude ; and Maud, flinging a wrapper about her, ran into Peggy's room with the large, square envelope addressed to the Misses Bulkley. Peggy had, however, long ago both risen and breakfasted, and was now seen rowing about with her father in a small wherry on the lake. Maud had accordingly no choice but to make Sally her confidante ; and she was scarcely disappointed when that cool and precise young lady received the announcement of the hunt without enthusiasm. Sally was not a good horsewoman, and could scarcely be expected to rejoice in an occasion which would afford her sister an opportunity to eclipse her. She regarded it as little short of immoral for a young girl to ride such a horse as Sultana, attracting attention by unladylike riding and a daring recklessness which savored of the circus. People would soon begin to surmise that, perhaps, Maud was a professional. No one in their position could afford to do anything too well ; for skill of any sort, beyond the point of amateurish dexterity, had a professional flavor, and would injure their social prospects. The only thing which a lady could afford to do professionally well, without danger of falling out of the ranks of elegant idlers, was playing tennis—an occupation to which the ladies of Atterbury accordingly devoted themselves with a zeal and assiduity worthy of a better cause, and attained a high degree of proficiency in.

Maud, however, who knew too well the animus of her sister's criticism of her horsemanship, was in nowise disturbed in her plans. She had two posts with a dozen holes in them set up in front of the stable, and upon these a movable lath was made to rest by means of pegs. Sultana, who had never been supposed to be a fencer, fairly distinguished herself in leaping; and, being put through her paces every morning for an hour or more, was made to jump two, three, and four feet without wincing, carrying the lath with her whenever she missed. Maud was so indefatigable in her efforts to induce her to jump five feet, that she was, in part, consoled for Philip's absence, and accused herself every evening of the basest treachery for not being able to persevere in her tragic mood. She had always fancied that she had a deep nature and was capable of the sublimest attachment. But, though she longed for Philip and wished him back, she was not as miserable as she had hoped and expected to be. The anticipation of the hunt, with the excitement of riding to the hounds, tingled in her blood. She fancied herself dashing across country in the front rank, leaving the field behind her, flying over fences, and astonishing everybody by her daring horsemanship. Sultana, in the meanwhile, learned to take her four feet and a couple of inches over, and showed up remarkably well both as to speed and bottom, in the experimental runs which Maud took on the sly across the moors, for the purpose of practising and to guard against startling surprises. In fact, Maud strongly suspected that she was not new to the business.

The meet had been fixed for Saturday, so as to enable that part of the Atterbury community which spent the week in New York to take part in the hunt. The September morning rose cool and sunny, with a stiff northeast breeze, and the atmosphere surcharged with exhilaration and ozone. While the Bulkley family sat at breakfast, grooms with blanketed horses were seen riding by, every three minutes, and there was an air of bustle and excitement about the quiet place which communicated itself to the dogs, who kept up a perpetual joyous barking in front of the stables.

And, apropos of dogs, permit me to remark that Mr. Bulkley hated dogs, and could not be made to see how they added to his dignity and social prestige. He appeared to take a satisfaction in appearing stupid when Sally and Maud tried to explain to him that it was the mark of a gentleman to keep high-bred animals, and, it was, no doubt, with a lurking malice that he intimated his preference for cats. He was emboldened to go so far in his opposition, because he well knew that Mrs. Bulkley detested dogs quite as much as he did ; though for social reasons she professed to share the sentiments of her daughters. She could talk dog laboriously by the hour, and admiringly exhibit her own specimens of dachshunds and bull terriers, which she privately thought hideous.

At half-past nine o'clock the groom Prellmann—according to report a cashiered German cavalry officer—had the horses in readiness, and Maud and Sally, in tall beavers and riding habits, appeared upon the piazza. They were both swung into the saddle, where they fussed a good deal while giving contradictory orders to the groom to fix them this way and that way, to lengthen and shorten the stirrup leathers, to tighten or loosen the saddle girth, and half a dozen other commands which were but the expression of a nervous apprehension in the elder sister's case, and of a nervous exhilaration in the case of the younger. Sally rode a handsome but rather sedate bay nag named Yuba Bill, who would, no doubt, refuse the first fence. But she knew, from report, that a number of other horses would do the same thing; so that there would be nothing ridiculous in her situation. She was constitutionally timid, and always felt unsafe on horseback. But rather than be missed on so "swell" an occasion as the present, I verily believe she would have faced the probability of a broken neck. She had always definite and well-formulated reasons for whatever she did. When the innumerable preparations were at an end, the two sisters, followed by the groom, started up the road toward the meadow where the meet was appointed for ten o'clock, for this was to be a morning (and not, as usual, an afternoon) run, and was to end gloriously with a one-o'clock breakfast, at which half the *élite* of the Long Island watering places were expected to be present.

There were twenty or thirty vehicles already on the ground, conspicuous among which were two four-in-hands drawn by stout coach horses, besides a great variety of other traps, drawn by as many varieties of horses. It was a very pretty spectacle, under the vast windy sky, in the clear, sunny morning. The bright liveries of the grooms, the gay parasols of the ladies in the carriages, the confused baying of the hounds, and the neighing and champing of the hunters produced an animated medley of sights and sounds which was marvellously exhilarating.

At the edge of the meadow, Marston Fancher, gorgeous to behold in a red coat, buckskin breeches and riding boots, met the two sisters, and saluted them in military fashion with his crop. His splendor almost took their breath away. He was simply dazzling. He rode a spare, clean-limbed gray hunter, and there was a look in his face of dignified responsibility, and perhaps, too, a consciousness of his faultless get-up. Maud's eyes flew instinctively over the field to discover, by comparison, whether her own " style " was equally irreproachable ; and she drew a sigh of relief when she had satisfied herself that nothing was amiss.

" Have you ever ridden to hounds before, Miss Bulkley ? " Fancher inquired, addressing himself with the utmost deference to the elder sister.

" No, Mr. Fancher," Sally replied. " I was just looking about to see whether you had provided ambulances for such cases as mine."

" Ha, ha, ha ! That's awfully good, don't you know ! " The master of the hunt laughed with a degree of appreciation which quite startled the perpetrator of the joke.

" You may think it good fun," she replied, with comical self-condolence, " but I doubt if it will strike me in the same light. However, I am willing to take my risks ; and if it turns out that Yuba Bill does not take kindly to fences and ditches, I'll join the rearguard or the provision train."

This flash of vivacity on her sister's part made so deep an impression upon Maud, that she had difficulty in concealing her surprise. Sally was one of those who rarely thought it worth the trouble to be agreeable in the bosom of her family, and who, therefore, was supposed not to possess the faculty. That she had, with cold-blooded deliberation, set out to captivate Fancher, was the conclusion which

Maud jumped at ; and though she had no immediate ambition to contest that prize with her, a spirit
of *diablerie* impelled her to enter the lists for the
mere fun of the thing. There could be no harm in
teaching Sally a little lesson of which, moreover,
she was greatly in need.

"I needn't ask whether you have ridden to
hounds before," Fancher remarked, turning to
Maud ; "I have seen you so much in the saddle,
that I really have forgotten how you look on your
feet."

"But you never saw me follow the hounds,"
Maud replied, with the insinuating sprightliness of
a girl bent on destruction.

"You don't mean to say that you never did?"

"Yes, unhappily; but I have made the acquaintance of all the fences within ten miles, and I'm not
afraid of them."

"Well, now, really, you don't say so," he laughed,
a little absent-mindedly, for a large barouche, drawn
by a superb pair of bays, came rolling up the road
and swung in at the gate. "I hope you'll pardon
me," he said, saluting as before; "my duties as
host call me elsewhere. You'll, no doubt, find
friends wherever you turn."

He spurred his horse and rode up to the barouche,
which was occupied by Mrs. Van Horst and her
recently divorced daughter, Mrs. Emmerick. The
elder lady—who was stout and rosy, with the complexion of a healthy infant—was spread out as if
she felt that her dignity demanded that she should
take up as much room as possible; while the

younger sat smilingly erect under her blue parasol, looking cool and sweet and distractingly appetizing. Maud and Sally both watched with strained attention the reception which these august ladies accorded to Fancher, and as they observed the dignified cordiality with which Mrs. Van Horst returned his greeting, a pang nestled in their hearts, and a sudden blight fell upon the bright and festal scene. This was the drop of gall in their cup of triumph ; and if they had not long been familiar with its bitterness, they would have yielded to an impulse, which they could scarcely repress, to invent an excuse for betaking themselves home. But that was out of the question. They knew what kind of reception awaited them at home if they yielded to such weakness. With a strange fascination they continued to watch the Van Horst carriage, and both marvelled why this lady, who was far from looking the haughty ogress she evidently was, had taken it into her head to make their life miserable. They fancied they discovered in Fancher's demeanor a studied and exaggerated deference, very different from the perfunctory politeness with which he honored his other guests ; and they even scrutinized, with malice prepense, the expression of his face, whenever it was turned toward them, determined to discover an unwonted animation and gratified vanity under the smiles of the beautiful *divorcée*. While they were in the midst of these miserable cogitations a horn was blown by somebody on the top of a tally-ho, and Sultana, startled by the suddenness of the blast, began to prance and pirouette in an alarming fashion. As it happened, Maud had her hands full, for a couple of minutes, in quieting the mare ; and when, after much backing and plunging, she finally got her under control, she found herself separated from Sally, and *vis-à-vis* with Mrs. Castleton, who hailed her from her carriage in the friendliest fashion.

" How do you do, Miss Maud ? " she cried, with a sweet cordiality which dispelled, as if by magic, all the bitterness in the girl's mind. " How lovely you look—if you'll permit me to be personal ! I venture to predict that you'll come in for the brush."

" I shall be content if I come whole-skinned out of the brush," Maud replied, laughing. " I am told it is going to be a frightful run through woods and underbrush, and over all sorts of obstacles."

" I don't believe it. That would be inviting accidents. But you have less reason to fear it than anybody else."

" You mean I have a good mount ? "

" Yes, I should say the finest in the whole field."

I believe nothing in the world pleases a man more than praise of his horse ; and in the case of a woman, it takes precedence of everything except admiration of herself. Maud flushed with delight at the compliment bestowed upon the capricious Sultana, and she had that feeling of light-hearted gayety, mingled with a vague pride and a keen zest in mere living, which in this reflective and dyspeptic age, no one experiences except in the saddle. The world swam about her in brightness and sunshine; the long brown moor, enlivened here and there with violet patches of blooming heather, stretched out invitingly before her; and the glorious sky canopied the glorious earth. She was young and had a right to be glad; and only the least touch of cordiality was needed to make her mind rebound from its morbid deflection to its natural altitude of youthful gayety and enjoyment.

"I am going to confide in you," she said, bending a pair of laughing eyes upon Mrs. Castleton. "I am awfully afraid of those snake fences. You've got to get into position in order to get a clean jump, and I don't see how you can do that when you are riding at full tilt."

"I wish I could tell you, my dear," Mrs. Castleton replied; "but in the days when I rode, drag hunting was not yet invented. Perhaps Mr. Castleton might give you a point. You see him over there on that big sorrel hunter."

"I shouldn't dare to ask him."

"I'll ask him for you."

She managed, within a few minutes, to catch her husband's eye, and in obedience to her signal he rode up to the carriage, and saluted Maud with that jocose cordiality which was habitual with him. He was a tall, portly man of forty, with a very pleasant face, but looked younger than he was. He was light-haired, wore a full blond beard, and was extremely handsome.

"Well, Miss Maud," he said, in response to his wife's query; "as regards the snake fences, I'll tell you, in strict confidence, of course, that they are all rotten. Don't bother about getting at them diagonally, but simply dash straight ahead, and the top rail will fly into splinters if your horse happens to strike it."

" Thank you, Mr. Castleton," the girl rejoined, " I am greatly obliged. I don't want to be left behind, you know; and there is nothing else I am afraid of."

" By Jove!" cried Castleton, admiringly ; " then you actually intend to come in at the death?"

" Yes, of the anise-seed bag."

" The anise-seed bag makes no difference as far as the run is concerned. You can ride quite as hard on a drag scent as after a live fox. And the drag has the advantage that it is sure to be there, while the fox is a ' mighty oncertain ' customer."

A bugle call now summoned the field, and from all parts of the meadow ladies and gentlemen were seen trying to wheel their spirited steeds into line. Maud, who had by this time learned all the tricks of the wayward Sultana, anticipated her plunge, and excited Castleton's admiration by her firm and gentle manner of controlling her. There were forty-four mounts and thirteen couple of hounds. A prettier sight is rarely seen than that field exhibited in the bright, autumnal landscape against the background of the forest, under the clear, metallic sky. There were twenty ladies, at least, all well mounted, and their fair faces lighted up with a pleasure which was healthy and beautiful. Presently, at another signal, the hounds were cast off ; and, after a few minutes' nosing over the ground, started in full cry westward over the moors towards the heathery Cockroach hills.

It was a very spirited start, and with a magnificent impetus the forty-four horses dashed away, Fancher and Maud well forward in the first flight, Sultana giving his hunter all he could do in keeping abreast of her. The wind whistled in Maud's ears, her nerves tingled, her pulses bounded, and her blood was stung with a strange thrill, an intoxication of joy, which was like a divine madness. She breathed more deeply, she felt more keenly, she thought more clearly than she had ever done in her life before. The possibilities of this earthly existence flashed upon her in ecstatic glimpses; and like a vague pang the reflection that this could not last, that she must again return to life's humdrum prose, flitted through her mind. The mad baying of the hounds —how merrily it sounded in the crisp air! Halt! there was a fence—of the villanous snake variety, too; and as the whole field bore down upon it—not in straight line, but in a long, irregular flight—the hounds were already fifty yards beyond, working over the ground with their loud, anxious yelp, and filling the air with their clamor. Maud's heart gave a big thump as she faced that ragged zigzag of sprawling rails, and her discretion would have gotten the better of her valor if she had not remembered Castleton's assurance. So, pulling Sultana back upon her haunches, she threw herself back in the saddle, dug her heel into the mare's side, and whiz! away she went like the wind, carrying the top rail with her and kicking it into splinters. It was a very pretty jump, and what was more, she was the first woman to land on the farther side. She heard a tremendous snorting behind her, mingled with shrill screams and half hysterical protestations.

"Beautiful, Miss Maud, beautiful!" some one cried close to her ear, and turning her head she saw Fancher, very much flushed, bending forward in the saddle, with his head set against the wind.

"Glorious!" she answered, a wild joy tingling through her nerves. She scarcely knew to what she was replying; but the exultation that hummed in her brain demanded a jubilant expression.

"That was a savage fence," said Fancher, after a minute's pause, now well abreast of her. "I thought it would play the mischief with the majority."

"Do you know what has become of my sister?"

"I think she has taken to the road."

"I was afraid Yuba Bill would refuse that fence."

"He was not the only one. Miss Bulkley has an abundance of company."

They went along thus, at a rattling pace, but taking good care to economize the strength of their mounts, even though they were passed by a half dozen whose enthusiasm hurried them on, without regard for consequences.

The pack here made a sharp double and then dashed northward, where the ground was encumbered with a dense underbrush of scrub oak and brier, and their cry rose louder and shriller than ever. "Now, here's the rub," cried Fancher, urging his horse through the tall shrubbery, though he reared and snorted and seemed determined to turn back. Maud, fired with feverish zeal, came crashing along at his side; and Sultana, rising to the occasion, behaved splendidly.   With fine intelligence she avoided the brier jungle, and was presently in the open, before Fancher's hunter had cleared the pestiferous bushes.   Maud had no time to look back, to count the accidents, but she noticed presently, as she glanced over her shoulder, that scarcely a dozen were visible on this side the jungle, foremost among whom were Castleton and Fancher. Then there came a country road, with two low board fences, and another clean run of a couple of miles.   Up and down, over the beautiful heathery hills, went the gay cavalcade, Maud and Fancher keeping neck and neck, exchanging brief remarks, which seemed to establish a delightful confidence between them, and feeling a kind of glorious comradeship in the distinction of leading the hunt. Presently a riderless horse was seen dashing past them; pausing, neighing, and running again with bewildered aimlessness.   Maud naturally wondered who the luckless rider was, and was rather gratified when her companion declared it was young Langley Van Horst.   The track doubled again and ran close along the bluff overhanging the water, where the turf was black from recent burning; and the dogs spread and puzzled out the scent with difficulty, owing to the strong burnt odor.   But they presently caught it again, and another tolerably straight run of a mile and a half brought them to the top of a round hill, where they stopped, tumbling over each other, and began to scatter, running in large and smaller circles, and yelping in a lost and bewildered way.   Maud made a dash straight up, comprehending that this was the finish; and whether from gallantry or from necessity Fancher failed to dispute her lead, and came galloping up with Castleton and a young sprig of a college boy, named Harlow, close at his heels. Then a bugle was blown; and all that was left of the Atterbury hunt—eight or ten horsemen in all, and Maud the only lady—was seen sharply silhouetted on that windy hilltop against the cold blue sky. They all congratulated Maud with profuse cordiality, and, as was proper, awarded her the brush, and she was so absurdly happy that she felt like shouting or embracing some one, or committing some other breach of propriety. She had never known what it meant to live until now.

She was seized with pity for herself, when she thought of all the gray, colorless years she had spent, and what crude notions she had had of what constituted pleasure. Here was a select little remnant of people, self-restrained and well-bred, who had reduced living to a fine art, and knew how to cull from the tree of life only the choicest and most fragrant flowers. Maud felt already as if she were one of them, and entitled to share to the full their refined enjoyments. The thought darted through her that Philip Warburton distinctly claimed not to belong to them, and professed to look down upon their pursuits as effeminate and frivolous. A faint echo of her conversation with Philip two months ago rang in her ears and caused a vague uneasiness. She could see from where she was the very bend of the road, near the overgrown clearing, where he had so earnestly declared his determination to work for the amelioration of the lot of his suffering fellow men, and to turn his back upon the pleasant things of life which dulled the voice of conscience within us. Now, curiously enough, Fancher and Warburton, friends though they were, became to Maud representatives of two opposing and irreconcilable views of life. She saw Philip, with his strong and earnest face, with that grave smile under his moustache, and it was undeniable that he was a more impressive personality than the eminently proper Fancher, whose thoughts rarely rose above horses, amusements, and creature comforts. But for all that, the latter appealed to that snobbish instinct which lurks in the very best of us. In style, Philip certainly could not compete with him; nor in that kind of distinction which consists in conscious superiority and a high-bred disdain for all that is "vulgah." There was something, to a woman, extremely uncomfortable in Philip's persistent self-questioning, and his tendency to see riddles and problems in the most common events. Maud could well fancy how much more dignified and serenely enjoyable life would be with a placid, aristocratic idler like Fancher than with a restlessly toiling plebeian philosopher like Warburton.

Strange thoughts will invade the human brain at most inopportune moments, and it was not Maud's fault that she could not banish the spectre of Philip during the homeward ride, nor could she make up her mind to a resolute choice between the two contending forces. She saw plainly enough the admiration in Fancher's eyes, and it amused her to think that it was her horsemanship to which she chiefly owed his now undisguised homage. Though he possessed none of his friend's eloquence, he managed yet to convey a sufficiently vivid impression to Maud that his heart drew him to her, even though his duties as host might compel him temporarily to desert her. He then left her in Castleton's charge; and thus she returned a little after one o'clock, arriving at the Casino, which was beleaguered by a Pharaoh's host of horses and chariots.

IT was the morning after the hunt that Mrs. Castleton sat at her writing desk, and wrote as follows to her friend in the wholesale drug business in New York:

"MY DEAR MR. WARBURTON,—Unless I am much mistaken, the young Lochinvar has come from a quarter where he was least expected. I won't tell you who he is, for there is a bare possibility that I may be mistaken; but I will leave it to your ingenuity to discover, when you come down here for a little autumn visit, as I have no doubt you will, before long. It was at the hunt ball yesterday that he startled the Atterbury clan by waltzing suddenly out of the region of the insupposable. He danced perpetually with the 'fair Ellen' and brazenly carried her off to the piazza, so that no one else should dance with her, when it suited his sovereign pleasure to converse in the dusk rather than to gyrate rhythmically to the noise of a piano and two violins. I am aware that this last revelation will cause you some discomfort, but, you know, it is not well for man to be too comfortable, and a little tender disquietude will do you no harm, and will, moreover, make you realize the significance of the following verse:

> ' He stayed not for brake and he stopped not for stone,
> He swam the Esk River, where ford there was none.'

Which, applied to your conditions, would read:

> ' He stayed not for business, but rushed to the tryst,
> He swam the East River when the ferry he missed.'

" Even Mr. Castleton, who is a trifle obtuse in such matters, suspected the presence of the young Lochinvar, and asked me quite innocently whether I didn't think the aforesaid gentleman was 'rather rushing it'? and it was this remark which confirmed my fears and made me mindful of my promise to warn you, in case anything in the shape of a suitor appeared.

" Mr. Castleton wishes me to tell you that your *protégé* Mr. McGregor is in a bad way, which will probably not surprise you. He offered the boat you gave him for sale, a few days ago, probably in order to buy the one thing needful. But Mr. Castleton has warned all the people here not to buy it, as the man's living depends upon it.

" By the way, I have a profound secret to tell you which you must not divulge : our Mildred has composed a waltz which she has named the Warburton. What do you think of that ? I hope you duly appreciate the honor. And Bertha, who, as you know, is trying to rival Paganini, has written out a violin score, and the two propose to play it to you as a duet when you come down here. If that will not bring you, you deserve to have the young Lochinvar carry off the fair Ellen ; for then I shall pronounce you a laggard in love and a dastard in war ; and remain,

" Cordially yours,

" HARRIET CASTLETON."

At the very hour when this missive reached Philip Warburton (Mrs. Castleton mailed her letters in her husband's pockets and had a poor opinion of the mail service), Marston Fancher, accompanied by his two huge mastiffs, Turk and Whiskey (who resembled each other as two drops of water), was seen wending his way up the gravel path to the villa of Thorn Hedge. He was greatly tempted to stop at the stable in order to ascertain whether it was properly kept, for he had ineradicable convictions regarding the proper way of keeping a stable. The hardwood box stalls, beautifully polished, were his particular pride ; and the great glass case, in which the harness was hung up, was an invention of his own which had afforded him the greatest satisfaction. As for the carriage house, it was so handsomely finished and (in his own day) so immaculately kept, that it could, at a pinch, serve for a ball-room; and, as a matter of fact, had frequently been used for that purpose. Marston Fancher claimed that he could always judge of a gentleman by the condition of his stable; and he had, in the present case, a suspicion that Mr. Bulkley did not come up to his requirements. That his tenant was an altogether objectionable party he did not question. His general appearance; his high, cracked voice, utterly devoid of modulation; and, above all, his ragged, yellow chin beard, stamped him sufficiently to make a closer acquaintance unnecessary. But then, on the other hand, the family (which was really very presentable) had so far succeeded admirably in keeping him in the background; and if Mr. Bulkley would consent to perpetuating this arrangement—being, as it were, permanently suppressed—the question of selecting him for a father-in-law might not be unworthy of consideration. Mr. Fancher had, during the last four days, made much progress in Maud's favor, having met her every morning on the beach, and promenaded with her along the dunes. He had been more than ever impressed with her cleverness, and found her vastly sympathetic on the subject of dogs, horses, and tennis. He discovered, too, that they were in the most beautiful accord with reference to drag hunting, which they both held to be an eminently manly sport, no whit inferior to fox hunting; and what was still more surprising, she entirely shared his sentiments on the subject of mastiffs as being a more gentlemanly dog to breed than setters and bull terriers. She gave unqualified adherence, too, to his cardinal conviction that an easy trot was the only proper gait for a saddle-horse, especially for long distances, and that cantering and racking were equally objectionable. In dog breeding she confessed herself a tyro, and accepted all his opinions with the sweetest docility and gratitude. What had particularly charmed him was her enthusiastic manner of receiving his remarks, as if they were very remarkable. Fancher had never known a girl who managed to put him in better humor with himself; and he was, indeed, far from suspecting any design in her guileless exclamations of approval.

Now the fact was, Maud had felt flattered at Fancher's attentions, being well aware what a great personage he was, and what an object of spirited rivalry among the fair denizens of Atterbury. She would have been more than feminine if the consciousness of the envy she excited on the beach, when she carried Marston and his mastiffs off in triumph, had not accelerated her pulse-beat and given a keener zest to existence. It was strange how he appealed to all the worldliness in her, and suppressed, by the mere sense of distinction she felt in his company, her aspiring self, and brought her lower, snobbish self to the front. In the case of Philip it had been exactly the reverse. All artificial divisions of society seemed in his presence of small account, and only the human worth, determined by character and aspirations, seemed of enduring value. But it was so long since she had seen Philip ; his words, if she heard them at all, sounded so remote. Her better nature—if indeed that was the better which he addressed—needed the constant stimulus of his voice, or it sank out of sight and allowed its snobbish twin sister to have full sway over her thoughts and actions.

This was the situation, as far as Maud was concerned, on that sunny afternoon in September when Marston paused outside the Thorn Hedge stable and wrestled with a mighty doubt as to the propriety of going in and inspecting the premises. But he concluded after five minutes' meditation that he would not himself fail to resent such an intrusion, even on the part of his landlord, and he therefore resisted the temptation and walked rapidly to the piazza, where he lifted a great bronze knocker, the reverberation of which brought the butler to the door. Marston handed his card to this dignified functionary and inquired for Miss Maud. He was shown into the parlor, which was furnished in the most exquisite taste with the spoils of a dozen European pilgrimages. All those beautifully carved Venetian pieces had their history to Fancher, and he almost begrudged the present occupants of the house their dearly bought right of absorbing the aroma of his treasures. He was reflecting vaguely upon the oddity of having other people live in an environment which was his and expressed him, profiting by the refinement of his taste, when the *portière* from the adjoining room was pushed aside, and Maud, dressed with intent to kill, slipped in with a furtive swiftness. She gave him her left hand with an adorable air of confidence, and sank into a Louis XV. chair opposite to him. What a marvellous change of attitude this implied, since the monosyllabic stiffness and shy reserve of their first meeting could not escape even Fancher's callous perceptions.

"Hush! Don't speak loud until he's gone," she whispered, with a breathless, laughing agitation.

"Until who is gone?" Fancher queried, much interested.

"Oh, it is a gentleman friend of—of—ours from the West!" she declared, with a fresh burst of suppressed laughter. "I fear he has come to spend Sunday; and if father sees him, he will be sure to invite him."

"But what did you do with him?"

"Oh, I saw him coming from my window upstairs, and I told the butler that I was not at home! But then he asked for Peggy, and she is sure to receive him. He's waiting for her out on the piazza."

In spite of the obvious preference for himself which this confession evinced, a slight uneasiness stole over the young man at the thought of this Western suitor. For unless he had been a suitor, how could Maud have known that she was the one he wanted to see; and, furthermore, who but a suitor would come all the way from the wild West to call upon a girl who was spending the summer on Long Island? Now what possible right could this presumptuous Westerner have to take it for granted that his visit would be agreeable? And did not the circumstance that he came, apparently uninvited, with the intention of spending Sunday, hint at an intimacy which Maud, for diplomatic reasons, now chose to disavow? These and a number of other uncomfortable reflections thronged Marston's mind, as he sat *vis-à-vis* with Maud, and beheld with the admiration of a connoisseur the style and charming effect of her garments. What an atmosphere there was about her, to be sure, and how beautifully she harmonized with the rich setting of the room! The tea-gown, of a pale lavender hue, which seemed as light as spider web, fell in soft folds about her noble form, and the pale-rose silk stocking, of which he caught a glimpse as it peeped forth under the hem of the miraculous gown, was like a little grace-note of color that emphasized the harmony. The whole girl had something wildly alluring about her which made him long to touch her, hold her, possess her for ever more. A truly artistic toilet has always an aroma about it—it expresses its wearer in a certain character, and usually the character to which her physique most fully lends itself. Maud had aspired hitherto to a certain stately statuesqueness, *à la* Romola, and her costumes had expressed dignity and avoided coquettish and kittenish suggestions. But to-day—possibly with an unconfessed desire to captivate Fancher, whose ideal of womanhood, she well knew, was not in the direction of the statuesque—she had donned this cobwebby and subtly insidious gown, so airily, fairily piquant, so tantalizing, as elusive in its effect as a fragrance, and as insistent-

ly and evasively assertive. The subdued light in the
room, shaded by the luxuriant vines without and
diaphanous draperies within, gave him a sense of
delicious privacy which was heightened by the
knowledge of that forlorn adorer who sat on the
windy piazza, shut out from the light of her countenance.

"I say, Miss Maud," Fancher began, ungenerously glorying in his privilege, "aren't you rather hard
on that fellow—what's his name—out there on the
piazza?"

It must not be supposed for a moment that he
underestimated his own worth, or was oblivious of
the distinction he conferred upon a woman by his
company, but he was yet masculine enough to feel
flattered by the favor of a beautiful young girl, and,
in the consciousness of her charm, to hold its own
importance in abeyance.

"I have simply nothing to do with him," Maud
declared with gratifying promptness. "I have not
invited him to come and see me."

"I—I—only hope Miss Peggy will take pity on
him," he chuckled, gazing with admiration into her
eyes, and fidgeting in his chair.

"Why should you care?" queried Maud, in a high,
flute-like note, letting her eyes wander about the
room so as to evade the persistence of his gaze.
The fact was, neither he nor she cared a rap about
the young man, but merely wasted speech upon him
in order to fill the awkward pauses.

"That was a fine run we had, the other day, over
the moors," said Marston with the most barefaced

purpose of making conversation; "that mare of yours is a stunning beast."

He had made this remark at least a dozen times before, but it might serve as well as any other as a substitute for silence. He had more than half made up his mind to ask Maud to marry him, and all he lacked was a fitting introduction to the subject, which somehow refused to suggest itself. The matter had been fermenting in his consciousness ever since the hunt; and he had come to the conclusion that, all things considered, he could not do much better. He needed ample resources; he required an establishment on a large scale, and his own means had of late suffered an intolerable contraction. He did not profess to be wildly in love with Maud—he was not the kind of character that could be wildly anything—but he was vaguely fond of her. He admired her, and he had a notion that she would make a comfortable and ornamental wife to any properly constituted man. As for the father-in-law, Marston fancied he could easily devise a plan for making him invisible. Some drawback there was bound to be in any affair of this sort. As a family skeleton Peleg was, on the whole, of a rather harmless and unobtrusive character.

These were the reflections which floated through the young man's brain, as he sat contemplating the lovely girl opposite him in all the glory of her youth, her beauty, and her Worth gown. He was a good critic, in a certain way, of those elusive phases of character and appearance that are the result of breeding and inheritance. His ambition was to lead a well-fed, well-clad, and commodious life, unvexed by the discomfort of thought, untroubled by cares or economic problems. He saw in Maud an aid to the accomplishment of this purpose; and though he had noted minor points in her toilet and manner which he meant, in his marital capacity, to correct, yet, taking her all in all, he approved of her, nay, found her, at times, altogether charming.

They fell to talking presently about McGregor and his mulatto wife, and seemed to be drifting farther away than ever from the topic which was closest to the heart of both.

"It is a deuced pity for a man of his family to have to put up with a woman of that sort," Marston was saying, leaning forward in his chair and clasping his hands about his knee.

"I should rather say that it was a pity for a woman, whether she were white or brown, to have to put up with a man of his sort," Maud replied with unexpected spirit.

Fancher opened his eyes in astonishment and ejaculated: "How so?"

"I am told he is a man of very bad habits," she rejoined warmly; "and it is simply touching to see the devotion of that simple creature, who seems to feel honored even by his abuse."

"Well, you mustn't judge that class of people according to your own standard. She hasn't been accustomed to anything better. She ought to feel honored. Whatever his habits may be, he is a gentleman; and it seems a shame for a man, born as he is, to be obliged to drag a mulatto woman through life, simply on account of some piece of boyish folly."

"If it hadn't been for her, he wouldn't have had any life to drag himself or anybody else through," Maud retorted bravely.

"Well, even if that were so, it isn't fair for her to claim his life because she saved it. It wasn't much of a gift on such conditions. I frankly told McGregor so when he asked me. I told him people might put up with his drinking, for there's many a man in good social standing who goes on periodic sprees; the only important thing is to do it as quietly as possible, and avoid making scandal; but a mulatto wife society would never tolerate, and it was the wildest absurdity for him to expect to be taken up by anybody as long as he stuck to that creature."

Maud hesitated a moment before replying. Another scene rose out of her memory, and another voice, with a ring quite different from that of her present visitor, sounded in her ears.

"Was it you, then, Mr. Fancher," she asked, with a sudden curious insistence, "who gave Mr. McGregor that advice?"

"Yes, to be sure. How did you know about it?"

"I? Well, only by chance."

She could not bear to describe to him that stormy afternoon, when she had overheard the conversation in the boat-house before she and Philip went sailing. She felt suddenly miles away from Fancher; and he perceiving a change in her manner, put it down to coquetry, and became the more zealous in his pursuit, as she seemed bent on escaping. He began to talk eagerly, defending his view of McGregor's relation to the mulatto woman; but Maud, though she answered with assenting monosyllables, scarcely heard what he was saying. She had felt from the moment he entered the parlor that he meant to-day to ask the fateful question; and she, though she had experienced a whimsical desire to put it off—to temporize—felt yet in the bottom of her heart a vague triumph, a joyous sense of conquest and gratified vanity. She had by no means made up her mind unalterably to marry Marston Fancher; but she had a dim fear lest in the decisive moment she might succumb to her baser self and accept him. She had loved to play with this dazzling temptation, to fondle it in thought, first, with the idea that it was perfectly harmless, and recently, with a sort of mental proviso that possibly she might come to view it in a different light. She might possibly, some day, grow sensible, as her mother expressed it; put romantic notions out of her head, and make a rational match with a man who by his social standing would advance her and the whole family. Such a match was now within her reach. She had, with a perfectly clear-headed calculation, labored to bring it within reach. And now, when the decisive moment was at hand, she wavered.

Never before had Maud seen the alternatives of her life so clearly presented. On the one side, a rich, comfortable existence, with fine trappings and daily gratification of vanity; a gradual loss of enthusiasm, perhaps, a gradual contraction of the horizon

of her interests, and a gradual flagging of the aspirations in which formerly she had gloried ; and in return a steeping in physical comfort, a stimulation of
that competitive luxury which is the most degrading concomitant of wealth in our American life.
You may say it was odd that so young a girl should
have seen the problem in this light, rather than
rejoice in the show, the glitter, the fascinating
pageantry of the fashionable existence to which her
admirer was about to invite her.   And the fact was,
she was fully alive to all the allurements of an
assured position and luxurious surroundings.   Siren
voices in her heart sang a most enchanting strain, to
which she could not help listening.   The kingdoms
of the world, with all their glory, lay spread out at
her feet, and she knew that they were hers, if she
would only say the decisive word.   But what made
her hesitate to utter this word, what produced this
fatal clearness of vision which saw the reverse no less
vividly than the obverse, was no precocious ingenuity of her own, but simply the memory of that
strangely solemn talk she had had with Philip, now
more than two months ago.   She recalled not only his
phrases, which now seemed far stronger and more
strikingly true than when she first heard them ; but
she remembered even the cadence of his voice as he
uttered them, the expression of his face, the insist-
ent iteration of the locusts' song, and the splendid,
spacious setting which the landscape supplied to his
tall, impressive figure.

It was while her visitor was developing his views
on McGregor's obligation, or rather non-obligation,

to his wife, and incidentally sketching his notion of what constituted a gentleman, that Maud found time to take fate to task for having placed her in such a cruel dilemma. She wished for a moment that she had never seen Philip Warburton and never heard the earnest ring of his voice, because she would in that case have had no higher standard by which to judge her present suitor and find him wanting.

"I fancy, Miss Maud," the unconscious subject of her criticism was saying, "that we agree pretty well, after all."

"Agree? Oh, yes!" she murmured faintly; for in her intense self-absorption his words had conveyed no meaning to her mind. But now the situation became painfully vivid, and she was again confronted with the cruel "either—or."

"I suppose, Miss Maud," he observed, resting a glance of vague entreaty upon her, "that—that —you like Atterbury rather better than the West?"

"Like Atterbury? Oh, yes, I am very fond of Atterbury!" she declared with perfunctory haste, while her thoughts kept laboring away with a feverish intensity. What should she do? What should she answer? Should she put him off so as to gain time, or should she give him that hearty encouragement which would precipitate the question and settle it forever? How could she know that Philip loved her? What obligation had she towards Philip? He had never told her that he wished to marry her. Perhaps she had merely deceived herself when she

11

fancied he cared for her. And her own love for him—might not that, too, be a piece of romantic folly, or a species of that self-delusion to which girls of her age, she had been told, were so fatally liable? Could she afford to dismiss Fancher merely because Philip might, at some time or other, take it into his head to love her? Did she not at this moment hold the fate of her whole family in her hand? It was with a feeble hope that something of this very nature might come to pass, that she and all the rest of them had invaded this aristocratic paradise by the sea. If her mother and Sally knew that the dearest hopes of their lives had been wrecked by her (and they would be sure to find it out), would they ever forgive her? Though she was remotely aware that there was a flaw in this kind of argument, she persisted in reënforcing it to the best of her ability. She launched presently into a vivacious discussion with Fancher, agreeing with the most enchanting cordiality to everything he said, and with accomplished coquetry inspiring him with admiration, and leading him towards the dangerous topic. The high-pitched key of her voice did not betray to him the agitation under which she was laboring; neither did he detect the occasionally forced note in her gayety, or her involuntary tremulousness, which she vainly tried to shake off. A glow of exhilaration, such as he rarely felt in the presence of a woman, sent his blood with a swifter impetus through his veins, and he rose to bold resolutions.

"Miss Maud," he began, with reckless ardor,

"I've got something — which—which — I've long been wanting to tell you."

"Indeed, Mr. Fancher? You make me excruciatingly curious," she exclaimed with adorable girlishness.

A perverse spirit seemed to be urging her to do the very thing which she had resolved not to do, for she was far from having settled the fateful question as yet. But, somehow, it seemed bent on settling itself independently of her volition.

"I wonder—I fancy—that is to say, I have a notion that I shall be awfully· sorry to have you leave this house," he broke out desperately.

"But I imagine it would be rather uncomfortable in winter," Maud observed with the air of a sagacious canary bird.

"Yes, of course—but—I meant—that's to say—I meant that I should like to see you back in it next summer—you look so—so—appropriate—so much in place, as you sit there in that wicker chair."

"Thanks, awfully, Mr. Fancher," she cried with a mock hilarity in which the strained note would have been audible to anyone but him. "You mean to say you want to make me a present of Thorn Hedge?"

She saw with inexorable clearness whither this was bearing, but the demon of perversity that had taken possession of her forced her remorselessly on.

"Yes, exactly," he replied, his face lighting up with a happy idea. "I will make you a present of Thorn Hedge, but only on one condition."

"And that is?"

"That you will take me into the bargain."

"You, Mr. Fancher? Why, you don't mean it? What should I do with you?"

She was now so violently agitated that she had to rise and go towards the window, for she felt in the clutch of a relentless necessity from which she could not escape except by physical motion. How could it be possible that she was so little mistress of herself that she had actually precipitated a proposal which she fancied she had intended to stave off, and was now on the point of accepting a man whom she had more than half made up her mind to refuse? Well, she could not reason about it. She seemed to be under a spell. An imperious force seemed to be driving her, willy nilly, toward the destiny from which she had half made up her mind to escape. Marston, on the other hand, had the beautiful fatuity of a man of limited intellect, who solves all problems with ease, simply because he does not suspect their intricacy. It was to him a charming exhibition of femininity and nothing more, this flight of Maud towards the window. As he approached her, full of masculine confidence, he saw through the shutters Peggy, wrapped in a shawl, but blue and shivery, conversing with the young man from the West, who had buttoned his coat up to his chin, but seemed too polite to tell her how uncomfortable he was. Maud, too, seemed absorbed in the same spectacle, and with a sort of numb apprehension felt Marston's arm stealing about her waist, and his breath, charged with cigarette smoke, enveloping her as in an oppressive enchantment. What was there in the sight of

the resolutely amiable Peggy and the dreary young
man in ill-fitting clothes, which, somehow, paralyzed
her will and made her submit, with a shivering re-
luctance, to Marston's caresses? Reduced to its
other alternative—was not that perhaps what her
life might be? This young man with his crudely
good-natured face and his free and easy manners,
was he not exactly the kind of young man she had
had to put up with until this year, and whose deficiencies she had never until this year suspected?
What a prince of gentlemen Mr. Fancher seemed, to
be sure, in comparison with him, and how very essen-
tial to her happiness were the mere superficial polish
and finish in which he excelled! From the bottom
of her heart she pitied poor Peggy, who had not yet
made this discovery; who was artlessly and unaffect-
edly delighted at seeing any friend of her childhood,
no matter how undesirable he might be from the
social point of view. Of course she did not mean to
compare Philip with this young drummer—she had
a dim recollection that he was or had been a drummer—but by some subtle mental process this loud-
speaking and offensively cordial fellow became a
representative of the life from which she had escaped
or was escaping, and from which Fancher seemed
her only refuge. For Philip was, after all, a most
elusive uncertainty, upon whose doubtful purposes
she could scarcely afford to stake her life's happiness.

She was yet standing in the embrasure of the
window, surrounded by some wide-spreading pal-
mettos on a raised stand, and with Fancher's arm

about her waist, when she was startled by the hilarious voice of her father, who was greeting the young man on the piazza. Anticipating the interruption of their *tête-à-tête*, Marston imprinted a kiss upon her cheek (at which she could not help giving a little shiver), and drew her back towards the lounge, where with a pale and half-frightened face she sank down passively at his side. He repeated here, more formally, his offer of marriage, and she replied; she never could quite recall what she replied, but that he took it to mean an acceptance of his suit was obvious enough from his satisfaction and the air of tender proprietorship with which he regarded her. But the conversation out on the piazza was now becoming so audible as to demand a share of their attention, much to the relief of Maud and to the chagrin of her admirer.

"Well, well, if it ain't Luke Perkins," were the words which they heard. "I'm awfully tickled to see you, Luke. How are your folks? and how did ye find us out, to be sure? But why do you sit out here on the piazzer spooning with Peggy? I kinder fancied it was Maud you was sweet on in the old times. Well, she'll be glad to see you, Luke. Guess she's around here somewhere. But come in, old fellow. It is too darned chilly to be sittin' here in this kinder weather."

It was quite in vain that Peggy tried by ocular telegraphy to convey the intelligence to him which she had received from the butler. Peleg was obtuse in such affairs, and failed to catch any sort of meaning from her troubled and warning glances. He even failed to catch a glimpse of her beautiful self-sacrifice in keeping the young man, who did not want to see her, occupied, for her sister's convenience. It was habitual with this plain and unappreciated Cinderella to play the most unheroic parts, as a sort of benevolent intriguer, in the little love dramas of which her sisters were the heroines. But her father, though he loved her dearly, was as blind as a bat to this pathetic phase of her existence.

Seizing Luke Perkins by the arm, Peleg dragged him with friendly urgency into the front vestibule, in spite of Peggy's pantomimic remonstrance; and pushing open the parlor door, exclaimed:

"You wait here, Luke, and I'll go and find Maud. Mighty comfortably fixed here, ain't we? Pretty snug box, I tell ye—though they keep it too darned dark for me——"

He had gotten so far when a formidable figure, arrayed in drab, rose out of a dusky corner, and with the utmost ceremony advanced to greet him. Mr. Bulkley, who wore a black alpaca coat, baggy black trousers (he had a notion that garments, in order to be decent, ought to be dark), and deerskin slippers, and was smoking a corn-cob pipe, was so taken aback by the unexpected appearance of this serious-looking young man that he stared at him with open mouth, and scarcely had the wit to grasp his extended hand.

"Well, I'll be blowed!" was his first remark; and there is no knowing in what strain he would have continued, if Maud had not suddenly collected herself and come to the rescue.

"I supposed you knew Mr. Fancher, father," she said, with a forced composure; "you know Mr. Fancher is our landlord."

"Oh, yes!" Peleg exclaimed, seizing the young man's hand, and staring at him with a frank curiosity which to anyone of less impregnable self-esteem would have been disconcerting; "glad to see yer, Mr. Fancher. I hope your agent is as prompt in handing over the cash to you, as I am in handing it to him."

"Mr. Fancher did not call to collect the rent, father," Maud explained, blushing with embarrassment. She thought she would sink into the earth with mortification, and was afraid of glancing at her *fiancé*, lest she should discover in his face a dawning regret at having connected himself with so vulgar a family. But she caught a glimpse in the mirror of his profile, and saw there a disgust so unmistakable that she lost heart even for making apologies.

Of course Peleg had not the remotest perception of the emotions which he aroused in his daughter and her visitor.

"I didn't know you was havin' company, Maud," he observed, addressing himself to his daughter; "but here is Luke Perkins—he has come all the way from St. Louis to see you. I reckon you'll be glad to see Luke, and he was a-sittin' out there on the piazzer gassin' with Peggy, and nearly bein' blown out to sea, because that blockhead of a butler didn't tell you he was here."

There was something almost touching to Maud

in the ignorance of social values which placed Luke
Perkins and Marston Fancher on the same level—
as merely marriageable young men—with perhaps
a leaning in favor of Luke as the better business
man of the two, and the most competent to make
his fortune.   Luke himself, however, though he was
not wanting in self-confidence, had a very much
livelier perception of the advantage "the swell" had
over him as an aspirant for Maud's hand; and he
felt decidedly uncomfortable under the rigid and
wondering stare which Fancher fixed upon him, as
if he were some curious freak of nature that had
escaped from a museum.   Maud, who in the meanwhile had come forward and, shaken hands rather
frigidly with her quondam friend, saw that an introduction was inevitable, and, concealing her embarrassment as well as she was able, performed the
disagreeable ceremony.   Fancher presented two
fingers to his rival's hearty grasp, and retired instantly into an adamantine shell of sulky reserve.
He felt simply outraged at having been brought
into contact with such vulgar people.   If he had
suspected that P. Leamington Bulkley was so glaringly objectionable as he had just now shown himself to be, it would have made a mighty difference
in his arrangements for the future.   How could he
make life endurable with such an impossible father-
in-law?   If he only had had a vice which might
finish him in a couple of years, he might perhaps
reconcile himself to a disagreeable necessity; but
Peleg was disgustingly healthy and virtuous, and
had obviously no intention of shuffling off this

mortal coil for at least a quarter of a century. It was, therefore, in no genial humor that Fancher got up and took leave of his prospective relatives. He looked abused and sour; but his good breeding was a second nature, and he omitted no ceremony which politeness demanded.

What incensed him most, however, as he walked back to the Casino, where he had left his tandem, was not Peleg's probable longevity, but his allusions to Luke Perkins as one whom Maud would like to see—one who had some sort of claim upon Maud's interest. The idea of such a creature daring to lift his eyes to the woman whom he—Marston Fancher —honored by his preference seemed too preposterous to merit consideration! But the fact that it did not strike Mr. Bulkley as in the least preposterous showed how barbarously innocent the whole family were as to the intricacies of civilized society, and how incapable they accordingly were of rating Marston Fancher, Esq., at his true value. He had a good mind to leave them with their Luke Perkins in their native slough. He writhed under a sense of outraged dignity, which was to him the keenest distress of which he was capable. Should he disavow the whole affair, and wriggle out of it as best he could? If the Luke Perkins episode had occurred before instead of after his proposal, he had a lively conviction that there would now have been no betrothal to wriggle out of.

Marston arrived, however, at no final conclusion as to what action he should take, and a dozen different aspects of the affair presented themselves to him in the course of the afternoon. And when all his chagrin had expended itself, two distinct and palpable considerations remained in his mind: first, that Maud was a beautiful, accomplished, and altogether desirable young woman; secondly, that P. Leamington Bulkley was a very rich man.

XII

WHEN Marston arrived home after this fateful expedition, he found a telegram from Philip, saying that he was coming down on the evening train, and meant to spend Saturday and Sunday in Atterbury. This was, on the whole, a grateful piece of intelligence, and Marston resolved forthwith to lay the case before his friend and profit by his disinterested counsel.

At about half-past six in the evening he drove down to the railway station to meet Philip, and expressed more than ordinary satisfaction at seeing him. The 6.30 train (particularly on Fridays) was the great event of the day in Atterbury, for then the majority of the "business husbands" returned, each usually bringing a guest or two ; and the platform about the primitive frame house that served for a depot was thronged with nice, sunburned girls and young matrons, in mannish caps and overcoats, who received with a charming, well-bred cordiality the fathers and husbands who dismounted from the train, carrying baskets of fresh fruits and boxes of Huyler's or Maillard's bonbons. It took some time, of course, to disentangle one's own dogcart, drag, or victoria from the huge snarl of glittering vehicles ; and this time was utilized in exchanging hasty greetings and in pleasant banter such as is apt to be heard wherever two or three Americans are gathered together. Philip caught a glimpse of Mrs. Castleton, surrounded by her husband and girls, just as she was taking her seat on the gay yellow buckboard, and the sweet smile and nod she gave him, so full of friendliness and good-will, went straight to his heart and sent a glow of pleasure through him. And there sat the lovely fourteen-year old Mildred at her father's side, hugging his arm, and glorying in having him next to her (for the two girls had had a little squabble as to which was to enjoy that privilege); and she, too, sent a shyly radiant nod to Philip, charged with delightful secrets soon to be revealed.

During the next half-hour the road from the depot to the beach presented as gay a pageant as the park drive on a sunny afternoon, and with the additional charm that the people in the carriages seemed to constitute one large family, all the members of which knew and felt kindly towards each other. Philip had never been so warmly conscious of the value of human good-will, and its power to beautify life, as he was during this short ride with Marston; and never had he realized more keenly the attractiveness of this highly refined and exquisitely civilized little oasis, with its tempered air and delight in its exclusion from the great American desert.

After dinner, which was served at half-past seven, the two friends were seated together in the so-called snuggery, which was meant to be a library, and would have been one if it had contained any books. But instead of that, it contained guns, swords, pipes, and a small teak-wood table of exquisite workmanship; the top of which, when removed, revealed a dozen compartments, filled with different brands of cigars. Philip confessed to a plebeian preference for the pipe, and the only brand of tobacco which he smoked was kept, for his special delectation, in a drawer of the same teak-wood table. Sunk in the deep embrace of leather-covered easy-chairs of the most delightfully indolent shapes, they had been smoking for ten minutes in silence, when Marston straightened himself up, began to pat the head of one of the big mastiffs, and after a while propounded this startling observation: "Look here, Phil, you are crawling pretty close on to thirty now, aren't you?"

"Yes," said Phil, "and so are you."

"Exactly. But that's neither here nor there. What I was going to say, Phil, was this. I should fancy a fellow like you, who has always been such a favorite with women, would pick out a nice girl one of these days, and go and get married."

"How do you know but what I have?"

Philip said this, not at all flippantly, but with a seriousness which would have told Marston that there was something under it, if he had not been too completely absorbed in his own perplexity. What Marston had in mind was merely to furnish a natural introduction to the confession which he was meditating. Therefore he made no immediate reply to his friend's indirect avowal, but remarked presently, as if he were introducing a new topic: "I

say, Phil, I'd advise you to get married; but, in the
meanwhile, I'm going to put a queer case to you, and
I want you to give your whole attention to it."

Warburton, taking his long pipe from his mouth,
turned his head and fixed upon Marston a look of
kindly scrutiny. He did not, from his manner, doubt
that it was a matter of much moment he wished to
lay before him.

"If it is an *affaire de cœur* you wish to confide to
me, Marston," he said, with quiet kindliness, "then,
I beg of you not to attach too much importance to
my advice. No man can really advise another in a
matter of that sort; and it is, moreover, a very ticklish thing to assume the responsibility."

Marston was obviously impressed with this view,
for he said nothing more for fully five minutes, but
puffed away at his cigar in meditative silence and
scratched the head of his dog Whiskey. "Well,
Phil," he began at last, "why don't you get married?"

"Perhaps I will," Philip answered soberly. "If it
depended upon me alone, I certainly should."

"Good for you, old fellow! You just go ahead,
and don't allow anything to discourage you. There's
no girl who can resist you, if it comes to that. If you
only make up your mind, there's no fellow that I
know of who would have any show in the same
quarter where you applied."

"Thank you, Marston, thank you. Not that I
hold your opinion in this case to be very valuable,
but I appreciate your friendly overvaluation."

"Then you have a romance in progress somewhere or other. You sly-boots, who would have suspected it?"

"Possibly. But it is a very one-sided affair as yet. It's all on my side."

He paused again, lighted his pipe which had gone out, and smoked for a while in silence. He was conscious of a strong impulse to confide in Marston, so as to find out, at least, who that young Lochinvar might be, and how far he might be dangerous. Marston knew everything that was going on, and was familiar with all the gossip of the beach and the Casino.

"Any strangers come here recently?" Philip inquired lightly, bestowing some friendly pats upon the head of Turk, who was standing in front of him, wagging his tail and begging to be noticed.

"No one of any consequence," Marston replied with a supercilious air, as he blew the smoke toward the ceiling.

"Well, then, who has arrived of no consequence?"

"A certain Luke Perkins from somewhere in the West. He is a drummer, I fancy, or something in that line; and I had the distinguished pleasure of making his acquaintance at the house of my tenants the Bulkleys."

"Ah," muttered Philip, with a sigh of relief, "the young Lochinvar!"

"What did you remark?"

"I was going to ask you whether he has come for a long visit? Is he staying in the house?"

"Yes, apparently."

"Is it to Miss Maud or Miss Sally he is chiefly devoting himself?"

"I should say the impudent beggar was trying to make himself agreeable to Miss Maud, though preliminarily he had to put up with Miss Peggy, who, as you know, is not a thing of beauty."

"Perhaps it is an old claim, an early attachment?"

"Why, no. She repudiated him up and down," Marston declared unguardedly. "She told me in so many words that she did not care a rap about him. She sent him out on the piazza to be entertained by Peggy, and sent word that she was not at home, when he inquired for her."

Philip's face grew very grave while he listened to this burst of confidence. He looked at the dog with a certain reflective intentness, whereupon Turk, much encouraged, placed his paws on his knees, and became disagreeably demonstrative. He was then pushed gently down, at which, visibly abashed, he slunk away and resumed his recumbent attitude, but beat his tail against the floor at the least indication of Philip's relenting. Marston, who was too absorbed in his own retrospect, too inflated with the vanity of fancying himself beloved, to have much regard for anybody else's feelings, continued presently, with a provoking reasonableness and serenity: "As I have told you so much, I might as well tell you the rest. The fact is, I am in rather an unpleasant position. You know, Miss Maud is a very handsome girl, and well-bred too. But there's no denying that she is—socially speaking—a trifle green. She has no perception of—of—the differences between people—don't you know? And that is, to a man of my position, rather a drawback, don't you see? And that old duffer, her father, he is simply impossible. He actually received me in deerskin slippers, and smoking a corn-cob pipe. Now, what can you do with such people?"

"Let them alone, Marston," said Philip with an almost fierce energy; "feeling as you do—and you can't make yourself over—you ought not to marry a woman unless—unless you approve of her."

"Ah, my dear boy! but there's just the rub, you know. I do care for her——"

"No, you don't. If you loved her, you couldn't speak of her as you do, and the difficulties which you complain of would vanish like smoke, or appear too insignificant to deserve a moment's notice."

"Good gracious, Phil, how you do take on! I tell you I do care for her; and, what is more, she cares for me. I suppose there's no indiscretion in telling you that——"

It was curious to observe Warburton's face while his friend, warming to his theme, continued his confession. Though he writhed inwardly with an. intolerable anguish, every muscle of his countenance was held in a tense placidity, and only the tightly compressed lips and a strained fixity in the eyes hinted at the struggle which was raging within him.

"Now, Phil," Marston was saying, after having recounted the tale of his woes, "what would you advise me to do? You know I set great store by

you, and whatever you say will be likely to influence
my action."

Philip knew perfectly that this was true. If he
should undertake to persuade Marston of the folly
of keeping his engagement, and enumerate to him
the disadvantages that would accrue to him from
such a plebeian connection, he could restore Maud's
liberty in less than half an hour. And this was the
temptation he was wrestling with, and to which he
was on the point of succumbing. For, with the deep
conviction of a strong and serious nature, he felt
that this was the one love of his life; while to
his vainer and shallower friend it was but a mere
episode, involving heart-burning, wounded vanity,
and a lively stirring of surface emotions. He had
no fear that Marston would suffer any serious dam-
age or fail to recover his equanimity within a reasonable time. Nor did he think that he was bound to
sacrifice what appeared to be his life's happiness to
any quixotic idea of friendship. But for all that,
there was one phase of the question which caused
him agony. If Maud really loved Fancher—and
Marston himself seemed to entertain no doubt on
that point—what right had he to sacrifice her happiness and his own? Granted that her love for
Marston was not very deep (though women are so
incalculable in that chapter that it is unsafe to take
anything for granted); suppose it were a mere social
ambition which, in the first place, had attracted her
to Marston, what right had he to interfere in her life,
to thwart such an ambition, and force upon her a
life for which she had not the nobility to aspire?

His host sat gazing at him with expectant intentness while he fought this battle with himself, and at last, being unable to restrain his impatience, asked: " Well, old man, how would you feel about it if you were in my place ? "

" If I were in your place," Philip responded desperately, " if ·I were you——"

Here he paused, and plunging his hands into his pockets stared with rigid gaze towards the ceiling.

"Well, if you were in my place?" the obtuse egotist repeated.

" I would thank God that I had been blessed beyond my deserts in gaining the love of so noble a woman!" Philip burst out ; and jumping up, paced across the floor, grabbed his hat from the stand in the hall, and walked out through the front door. The wind made it necessary to struggle for a moment with the door, and before he succeeded in closing it, half a dozen other doors slammed and banged, and a cloud of smoke and ashes escaped from the fireplace and swept along the floor.

"Good gracious! what an extraordinary proceeding!" Marston murmured. " Perhaps he wasn't feeling well."

He lapsed into peaceful meditation, and the more he thought of Philip's advice the better he was satisfied with it. It did imply, of course, a slight undervaluation of his own social position ; but he was accustomed to that in Philip, and had long since accepted it as a curious eccentricity in an otherwise clever and level-headed man. But Phil's appreciation of Maud had something strangely inspiring in it, investing her, as it were, with a new charm. It made her doubly precious in Marston's eyes. It was so immensely satisfying to know that Philip thought well of her.

Philip strode along the road towards the beach, in a terrible tumult of spirit. It seemed as if a blight had fallen upon his life; as if the future contained nothing which had the power to move him. Wherever he turned, blank, cold, barren vistas met his gaze. What quixotic magnanimity had impelled him to throw away that which was to him most precious, and give it to one who had not the wit to appreciate its value? Why was he strong, if not to assert his strength and use fairly the advantage of mind and will with which God had equipped him? Again and again he stopped and cried out in fierce protest against that sense of duty which had induced him to thrust away the cup of joy when it was held to his lips. The wind yelled and howled in his ears; all the wide vault of the sky seemed alive with tempestuous demons, and tempestuous spirits in his own soul responded with a wild clamor of lamentation to the stormy chorus without.

Never had Maud appeared so supremely desirable to his fancy as she did in this moment. Never had Marston seemed more pitiful with his obtuse condescension and his prating about his social standing. Sometimes the anger blazed up within him, and the blood beat in his temples with the impetus of rage. It was not so much the bitterness of his disappointment which urged his hurried steps along the top of the dune, but rather a wild rebellion against the whole order of creation.   He cried out against what he termed the weak conscientiousness which had made him surrender what, according to Nature's oldest law, was his.   Violently swayed by these emotions, he dashed onward, with his forehead set against the wind, hearing, as in a dream, the roar of the surf at the base of the dune.   Now and then a whirl of spray rose into the air and flung itself in a lashing shower against him ; while from every little hillock the sand streamed on the windward side, like the hair of some grotesque head, with brow bared to the storm.   While thus fleeing from his own fancies, seeking relief in motion from the torment of thought, Philip was suddenly arrested by a sweet strain of music, which for an instant blended with the howl of the wind ere it swept heavenward. It was the sound of a violin and two piano parts. Right above the brow of the dune a friendly glow radiated from a row of unshaded windows, through which he saw the whole parlor of the Castleton villa illuminated by the steady sheen of the large lamp on the brazen tripod.   There sat Mrs. Castleton herself at the piano, playing the bass, and counting one, two, three ; one, two, three ; and at her side her lovely juvenile counterfeit Mildred, struggling earnestly with the treble, while the thirteen-year-old Bertha was accompanying the performance with the dulcet strains of her violin.   Mr. Castleton, looking the very picture of contentment, was sitting in one of the capacious arm-chairs, smoking a cigar, and watching with a smile of paternal tenderness the benign countenance of his wife and its charming variations in the two daughters. There was something very amusing to him in the zealous determination and energy visible in their flushed and animated faces, as they prosecuted their melodious task in the sweat of their brows, and every now and then he clapped his hands in recognition of some particularly well-rendered passage, and cried bravo.

"I envy Philip Warburton; that is all I can say!" he exclaimed, loud enough to make himself heard above the music. "If you had composed a waltz like that in my honor, it would—it would make my hair curl," he finished, laughing.

Philip could not distinguish what Mrs. Castleton and her girls answered, though he heard their voices in a sweet and vivacious medley as the waltz came to an end. The next he saw, as he passed the windows, was Mildred hugging her father in recognition of his compliments for her composition, and Mrs. Castleton striking the *g* and *a* on the piano, while Bertha tuned her violin. This little domestic interior touched him so deeply that the tears rose to his eyes. This represented his idea of happiness —the highest happiness of which man is capable here on earth. It had risen in many a lonely hour before his mental vision, as a glimpse of the unattainable paradise from which he was now shut out forever. For Maud had occupied the place of Mrs. Castleton in all his dreams of domestic bliss; and he had noted with delight a certain sweet matronliness in her, which made her readily adapt herself to the part his fancy assigned to her as the centre of a happy houshold and a "joyful mother of children." He felt, too, a great capacity for loving in his own heart, and a fund of potential tenderness which would now be wasted. He had imagined that he had the genius for being a father—a kind, loving, sympathetic father—upon whose neck, daughters would trustfully hang, and to whose arm they would affectionately cling.

Though it was a bitter-sweet pleasure he experienced in standing like the disconsolate Peri at the gate of Eden, the sight of this little domestic paradise yet took the keenest sting from his grief. The idea of the little girl (who secretly admired him) composing a waltz in his honor, and practising it with much perspiring industry, so as to be able to play it for him before his return to the city, was so ineffably sweet to him, that he found himself unable to despair. It was like a warm hand stealing silently into his, and giving it a pressure of affectionate reassurance. A mellower light diffused itself over the world, and there were yet things worth living for, even though the supreme prize of existence were beyond his reach.

With this feeling he rang the bell of the Castleton villa, and had no sooner been admitted than he was hailed with a joyous chorus of welcome. They scarcely knew how they could put themselves out sufficiently for his comfort, those dear people! Now his chair was not soft enough; now he had to draw nearer to the fire; now he was offered tea; now he was urged to smoke, and a choice of cigars was pressed upon him; now the lamp was moved so as not to annoy him with its glare. Philip fancied he detected just the minutest shade of compassion in Mrs. Castleton's solicitude for his well-being ; and so far from resenting it, he felt grateful for it. It afforded him another glimpse of the rare and generous nature of that glorious woman, who was continually giving of her soul's abundance and feeling the richer for it.

After some preliminary talk the secret of the *Warburton Waltz* had to be gradually communicated to him, and he to feign a proper amount of surprise at having been made the recipient of such an honor ; but he surely did not have to feign the gratification which he expressed at the sentiment which the dedication conveyed. Then came a little coaxing, so as to overcome the composer's bashfulness ; and beautiful it was to see how instantly she dropped the awkward air of self-consciousness when her mother said, with grave kindliness: "Why, Mildred dear, you play it very well. We'll all play it together for Mr. Warburton."

And, in spite of his grief, it was a happy half-hour Philip spent listening to the *Warburton Waltz.* Then it was time for the girls to go to bed ; and as they stumbled along with the adorable clumsiness of their age, kissing their parents good night, Philip, too, came in quite naturally for a kiss, which was duly appreciated.

When he walked home, after eleven o'clock, he often turned back to watch the friendly yellow light which poured out into the blackness of the night from the windows of the Castleton villa.

XIII

FOUR months elapsed without any noteworthy incident, except the desertion of the seaside and the return of the fashionable world to New York. The Christmas holidays were over, and the Bulkleys had, through Fancher's influence, begun to be recognized by society as people whom it was proper to know. They had ventured to give a few dinners, every detail of which was submitted in advance to the future son-in-law, and it was entirely due to him that Knickerbockers of unquestioned social eminence accepted their invitations. Peleg, accompanied by his daughter Peggy, went on a pretended business trip to the Northwest, lest he might by his appearance and cheerily unceremonious manners bring confusion to the carefully prearranged programme; and it must be admitted that he amused himself admirably, and was in no haste to return. He met no end of old friends whom he was glad to see, and whom, in his artless manner, he liked to impress with his magnificence, even though privately he detested it. He bragged a little, in a gentle and harmless way, of things against which, at heart, he rebelled, and in the admiration of these simple folk found a guileless satisfaction. He begrudged in nowise his wife the privilege of dining with the big-wigs, and rather congratulated himself on his escape from the ceremony and restraint of such lugubrious occasions; but that did not prevent him from expanding with an agreeable sense of dignity in the company of people in whose eyes that privilege was a claim to distinction.

It was one day early in January, when Mrs. Bulkley was returning from a ride in the park with her daughters and Fancher, that the servant handed her half a dozen cards on a silver salver. She glanced at them first carelessly, then suddenly clutched one and held it up before her eyes, staring at it with an air of fierce triumph. "At last," she said, with a deep sigh of relief, as she crumpled the card in her hand, having first made sure, however, that there were two more, bearing the same name, upon the salver.

"Upon my word, Gussie," her husband exclaimed (he had returned a few days since from the West), "what's the row now? I never saw you so excited about anything as long as I can remember."

Mrs. Bulkley said nothing, but with the same fierce *empressement* handed him the crumpled card.

"Mrs. P. Stuyvesant Van Horst," Peleg read. "Gimme-crack-corn, you don't say so? Well, I'll be blowed if I would have cared a tinker's darn, if I had been you. I had no idea you was hankerin' so for her acquaintance."

"Hankering, Mr. Bulkley! Hankering! You'll see presently how much I hanker, as you express it, for Mrs. Van Horst's acquaintance. I do not intend to return her call——"

"Why, mother!" both the horrified girls ejaculated in one breath.

"That is to say," Mrs. Bulkley continued, as the soberer second thought prevailed, "I intend to take my time about it."

It was, of course, Maud's engagement to Fancher which had induced Mrs. Van Horst to take the very serious resolution to break through her wall of tradition and prejudice, and admit an outsider to her charmed circle. She felt it herself to be a terribly revolutionary proceeding, and had debated it exhaustively with all the members of her family, individually and collectively, before she could make up her mind to take the fateful step. But she regarded Marston Fancher as such a high-bred young man, that she could not conceive of the possibility of his falling in love with a girl, unless she were from a social point of view unexceptionable. When Maud, within the prescribed week, returned her call with her sister and mother, Mrs. Van Horst took quite a fancy to her, and pronounced her altogether charming. She even, during a temporary attack of generosity, resolved to give a dinner party in her and Fancher's honor, and about the middle of February actually issued the invitations.

But before arriving at this significant event, I am obliged to divulge a little *histoire intime*, a sort of heart chronicle, relating to Maud and Fancher. An engagement, as everybody knows, is a very ticklish affair, dependent for its health and longevity upon all sorts of impalpable and insidious influences, which no one can forecast, and which are as uncertain as the prognostications concerning the weather. The fact was, Maud was not as happy as she had anticipated in her fashionable and socially distinguished engagement. Though this was what she had aspired for, and what the whole family had united with her in aspiring for, she was conscious of no triumph in having secured so great a matrimonial prize. An intolerable sense of vacuity and a listless *ennui* oppressed her, and there were days when she spent the entire afternoon in her room, on a pretext of illness, in order to avoid meeting her *fiancé*. He was devotion itself—that is, in a mild and proper way—called with undeviating regularity to inquire for her health, sent her daily baskets of flowers, and conducted himself in every way as an engaged man should. And yet, with every week that passed, she seemed to be growing farther away from him. His rigid, self-respecting propriety, which formerly she had admired, became now (when the perverse mood seized her) odious and wildly exasperating: and that blank, uncomprehending stare which he fixed upon her, as if he privately questioned her sanity, made her despair of ever drawing any nearer to him. If he had grown angry and berated her roundly when she tormented him, she would have been grateful; for it would have furnished a ground of common humanity upon which they might yet possibly meet. But that air of being mildly shocked, and the rather supercilious look of rebuke with which he contemplated her " tantrums," aroused in her a spirit of perversity, which made her say and do the very things which she knew would shock him.

What made the situation doubly intolerable was the fact that the whole family knew of their differences, and both her mother and Sally sided with him against her. It turned out that Sally was his special confidante and gave him all the sympathy which he craved in his tribulations. There never were two people who were so naturally sympathetic as Marston and Sally; and it seemed to Maud a vast pity that they had not discovered before that they were kindred souls. Then a good deal of misery might have been avoided.

Though Fancher was by no means a demonstrative lover, he was yet too affectionate for Maud. There were times when she could scarcely bear his touch, and a caress made her flesh creep. She was so sensitive in this respect, that when necessity compelled her to put up with tender approaches, she had to steel her nerves beforehand, as for an ordeal. This strange abhorrence for physical contact had surprised her from the very day of their engagement. He was almost obtrusively clean and immaculate, and in his outward appearance altogether attractive. She was quite at a loss to account for her capricious aversion, and yet she seemed to herself blameless; for she could not possibly have foreseen the complication which actually arose. For this very reason it made her unhappy; for it seemed to preclude any possible approximation between them in the future. When, on the other hand, the image of Philip rose up before her mind, a yearning tenderness filled her breast, and she strove resolutely to chase away the visions which her lawless fancy conjured up at the thought of what might have been, had she but been nobler, braver, more worthy of his love ; had she but been strong enough to conquer her baser self, and strive for a loftier ideal.

If Maud had been left to her own devices, she would soon have made an end of the struggle, by giving Fancher his *congé*. But her mother, who would listen to no " nonsense," as she phrased it, used every manœuvre in her power to cut off her retreat. She made Maud feel every hour of the day that she was the one hope of the family ; that all their expectations were centred in her ; and that if she disappointed them, she would have a terrible responsibility upon her conscience till the end of her days. When the daughter cautiously hinted that Sally was far better suited for Marston than she, and that, by a little clever managing, he might be made to transfer his affections to the elder sister, Mrs. Bulkley declared, with the most ominous emphasis, that it would be madness to run so great a risk. You are not apt to catch twice the bird phœnix, she intimated ; and if you have caught him once, make haste to cage him, and give him no chance to escape.

It was frightful how dull, narrow, and woefully uninteresting the whole world grew to her in Marston's presence. He seemed gradually to be closing all her avenues of thought and vision one by one, leaving open but one excessively dreary and cramped one, viz., society. She had to learn to view things as society viewed them ; to acquire, as

he put it, the point of view of well-bred people.
But if he himself represented this point of view, she
would rather perish than acquire it. That mind-
dwarfing, soul-crippling competition in futile vani-
ties, unelevated by inspiring ideas, guided by arbi-
trary rules of narrow propriety—that was indeed a
worthy object to which to devote her life, and that
was the life to which Marston was inviting her.
The fact that she had aspired to it as long as it
dazzled her from afar by its glitter, its gayety, and
freedom from care, had now no more influence with
her. She knew it now fairly well, though she did
not pretend to be initiated in its inner mysteries.
All the future seemed to be stretching out before
her like a desert.

As the day appointed for her marriage drew
nearer and nearer (being now but seven weeks
distant), she seemed to herself like the prisoner who
saw the iron walls of his cell contracting slowly,
but inexorably, until with a creeping horror he
felt himself strangled and crushed in their deadly
embrace.

At the beginning of Lent there was a pause in
the round of social gayeties. After the Van Horst
dinner Maud was invited everywhere, and her
beauty and toilets furnished an endless variety of
items to those weeklies which live on that kind of
inanities, and in New York take the place of the
peripatetic gossip. She was in a fair way of becoming a celebrity. Her picture, extremely *decolleté*,
was seen for a whole week, nailed up on the news-
stands of the Elevated Railroad, among the " Belles

of the Season Series;" and one of the great dailies reproduced her counterfeit, much distorted, on horseback, among the notable horsewomen in the Central Park. In the midst of this whirl of distracting amusements, and buoyed up by the success which she everywhere encountered, she may, perhaps, be pardoned for swimming thoughtlessly with the tide until Lent swung her into an eddy of solemn reflection. The prescribed solemnity of this season induced rather a contemplative mood, and afforded her the opportunity to take an invoice of the contents of her soul and make up her account with the future. This renewed the struggle, which was the harder because she had to fight it alone, having no one to whom she could resort for counsel or sympathy.

It was during the second week of Lent that she casually read the death of Philip's father in the papers. Though she had never seen the crusty old Scotchman, she resolved forthwith to go to the church from which his funeral was to take place the following day. She had not seen Philip a single time since he left Atterbury; and, though Marston sometimes talked about him, and even offered to bring him to the house, she learned afterwards that, for some reason, he had declined to come. The fact was, his friend declared, the old gentleman had gone into partnership with a rascally contractor uptown to put up two apartment houses at an enormous cost, and the partner, having in some way outwitted him, had retired from the bargain and left him to finish the job alone. The old Scot, who was terribly sensitive regarding his commercial honor, had done his level best; but, becoming at last hopelessly involved, had been forced to the verge of bankruptcy. This had preyed so upon his mind that he had become a trifle unbalanced, and had finally died. Philip, forgetting all past differences, had hastened to his father's side as soon as he learned of his troubles. He had offered him his own scanty savings (which probably had been swallowed up in the efforts to stave off ruin), and had been the old man's comfort during his brief illness. This, Marston averred, was the reason why Philip was, at present, disinclined to accept invitations of any kind.

To Maud, weary of shams, and hungering for realities, there was something profoundly moving in this very common experience. It was not merely the vague fear and revulsion she felt at the thought of her own future which made her hail the misfortune of another as a welcome diversion, but it was a passionate yearning, which she could not suppress, to be at Philip's side, with the right to share his sorrows. Poverty which united two hearts in a common privation seemed to this pampered child of luxury a beautiful, an enviable thing. What deep, genuine, and unaffected emotions such a relation would call forth! And how she longed, after the vivacious contortions of society, for a true, strong, unmistakable feeling! If she disregarded this love of hers for Philip, which was the only strong sentiment she had so far experienced, could she ever hope to rise out of the slough of shams and vanity and oppressive mediocrity to which, by her marriage to Fancher, she would doom herself?

Marston presented himself with his carriage and coachman on the morning of the funeral, and Maud, though she would have much preferred to go alone, had no choice but to accept his escort. They found the church about half-filled with Masons in regalia, and representatives of other benevolent orders to which the deceased had belonged. The rosewood coffin was borne by Masons, and behind it walked Philip as the solitary mourner. Maud stared at him as he came nearer and nearer. The organ was playing " Nearer, my God, to Thee," and she felt as if each separate strain of the music were vibrating through her nerves. Philip's face, which was now but a few feet distant, had undergone some marvellous change. It was nobler, stronger, and more austere than when she last saw it. There was a moving solemnity in it which appealed strangely to her. A dull heartache, a queer burrowing pain nestled somewhere in her bosom, and she had to make an effort to draw breath. It came over her like a flash, that, in comparison with this man, all the rest of the world was of small account to her. Nothing in time or eternity was desirable without him. It seemed the most inconceivable folly to have allowed anything else to outweigh her yearning to spend her life at his side, in his companionship.

The coffin was now deposited in front of the altar, and in the startling silence which followed the cessation of the chant, the glorious words, "I am the Resurrection and the Life," rang out with solemn distinctness. Maud, being no longer able to restrain her emotion, burst into tears. She stooped down, burying her face in her hands, and, to Marston's great annoyance, wept as if her heart would break.

"Good gracious, Maud," he whispered, "do control yourself!"

But now that the flood-gates had once been opened, she had to weep her fill. There was a half-painful luxury in being able, after her long, enforced propriety, to surrender herself to an unrestrained grief. It was not for Philip's father she wept, nor for Philip. It was for herself—for her paltry and contemptible worship of Mammon; for her subjection to her baser self; for her faithlessness to that which was best and noblest in her. They were tears of penitence, tears of sorrow, tears from which sprang a new resolution.

The service, which was very brief, soon came to an end, and she rose with the rest, and walked at Fancher's side out of the church. The great, noisy world, with its glare of sunshine, seemed scarcely the same as the one she left, half an hour ago, to enter the church. She breathed more freely, from deeper down, and her thoughts moved with a vigor of which for months she had not been conscious. She seemed to herself a saner, stronger, and wiser being than she was when she left home with Marston. It was as if an incubus had been lifted from her breast, and the problem of her life seemed simplified.

"What made you cry so for that old codger whom you had never seen?" asked Marston, when they had both taken their seats in the carriage.

"It was not for the old man I cried," she said with a sunny frankness, which differed much from her ordinary manner towards him; for she had, indeed, tried his exemplary patience severely.

"For whom then? Was it for Philip?"

"Well, no; I am not even sure it was for Philip. But don't you know, Mr. Fancher, that it is possible to cry from a mere general sense of misery—without any more definite reason?"

"Then you wish me to understand that you are miserable?"

"Yes; why should I conceal it from you? You would be sure to discover it."

She spoke with a grave friendliness which made her more fascinating than ever in Marston's eyes. She could, indeed, when she chose to be amiable, twist him about her finger. And, strangely enough, she felt kindlier towards him than she had ever done before, though she had made up her mind to break with him. As he appeared now, no longer as the tyrant and oppressor, she began to discover what there was good in him; and she was even vaguely sorry for him, and admitted to herself that she had treated him shabbily.

"Am I to take that, perhaps, as a hint?" he queried, as the idea slowly penetrated his intelligence.

"It would save me much trouble if you would."

He straightened himself up in his seat, bowed to an acquaintance in the street, and grew very red in the face.

"If you intend to make a row, I hope you'll

wait till we get home," he said with an ominous sobriety.

" You need have no fear of any excitement, as far as I am concerned," she replied, almost cheerfully ; " but since we are discussing this subject, I should like to get it out of the way, so that we never need refer to it again."

He opened his eyes with that rigid stare which she found so trying, as if he questioned her sanity, and observed with supercilious condescension : " It would not be fair to take you at your word."

" Yes, it would. I beg of you to consider it as final. I am sure it is for your benefit, as well as for mine, that we should part company now."

Carriages rolled by in an endless procession up and down the sunny avenue ; and as his acquaintance was numerous, he was kept saluting every minute, and distributing nicely graded smiles and greetings, exhibiting just the intended degree of cordiality or condescension. Maud's face, too, was wreathed in her acquired society smile, as she returned the bows of the fashionable acquaintances she had made through this very engagement which she was now breaking. She remembered the lost and envious feeling she had had but a year ago, when she tramped the smooth pavement with Peggy, never once meeting a friendly face or hearing a cordial greeting. She remembered with what eager avidity she had gleaned fashionable intelligence from the society weeklies, and obtained from her riding master approximate identifications of the bearers of august names. She was perfectly well aware that her position in this charmed circle was insecure, and that when she dropped Fancher, society would very likely drop her. As the wife of Philip Warburton (if she ever reached that goal of her desires), she would surely have no place in the exclusive set ; and she would have to relinquish forever her ambition to ride to Tarrytown on the top of a tally-ho, and dance the German among the favored Four Hundred. But these temptations which but yesterday had been so potent had to-day lost half their power to allure her. And though, truth to tell, the horn that was blown from the top of a passing four-in-hand coach sent a vague pang to her heart, she conjured up Philip's strong and earnest face, with its stern resolution, its mournful tenderness, and its deep sorrow. There was a vigor and sincerity in his bearing, a manly simplicity, which took no note of artificial values, but expressed with frankness his personal feeling and his estimate of your worth. With him "it was good to be," for with him were life's vivid realities ; its joys and griefs ; its stimulating, vitalizing, ennobling experiences. And compared to Fancher, with his serious absorption in a thousand petty shams which he had not the wit to rate at their worth, how great Philip seemed, how true, how refreshingly forceful and virile!

It was not in a jubilant frame of mind, by any means, that Maud, with Fancher's aid, dismounted from the carriage in front of the spacious mansion on Fifth Avenue. Marston seemed determined to gather glowing coals upon her head, first, by the

punctilious politeness with which he assisted her;
and, secondly, by refraining from all allusion to the
unpleasant topic of their discussion. He had acquired a sense of proprietorship in her which he
found it extremely hard to relinquish; and, perhaps, too, he had surprised himself by growing
fonder of her than he had fancied himself capable
of. He was dimly aware that she was a far finer
and cleverer person than he. There was no denying that, as his *fiancée*, Maud had been a great
success; and Marston had warmed up to an appreciation of her worth by the admiration she excited
in his set, and the enthusiastic praises of her which
he had heard from the most exclusive people. He
could not, therefore, accept as final what was, very
likely, a mere emotional outburst, and he thought
the best way of getting over it was to ignore it
altogether. He was therefore taken by surprise
when Maud, as he was about to leave, returned to
the subject, and remarked: " I hope, Mr. Fancher,
that you will not think it necessary to break off all
connection with the family because our engagement
has come to an end. I shall not object to seeing
you, and I have no unpleasant feelings towards you.
Of course, I am not urging you to remain on any
terms but those of your own choosing. I merely
wish to leave the matter entirely to yourself."

XIV

PHILIP WARBURTON had good reason to mourn his father's death. Though it was a consolation to have closed the old man's eyes, and to have re-established their bond of love and confidence, it was doubly hard to lose him just as each had discovered the possibilities of happiness which he might derive from the clearer and warmer relation to the other. Philip reproached himself for having allowed a pique, however apparently justifiable, to rob him of his father's friendship, and deprive the latter of the comfort and pleasure which his son's company would have afforded him. Then, to a thoughtful and conscientious man like Philip, there was something very bitter in the reflection that he had permitted a mere infirmity of temper and an occasional crustiness in intercourse to obscure from his view the sterling, nay, heroic qualities of his father. When he recalled, word for word, the broken sentences which the old man had spoken during the day preceding his death, he felt proud of being his son. For such sturdy uprightness, such a delicate sense of honor, such nobleness of soul as this rugged and taciturn man betrayed in his last directions to his only heir and mourner, were like a voice from a purer and sterner age, when men held truth and honor in higher, and paltry pelf in lower, esteem. Philip felt humbled in his heart at what he termed his own lapses from the ideal of manhood which his father's rigid, self-denying life had presented; and he resolved to honor his memory by straining every nerve to avert the bankruptcy which had haunted his dying thoughts.

"No man ever lost a dollar by me, Philip," he had kept repeating, even while gasping for breath; "and—God willing—no man shall. My word—was always as good—as my bond. You have—got good Scotch stuff in you,—Philip. You will take care—that—that—no man—can say—he lost a dollar through—James—James Warburton."

It was this terrible problem, how to pay each creditor his due, according to the most rigid requirements of honor, and without ignominious compromise—it was this problem which was perplexing Philip. The law, as he well knew, permitted a man situated as he was to escape on very easy terms, paying perhaps forty or fifty cents on the dollar. But it was in order to save himself from this (as it seemed to him) disgraceful predicament, that the old man had spent "long days of labor and nights devoid of ease," and finally exhausted his vitality and lain down to die. Philip could not think of resorting to an expedient which had appeared to his father so hateful.

What made his situation doubly difficult was the fact that he had, some six months before the calamity overtook him, been admitted to partnership in the wholesale drug firm in which he had for years been the chief bookkeeper. It would, of course, injure the credit of the firm if one of the partners were to go into bankruptcy, and legal complications might arise regarding the liability of the firm for the private indebtedness which he had voluntarily assumed. To Philip, with his proud and sensitive spirit, this prospect of bringing discredit upon the men who had trusted him, and of their own accord advanced his fortunes, was the last drop which made his cup of gall overflow. Another trouble which haunted him with persistence was the necessity of selling the house in which he had been born, in which his parents had lived and died, and which had been solemnly deeded to him in the presence of his sponsors on his christening day. He clung to this home, every nook and corner of which was crowded with memories, with a tenacity of affection which was truly Scotch. The front room on the third floor, of which, with proud sense of proprietorship he had taken possession on his twelfth birthday, seemed so much part of himself, that the mere thought of its being inhabited by a stranger cut him to the quick. The plain old book-case, in which were the romances of Captain Marryat, Oliver Optic, Jules Verne, and later and maturer favorites, marking, shelf by shelf, the processes of his mental growth, seemed like a familiar friend whose breast was stored with boyish confidences. The gun-rack, the antlers over the door, the cases full of beetles and butterflies, were so many chapters recording each juvenile hobby which he had cultivated, and there was not one of them which he regretted ; not one from which he had not derived some permanent benefit.

However, the question to his mind scarcely admitted of debate. Dear as it was, his childhood's home could not remain in his possession. The twenty-five or twenty-six thousand dollars which it would bring would enable him to settle the most urgent claims and gain time on the rest. Accordingly he gave it into the hands of an auctioneer, and the auction was fixed for the first Tuesday of the following month. On Monday the red flag of anarchy, which in this connection seemed symbolic, was hung out over the front steps; and Philip, who could not endure the sight of it, roamed, in a state of deep dejection, up one street and down another, scarcely heeding whither his steps led him. It was about four o'clock in the afternoon when, by chance, he found himself on Madison Avenue near Fifty-seventh Street. The glare of the sunlight hurt his eyes, and the heartless gayety of every one he met gave him a pang.

Of all sorrows to which flesh is heir, none is more painful than humility—the sense of one's own insignificance. Philip was not frequently subject to moods of this sort; but to-day all the world seemed to have entered into a conspiracy to remind him of how little account he was, after all, in the great cosmic economy. He was well aware that no man would hold life worth having, if he could for a moment realize his true relation to the universe at large, and the enormity of his own insignificance. Self-deception is what gives its chief charm to life;

nay, what makes it possible. Therefore the blessed curse of work has been laid upon us; and that beneficent but mendacious demon Ambition sits on our shoulder and prods us on to activity, whispering all the while the most flattering lies in our ears. Philip knew this demon well, but had enough of that unprofitable self-knowledge which is the beginning of wisdom to discount his statements—to take them, as it were, with a grain of salt. He had a remorseless habit of going to the bottom of every question, and not blinking at the things he saw, however terrifying. Why was he torturing himself and making his brief span of days bitter for the sake of that figment of the brain, that fantastic idea which men call honor? What would it matter to the world at large whether he surrendered his property or not, compared to what it would matter to him personally, in the way of comfort and social importance?

He was sauntering along with a dogged recklessness, staring at the ground, and kicking viciously out of his way a piece of coal which lay on the sidewalk. As he came to the street crossing, where he was obliged to take note of his surroundings, he became aware of two earnest blue eyes gazing at him with a half-distressed sympathy. At his side, waiting for a huge red furniture van to pass, stood Mildred Castleton with a roll of music under her arm. Philip returned in a rather absent way her shy greeting; and, absorbed as he was in his own gloomy thoughts, was about to press on, paying no further heed to her. But, as a pair of fast trotters attached

to a light wagon came dashing down the avenue,
Mildred had no choice but to seize hold of his arm;
and with an apology for his neglect, he piloted her
across the street. This trifling incident, somehow,
broke the current of his sad reflections, and with
something of his old friendliness he looked at the
little girl, and was vaguely touched by her adorable
awkwardness, her two blonde pig-tails, and the lovely expression of her face. It is a sweet thing to be
a little girl's hero; and Philip knew that this shy
and bashful Mildred cherished in her heart an extravagant admiration for him. As he recalled this
fact, he made an effort to shake off his oppression,
and engage in a conversation on things which he
fancied would interest her. He asked her about her
music, her studies, how she was getting on at school,
etc., with the jocose condescension which one is apt
to adopt toward maidens of fourteen; and she,
though not particularly pleased with his manner,
was yet conscious of a fluttering felicity in walking
at his side, and being seen by envious comrades
in his company. She managed to impart to him,
in a hushed and girlish way, that she had a German
teacher, who one day had exclaimed dramatically:
" Leddies, you make me ashamed off your interpunction." The girls had all been dreadfully shocked
at this, fancying that "interpunction" had reference to some grave moral delinquency; and they
were much relieved to find that he meant "punctua-
tion." Philip laughed at this, in a hollow and
perfunctory way, to disguise the fact that he had only
listened with half an ear, and then plunged in boldly

to make conversation. But his success was not brilliant. The forced note in his talk was audible even to himself ; and walking along at the girl's side he finally lapsed into silence, feeling all the while the look of candid distress in the glance which now and then she stole at him. Her vivid blush told him that she was struggling with something to say— something kind and sweet as her own dear self—but could not master her bashfulness sufficiently to say it. And thus they reached at length Mr. Castleton's house, and Mildred, though she had made several tentative starts, had not yet ventured, as she yearned to do, to offer him her consolation in his troubles. She belonged to the class of little pitchers who have very sharp ears, and she had gleaned enough of Philip's romance at Atterbury to loathe and detest Maud Bulkley for treating him so cruelly. This did not prevent her, however, from regarding their alienation with a certain satisfaction ; because, in a secret recess of her heart, she cherished an unconfessed hope that Philip would marry no one until she, Mildred, had got into long dresses, and could show him what a true woman was.

"Won't you come in, Mr. Warburton ?" she asked, as they paused before the front steps; "mamma would be so glad to see you."

"Thank you, Mildred; but I am not agreeable company for anybody to-day. I will rather call some other time."

He took her hand, held it for a moment, and was about to go, when she called him back.

" Mr. Warburton," she said, with a sweet embarrassment, " I wish you wouldn't go. You haven't called on mamma for so long, and I know she would like so much to see you."

Philip saw the motive of this friendly urgency. The child was distressed at his distress, and she knew that mamma was a prince of comforters. She had a balm. for every wound, and solace for every sorrow. He was deeply touched. A warm current diffused itself through his frame and thawed the icy despair which had chilled his heart.

"Very well, dear ; if you are sure that mamma would like to see me," he answered cordially, "then I am sure there is no one whom I would rather see than your mamma."

In the next moment the door was opened by a servant, and Philip was ushered in. Mildred bounced up the stairs excitedly to tell the important news to her mother, and presently the servant invited Philip to walk up stairs, where Mrs. Castleton would receive him ; for Mrs. Castleton saw only formal visitors in the state parlor on the first floor. But friends whom she had admitted to her intimacy were received in a large, light sitting-room on the second floor, lined with book-cases, draped with *portières* in old gold and blue, and provided with a large fireplace in which a merry hickory fire was blazing. It was a room which was instinct with the sunny, beautiful spirit of its occupant ; a room not to look at, but to live in, a room that furnished a soft and unobtrusive frame to the pretty domestic scenes that were daily enacted in it.

"Well, this is a rare guest, indeed," said Mrs.

Castleton, coming forward with a lovely *empresse-ment* to shake Philip's hand; "we thought you had deserted us, Mr. Warburton."

"Well, he had, mamma," Mildred broke in vehemently; "it was I who made him come in."

"I have to plead guilty," Philip responded, with his grave smile; and Mrs. Castleton, noting the mourning band upon his hat, grew more subdued in her manner as she added, with gentle seriousness:

"We were deeply grieved to hear of your loss, Mr. Warburton. Permit me to offer you, once more, my deepest sympathy."

"Your letter was the only one of all I received which did me good," Philip replied, after a pause.

They talked for some minutes of indifferent topics, while the young man's eyes dwelt admiringly upon the sweet and gentle face of the hostess, who seemed to him to grow more beautiful with every year that passed over her head. He came to the conclusion, as he sat rejoicing in her presence, that hers was not the mere external perfection of form, but it was the breath of the noble spirit that animated her which gave to her features their wonderful charm. Her face was beautiful, because it bore the record of a beautiful life. A weight of woe was lifted from Philip's breast, and he breathed once more freely and looked the world fearlessly in the face. All that was good in him was strengthened by the mere sight of this woman, by the touch of her hand and the sound of her voice. Before he knew it he found himself confiding to her his perplexities, and drawing comfort and courage

14

from her sympathetic questions and responses. She knew so much already, that he did not have to be explicit, and she possessed in a rare degree the womanly faculty of divination which gives assurance of a complete understanding when but a few words have been spoken. There was to him such a deep comfort in this sense of being understood and rated at his highest worth. It was not conceit, but a far different sentiment which made him expand with a warm glow of satisfaction. It is not good for man to be alone in his thoughts and feelings, and Philip had been too much alone. With Mrs. Castleton he always met naturally in the higher regions of himself—as naturally as with his other acquaintances he met merely in the lower planes. There was an exquisite tact in her expressions of sympathy, which was like the reassuring pressure of a friendly hand—more eloquent than speech. He was in doubt no more now as to his line of action; and his only wonder was, that he ever could have wavered. But, being afraid of appearing to pose before her as better than he was, he was desirous to let her know that he had been sorely tempted to take advantage of the law and ignore the higher obligations.

"The fact is, Mrs. Castleton, I find it very hard to sell my house. You can never know what that house has been to me. All those friendly claws of griffins on table-legs, bed-posts, and bureaus; and the brazen lions' heads in the handles of the sideboard; and the figures of the wall-papers, out of which I made monsters with tails and fantastic faces, when, as a boy, I was ill with scarlet fever—why, to lose these things—it is like parting with my whole past, with half of my own individuality. If you will only allow me to make a fool of myself to the extent of confessing this, I know I shall brace up afterwards and feel less sore about it."

The tears came into Mrs. Castleton's eyes as she divined the pain which he was trying to disguise under these careless and half-jocular reminiscences. His reference to the wall-paper especially moved her, because she had vivid recollections of similar experiences from her own childhood.

" And the closet door, which I always got up and shut before creeping into bed, because of the horrible things that crawled out of it in the dark, and stretched long arms towards my bed," Philip continued, with a lugubrious laugh ; " how can that by any right belong to any one but me ? What will a stranger be able to do with such possessions, the worth of which he can never discover ? And how can I ever again be my whole and undiminished self when so large a share of me is put up at auction, sold to the highest bidder, and scattered through pawnshops, second-hand furniture stores, and boarding-houses ? "

" But can you not prevent its being scattered ? " asked Mrs. Castleton sympathetically. " Could you not induce some one to buy the house furnished and let it, until you are in position to buy it back ? "

" I have thought of that, and in a sort of quixotic humor I told my auctioneer to make the attempt. But it is only in fairy-tales that such charming things happen. I lost track of my fairy godmother at an early age, or she lost track of me, and she has not been importuning me with favors recently. But you know there is a superstitious streak in most of us, and we like to offer these blind chances to Fate, with a sneaking hope that Fate will see her opportunity to do the handsome thing and jump at it."

The conversation presently drifted into other channels, and at the end of half an hour Philip got up to take his leave. But it was no easy matter to tear one's self away from Mrs. Castleton; and, in accordance with his wont, he lingered at the door, hat in hand, then strolled back towards the mantel-piece, and stood leaning against it, yielding to a soft enchantment which wrapped him in a thousand invisible meshes. This invisible netting he had to break through violently before he could depart. If Fate had bestowed upon him an elder sister like Mrs. Castleton, he thought, how harmless would " the slings and arrows of outrageous fortune " have seemed to him now? He was talking on, half in-consequently, in a reminiscent way, only to postpone the unpleasant necessity of betaking himself away, when an electric bell began to jingle, and the servant was heard to open the front door. " Well, I must be off," Philip observed, starting up at the sound of the bell; " I hope, when we meet next time, I shall be more agreeable company."

" Pray, don't wait for so remote a contingency," replied his hostess with her radiant smile. " You deserve just such a reply, when you make such stupid remarks to me," she added in a tone of gentle reproof. "Only remember this, please, that both my husband and I are always glad to see you."

They shook hands, and Philip was just descending the stairs, when, to his amazement, he found himself face to face with Maud Bulkley, who was being piloted in the opposite direction by Mildred. Their eyes met for an instant in a startled and, on his part, as it seemed to her, reproachful glance. Mildred, who was simply tingling with the dramatic intensity of the situation, stared hard at both, with the undisguised interest of a child; and when they bowed, and then passed on, she up and he down, without exchanging a single word, the distress in the benevolent little plotter's face was so keen that it seemed as if she must burst into tears. Hearing Maud's voice in the hall, she had taken the responsibility of conducting her up, without an announcement, so that Philip should not have an opportunity to escape, as he surely would, if Miss Bulkley's name was mentioned. What she intended to accomplish by this manœuvre was by no means clear to her mind; but she had a vague hope that, by a meeting between the estranged lovers, things might in some way be straightened out, and her admired Philip might once more show her a smiling countenance.

XV

"WELL, my dear, and how is the *fiancé?*" inquired Mrs. Castleton with the conventional degree of interest, after having turned Maud about, and expressed admiration for her hat and jacket, which were, indeed, a most pronounced success. There was something breezy and exhilarating in her entrance into a room. She seemed to bring such a lot of fresh air with her, and such prosperity and general contentment. She moved with a consciousness of style which, with the marvellous adaptability of her kind, she had acquired to perfectness in one or two short years. She seemed to fill the room with the rustle of rich garments and friendly bustle, and an atmosphere of girlish flutter and inconsequence. She conveniently ignored the question about the *fiancé;* and she did it, as only a woman could, without the least rudeness, talking all the while about twenty different things, and skipping from one to the other as naturally as a bird skips without premeditation from bough to bough. And then, at the end of ten minutes, when she had touched upon all topics she could think of, without conveying an atom of information, she lighted upon the subject of the *fiancé* as if the thing had just occured to her; while the fact was, she had only been working off her excitement at meeting Philip, and

nerved herself to attack the difficult theme. "Oh,"
she said, cocking her pretty head, thoughtfully,
"you were asking about Mr. Fancher? You know,
I suppose, that we are not engaged any more?"

Mrs. Castleton opened her eyes in candid amazement, and at the end of a considerable pause,
observed: "Without intending any unkindness, permit me to congratulate you both."

Maud was a little puzzled at this diplomatic form
of felicitation; but, good-humored as she was, could
not believe that Mrs. Castleton intended to offend
her.

"You mean to say," she began with a vaguely
anxious air, and then paused inquiringly.

"That I am glad both for your sake and for
Marston's," Mrs. Castleton finished; "for I never
thought you were suited for each other."

Maud's uneasiness was not allayed by this assurance, and after a little distressed meditation she
said sweetly: "You are very fond of him, aren't
you?"

"Yes, but not so fond as to be blind to his limita-
tions. Marston is what men call a nice fellow, but
he is very little else. I was sorry when I heard of
his engagement to you, but more on your account
than on his."

A glow of satisfaction warmed the girl's chilled
soul at these friendly words. She hungered for
praise and approval, after the scoldings, the wounding
sarcasms, the bitter upbraidings which she had had
to endure at home since she broke her engagement.
Her mother had surpassed herself in the ingenuity

of the torture to which she had subjected her recreant daughter, who refused to realize her ambition, and threw her back into her former cruel uncertainty. Only Peleg had furtively signified his gratification, but he was too fond of domestic peace to declare himself openly. Even Sally, who did not like to miss a chance of being disagreeable, joined forces with Mrs. Bulkley, and administered neat and ladylike little stabs to Maud at breakfast, luncheon, and dinner, until the poor girl had many a time to leave the table, and cry out her misery in her own room. She was therefore sore from many hurts when she came to Mrs. Castleton, in all the glory of her fashionable toggery, and having by this time become an expert in the civilized art of dissimulation, she had imposed even upon so astute an observer as her hostess, who had fancied that she was in high spirits. Now Mrs. Castleton was beginning, however, to detect the symptoms of agitation in her manner; and seeing that she was far from heartless, she naturally adopted a more cordial tone.

"I fancied," she went on, as if to explain her remark, "that you were made for something better than the companionship of a man of such narrow sympathies as Marston Fancher."

"It is very sweet of you to say that to me," Maud ejaculated in a staccato full of suppressed emotion. "I don't know why it was that we didn't get on any better—unless—unless—it was that I never really cared for him."

"Well, I should say that was quite a sufficient reason."

"I really don't understand, myself. I must have been bewitched. I don't to this moment comprehend how I came to accept Mr. Fancher, just as I had made up my mind to refuse him."

"It was probably what my husband calls the double combination back action of the feminine mind, which always may be depended upon to produce the unexpected."

"It must have been something of that sort," the girl observed vaguely, without appreciating the point of the joke ; for women never quite comprehend witticisms at the expense of their sex. She was so absorbed in the thought of Philip, and racking her brain to find a natural way of inquiring about him, that she had but a small share of attention to spare for her conversation. Mrs. Castleton, who began to divine her state of mind, experienced a thrill of sympathy as the situation dawned upon her.

"I think I met Mr. Warburton on the stairs," Maud ejaculated with a fine assumption of indifference; but the consciousness of her hypocrisy manifested itself in a sudden sense of awkwardness, and a treacherous blush which she felt spreading like a warm wave over her neck and cheeks. She knew then that further dissimulation would be vain, and that she might as well make Mrs. Castleton her confidante.

"Yes," the latter replied, with a look full of pointed significance. "You know his father died a few weeks ago, and he takes his loss very hard."

"I noticed that he looked sad. Does he come often to see you?"

" Not so often here in the city.   He has so many serious troubles at present.   You know his father died really bankrupt ; but Philip is trying to pay off all his debts, and will accept no—compromise, I think they call it—which Mr. Castleton tells me he could easily get on his own terms."

They talked on for five or ten minutes about Philip and his affairs, Maud with a hungry avidity to absorb every detail relating to him and his sorrows, and Mrs. Castleton with a tender elder-sisterly considerateness which would have made confidence easy and natural.   And yet there was a thought in Maud's mind which restrained her from speaking as freely as she would have liked.   It was the fear lest Mrs. Castleton, being Philip's intimate friend and knowing his heart-history, might suspect a desire on her part to have her confidences communicated to him.   And Maud respected herself and her love for Philip too much to be willing to expose herself to such a suspicion.   Nevertheless, in spite of all her efforts to remain unmoved, she betrayed her secret, and felt that she was betraying it, when Mrs. Castleton repeated what Philip had just told her about his fondness for his house, and the pain it cost him to sell it.   Then the tears began to course, one after another, down her cheek, until with an abrupt movement she arose, bade her hostess good-by, and hastened down the stairs. Mrs. Castleton would have liked to kiss her, for her heart was overflowing with sympathy.   But she knew that if she made even the lightest attack upon her beautiful reserve, all resistance would crumble, and

Maud would have surrendered herself to the luxury of tearful confidence; and that, for some reason, Mrs. Castleton did not now desire. She abhorred the *rôle* of the officious match-maker, and had no intention of doing any benevolent plotting for the benefit of the estranged lovers. Though she ardently desired their happiness, she hoped that they would find each other without her or any one else's intervention. Maud was surely not a girl who had to " be provided for ; " and Philip was a sufficiently manly man to do his own plotting, slay his dragon, however venomous and formidable, and carry off his princess, who was well worth the trouble of an arduous wooing.

XVI

ABOUT half past nine o'clock on the morning after Maud's call upon Mrs. Castleton, a brougham of an extremely stylish appearance was seen to halt at the curbstone in front of the mansion in Fifty-seventh Street. A tiger jumped down from the box, rang the bell of the house, and opened the door of the carriage. To the astonishment of the host-ess, who at that time of day was rarely visible, Maud Bulkley ascended the steps with a nervous haste which betrayed excitement, and, on being admitted, asked the man-servant with almost plead-ing urgency to be allowed to see Mr. Castleton. When the servant informed her that Mr. Castle-ton had started for Washington on business, the night before, she seemed distressed, and was about to take her leave, when Mrs. Castleton appeared in a blue wrapper at the head of the stairs, and inquired if she could be of any service. Maud then sat down on the lowest, and Mrs. Castleton on the topmost step, and began the following conversa-tion:

Mrs. Castleton. " Please don't look at me, dear. I am in a shocking state of *dishabille.*"

Maud (with a tremor of excitement). " Why, you look perfectly lovely, Mrs. Castleton ; indeed you do. I only wish I looked half as well at this time in the morning. I hope you will pardon me for calling upon you at such an unearthly hour. But it was really your husband I wanted to see."

Mrs. Castleton (playfully). "And may I be permitted to ask what designs you have upon my husband? Do you want to elope with him?"

Maud (with an unsuccessful attempt at playfulness). "Yes, that is just what I want; and I am heart-broken at not finding him."

Mrs. Castleton. "And I suppose there is no chance that I might do as a substitute?"

Maud (eagerly). "Why, yes, if you will be so kind—though I wish you were a man. It is a man I want; a good, sensible, reliable, and gentlemanly man like Mr. Castleton."

Mrs. Castleton. "Thanks for the compliment. I'll report it to him, and it will be highly appreciated; but in the absence of such a man, might not a good, sensible, reliable, and gentlemanly woman do?"

Maud (with breathless excitement). "Yes, dear Mrs. Castleton; only, how can you possibly get ready in time? The auction is at ten—Mr. Warburton's auction. I've *got* to be there. Will you go with me?"

Mrs. Castleton (seeing a great light, ecstatically). "Will I? Why, my dear sweet girl, indeed I *will*. Only wait for me for ten minutes, and I'll be ready. Come up, dear; don't sit there on the stairs. I don't mind you a bit—now, don't say anything, but come up."

Mrs. Castleton gave Maud a little hug and kissed her cheek; then she pushed her in through the open door into her sitting-room. Mrs. Castleton's *boudoir* had been aired and swept and garnished, and the vague chill and fresh dampness of the winter morning had not yet been dispelled by the genial glow of the wood fire. There were recent traces of the broom upon the Axminster carpet, and a symmetrical order in the arrangement of books, paper-cutters, etc., upon the table, which never lasted beyond the hour of the children's return from school.

Maud was in such a state of agitation that she found it impossible to sit still while waiting for the completion of her friend's toilet. But Mrs. Castleton was as good as her word. She emerged from the adjoining room at the end of ten minutes, flushed with health and pleasure, and beaming forth a kind of morning brightness which made it difficult to be sad in her presence. In a few minutes the two ladies were seated together in the brougham, talking with a sort of perfunctory vivacity about everything under the sun except what they both had at heart. Maud had given instructions to the coachman to drive fast, and scarcely twenty minutes had elapsed when they found themselves in Ninth Street, between Fifth and Sixth Avenues. Here the carriage stopped before an old-fashioned, high-stooped brick house, three stories high, with a white-painted door, flanked with fluted Corinthian pilasters of wood. It was the kind of house New Yorkers built fifty or sixty years ago, and which yet abounds in the lower part of the city, something half-Dutch, half-Puritanic in its severe simplicity. But it had character and individuality, which is more than can be said of the vast, featureless, brown-stone nightmare that belongs to the next following period.

Mrs. Castleton strove hard to banish from her heart that feeling of condescension with which the denizens of the fashionable avenues visit the haunts of decayed and departed elegance in the lower city. She was fond of Philip; but, in spite of all her good will, the brass plate on the door, with the name Warburton in florid script, awakened her pity. Maud was tremulously intent upon her errand, the thought of which affected her alternately with a glow of heroic courage and a chill of despairing timidity. She saw a crowd of people surging through the rooms, and in a spirit of heartless and irresponsible exploration peep into closets, examine the furniture, tap the china, and indulge, without restraint, that vulgar curiosity, to gratify which auctions, probably, were invented. The biographical interest predominates largely in women, and that is, no doubt, the reason why they are always in the majority at auctions. Here, though they may have no intention of buying, they can ruthlessly tear away the veil of privacy, and decipher many a piquant chapter of domestic history. It is astonishing how much information of this sort furniture, closets, and crockery will supply, when skilfully cross-questioned.

Mrs. Castleton and Maud, being women of a different mould, entered Philip's house rather shrinkingly, and could not quite rid themselves of the feeling that they were intruding. They took their places in the remotest corner of the large, dismantled parlor, and having pulled down their veils, sat in

silent expectancy until the auctioneer mounted a
chair and read a document of which they did not
understand the purport. Behind him stood Philip,
who had evidently just come in, as they saw him
pushing his way through the crowd. His face, in
spite of his determination to show a bold front,
bore the traces of suffering. There was a haggard
look about his eyes and mouth which told of sleep-
less nights, but he held his head high, almost defi-
antly, as if he had resolved, come what might, to
bear himself like a man.

The auctioneer, a small, dapper man, named Culver, with a shrewd and vulgar face, here stooped
down and held a whispered conversation with Philip.
As soon as he had regained the perpendicular, he
surveyed the crowd with visible satisfaction, and
began to speak as follows: " Ladies and gentle*men !*
An opportunity will be offered you to buy this elegant mansion as it stands, luxuriously and tastefully
furnished. If no satisfactory bid is made which the
owner is willing to accept, I shall proceed to sell the
house and lot first, and then the fixings and furniture in separate lots to the highest bidder. Now
what is your pleasure, ladies and gentle*men?* I
offer you here a rare opportunity, which will probably not recur in the lifetime of any of you, to buy
at a low price a solidly built three-story brick mansion, twenty-two feet wide—think of that, ladies
and gentlemen, twenty-two feet wide—with complete and elegant fixings, and furnished in a comfortable and homelike style. No sham or shoddy here,
but everything genoo-ine, designed for use, comfort,

and durability; for, as the divine Bill Shakespeare pertinently remarks :

> ' The cloud-capped towers, the gorgeous palaces,
> The solemn temples, the great globe itself,
> Yea, all which it inherit, shall dissolve,
> And like this insubstantial pageant faded,
> Leave not a rack behind ! '

" But if you will permit me to differ with the justly celebrated Bill, I venture to say that this house is so substantially built from the foundation up—none but the best Portland cement used—that it will neither dissolve nor fade away even at the last trump. It would not surprise me if it were to remain standing amid the general ruin, a monument to the sound workmanship of the late lamented James Warburton, who built it for himself, and lived in it until the day of his death."

He went on in this jocose strain for some minutes more, to the visible annoyance of Philip, who stood behind him, nervously twirling and biting his moustache. But Mr. Culver knew what he was about, and Philip, who respected his skill, though he disliked his manner, did not interrupt him. Finally, with quite a sudden transition, he abandoned poetry and asked for bids. After a pause of nearly five minutes, which had been filled with encouraging remarks by the auctioneer, an elderly man, who looked like a retired capitalist, offered twenty thousand dollars. Mr. Culver pretended to regard this offer as an insult to his profession, and was so shocked that he came near tumbling off his chair. He made now a second speech still more amusing than the first, and

15

got his audience into a sanguine and optimistic humor. Once more he called sharply for bids, and an offer of twenty-one thousand was made by a real estate dealer who stood looking out of the window. No one heard it except Mr. Culver, and there were many who doubted whether he heard it. But it had the effect of making the first bidder add another five hundred to his bid ; and thus the price kept crawling slowly up, until it reached twenty-five thousand. There it stuck, and no amount of coaxing, apparently, would avail to make it mount higher. The auctioneer turned again to Philip, consulting him as to whether he should accept or reject the offer.

Maud, who sat unseen in the corner, squeezing Mrs. Castleton's hand until she was on the point of screaming, witnessed these repeated consultations with a painful, quivering agitation. Every time a bid was made, the higher figure she desired to offer trembled on the tip of her tongue, but the word somehow remained inaudible ; she simply could not utter a sound. Mrs. Castleton. who grew more and more mystified, got an uncomfortable questioning look in her eyes, as if a suspicion was beginning to dawn upon her which she strove in vain to dismiss.

It was obvious from Mr. Culver's manner, when he resumed his elevated station, that Philip had rejected the twenty-five thousand dollars, and Maud was now in mortal terror lest he should offer no further opportunities for bidding. Therefore, as soon as the auctioneer had announced that the offer was not acceptable, she half arose in her seat, gave

Mrs. Castleton's hand a desperate squeeze, and called out tremulously : " Thirty thousand."

That bid made a sensation. For a full minute a sort of enchantment seemed to have taken possession of the assembly. The silence was full of breathless suspense and anticipation. Philip, at the sound of her voice, had turned sharply about and started forward. He was staring with an anxious frown towards the corner where Maud and her friend sat disguised behind their veils. The poor girl, now that the heroic deed was done, seemed on the point of sinking through the floor. She seemed to feel every eye in the room fixed upon her with a burning intentness ; while the fact was, that not a dozen people of those who had heard her bid had seen her, or knew where she was sitting. But the auctioneer soon made an end of her *incognito.* As soon as he recovered from his surprise, he despatched an assistant towards her corner and asked for her name. She fumbled for an interminable minute for her pocket, which was safely hidden from discovery, and finally found the card-case, which she had been seeking, in her muff. Selecting a card, she gave it to the young man ; and, being anxious to escape from the interested gaze of the crowd, she gave Mrs. Castleton an admonitory pinch (for she did not dare trust herself to speak), and slipped quietly out of the door. But here she was once more overtaken by the importunate young man who, this time, wished to know if she was of age. She gave an affirmatory nod, though she was at a loss to know the reason of his impertinence ; and it occurred to her afterwards that she was not of age. Before Philip could make his way out after her, the tiger had slammed the carriage door, and the two friends were being whirled towards Fifth Avenue, with an exciting sense of being pursued and a prodigious clatter.

Mrs. Castleton had a hundred things to say, but refrained from saying them, and Maud was grateful for her silence.

The auctioneer, in the meanwhile, was making a feint of asking for higher bids; and when no one seemed inclined to avail themselves of the opportunity, the house, with all that it contained, was knocked down to Maud Bulkley.

XVII

IT was about four o'clock in the afternoon of the day following the auction, that Philip Warburton's card was handed to Maud by a liveried servant. She had not quite recovered her composure after yesterday's agitation, and her first thought was, that Philip, refusing to be under obligation to her, had come to declare the sale cancelled. As she stood surveying her fine, straight back in the mirror, and bestowing little ornamental touches here and there upon her toilet, she resolved that if he chose that tack, she would prove herself a match for him. Not all the king's horses and all the king's men should wring from her the confession that she had been influenced by any other than business considerations. At the same time she exulted in her heart at having established some sort of relations with him which compelled him to seek her. He could no more ignore and avoid her, and she had sufficient confidence in her own attractions to hope and believe that she would bring him in time to her feet. What had caused her such a torment of unrest was the fear that he had resented her engagement to Fancher; that, being an obtuse masculine creature, he would not be able to comprehend such an intricate affair, and might accordingly judge and condemn her hastily.

When she had, at the end of fifteen minutes, complcted her elaborate armament, she descended the stairs, but had to stop twice on the way to compose herself. She pressed her hand against her left side, and could distinctly feel her tumultuous heart beat. The scene of the wide, beautiful hall, with the two odalisques of black marble at the foot of the stairs, carrying gas-globes for torches, impressed itself with a strange insistence upon her mind. She had a feeling that this was a significant moment in her life. But how helpless she was! How confused and blindly impulsive! And how stanch and reliable Philip seemed, with his clear and quiet speech and his unflinching resolution! She had almost lost all her good opinion of herself when she reached the lower hall; and, as was always the case at such times, a kind of breathless and exaggerated cordiality gave a touch of over-emphasis to her manner. She noted, as she shook hands with her visitor, that he looked portentously grave. A vague pang had located itself somewhere in her breast. She talked on rapidly about Mrs. Castleton, Atterbury, the Van Horsts, and a dozen other things, before she gave him a chance to state his errand. She had seated herself in a *tête-à-tête*, and he was sitting in a brocaded easy-chair opposite. He was leaning forward, resting one hand on his knee, and looking at her with a melancholy wonder, reflecting that she was more beauti-ful than ever, but singularly discursive and in-consequent. What he had admired so much in her before was a certain boyish candor and good fellowship, and a freedom from all the intricate arts of feminine diplomacy.

"I hope you will not misunderstand me, Miss Bulkley," he began, in the first available pause, "if I have the effrontery to ask you some disagreeable questions. My own sense of honor demands that I should know certain things before I can make up my mind to accept your bid on my house as final."

Maud saw that she could temporize no more. It was as she had feared. He objected to being under obligation to her.

"I supposed," she said, catching her breath, and wringing her hands in her lap, "that that was all settled. I have already sent my check to the auctioneer, and—and—I supposed that was the end of it."

"The final decision rests with me," he observed with a touch of severity. "I think I can appreciate your motives, and be grateful to you for your kindly feelings towards me. But before I avail myself of your offer, permit me to ask you whether Mr. Fancher—your *fiancé*—knows what you have done and approves of it?"

"Mr. Fancher is not my *fiancé*, and it is a matter of no consequence whether he approves or disapproves," Maud replied, with blazing cheeks.

Philip sat for a moment as if petrified, gazing at Maud as if he were in doubt whether he might dare believe her. Then, with a slight start, he straightened himself up, and it was impossible not to detect the change that came over his face and manner. Maud's heart gave a leap, and, disguise it as she might, she felt that that single magic word she had spoken had laid the ghost that had sat between them.

" Permit me, then, to ask you," inquired Philip, with a visible attempt not to show the relief he felt, " whether your father approves of—of your purchase ? "

" I have not told him yet, but I intend to do so ; and I have no doubt whatever that he will approve. My father is an excellent judge in business matters, and he cannot fail to see that this is a safe and promising—isn't that what you call it?—investment."

" Pardon me if I appear inquisitive, but it was purely as an investment, then, that you bought my house ? "

" Yes, certainly ! Why else should I have bought it ? "

" I don't know. But I fancied that perhaps Mrs. Castleton might have told you how much I loved that house—how hard I found it to part with it."

" Well, perhaps she did. But that had nothing to do with it," Maud declared brazenly ; " I have some money in my own right which father requires me to invest and manage myself, and it has been the burden of my life to keep from losing it. Whenever an absolutely safe investment is brought to my notice, I am always grateful for it, because it relieves me of just that much anxiety."

Philip sat pondering this new aspect of the question for a while, evidently weighing in his mind whether he might believe her. He had heard that women were experts in the art of prevarication ; not that crude mendacity which consists in misstatement of facts, but a sweet and guileless equivocation, uttered with a charming candor which made it, artistically speaking, a more valuable product than truth itself. Philip could not decide for the moment whether Maud, from the most generous motives, was practising this refined art of dissimulation upon him.

"I may as well tell you," she continued with a fresh burst of candor, "that father has a sort of hobby on the subject of girls learning how to manage their own finances, so as not to be entirely at the mercy of their husbands when they marry. He has given me lectures on the difference between railroad stock and railroad bonds; he has made my head swim with mortgages, dividends, securities, collaterals, and I don't know how many other dreadful terms. And I am ashamed to say that I know no more about it all than I did before. But my sister Sally, she is a great financier, and a match for father himself."

The young man listened with the liveliest interest to this discourse, and the conviction stole upon him that Maud had been governed, as she said, by business considerations. There was no question but that the investment was a good one, and he had no right to interfere in affairs which did not concern him. He saw the situation clearly, and smiled to himself at the idea of Maud on the alert for safe investments.

"May I ask what disposition you intend to make of my—I beg your pardon—your house?" he asked in as business-like a manner as he could produce.

"H'm!" Maud replied, seizing hold of her chin and frowning portentously, "I—I—don't know but

—but—that I—will have the police evict you, and —secure a more profitable tenant."

Her spirits rose high as she felt that she had successfully imposed upon him, and she looked so adorable as she mimicked his masculine voice and burlesqued his manner, that he had to join in her laugh; and, somehow, the world wore, from that moment, a brighter face.

"Or, perhaps," she ejaculated gayly, "I will conclude to keep you—only on probation, you understand—and you are to pay rent to me, and I am to be your landlord. Isn't that too amusing?"

She laughed again with a happy abandon, and then gazed at him with an engaging frankness as she added:

"I believe tenants always hate their landlords, and think them mean and horrid. I hope you won't hate me, Mr. Warburton."

"I will try not to," was his smiling reply. He felt more than ever how deeply he loved her; and though he did not like this complication of business with sentiment, he saw that he had no choice but to accept it. It was not a reckless passion which throbbed in his veins and set his pulses tingling; but an infinite tenderness spread like a warm glow through his being, lifted the load of his sorrows, and filled his soul with bright visions. She seemed so precious; no words could express how dear, how noble, how adorable she was to him! It was not this or that which he admired in her, but all that appertained to her was rare and beautiful, because it was hers. And now he had something to live for, indeed. His misfortunes had not been in vain, if they had been the means of restoring once more this goal for which he was to strive—this delirious hope of which he had so long been deprived.

He rose to take his leave, but stood lingering, as was his wont, punching his boot with his stick, or hitting his leg. A sense of duty, a fear of abusing her hospitality, impelled him to go ; but the sight of her was so grateful to him, that he seized every excuse for tarrying.

They had just shaken hands, and he was slowly backing towards the door, when Maud, encouraged by his obvious admiration, said with a confidential air:

" Now, tell me, Mr. Warburton, why were you so very anxious to know my motive in buying your house ? If I had had the least desire—which I don't say I had—to do you a kindness, would you really have deprived me of that pleasure ? "

Her voice was sweet and low, and she spoke with a cooing, insinuating cadence which was simply irresistible. But for all that, the doubt which he had dismissed leaped up again in his mind, and the happy light in his eyes was quenched. " Then you mean to say—that—that—it was not on your own account, but on mine—that you bought the house ? " he queried, with an almost menacing insistence.

" Not at all—nothing of the kind ! " cried Maud, heartily regretting what she had said ; " but it just occurred to me, as an interesting question, why you men—even the best of you—should be so afraid to be indebted to a woman. Why is it any more

humiliating for a man to be under obligation to a
woman than for a woman to be under obligation to
a man ? "

" I don't know that it is. Only there is a super-
stition of that sort—a prejudice—and I, like the rest,
am not free from it. In fact, we are fearfully and
wonderfully made, and we shall have to be made all
over again, before it will appear right to us."

She heaved a little sigh, as if she were a trifle disappointed. Then they shook hands once more, and
he promised to avail himself of her invitation to
repeat the call.

Her voice rang in his ears all the way down the
avenue ; and the look of her eyes, as she bade him
good-by, shone like a star in his memory. They were
good, honest eyes, and they gave glimpses of a sweet
nature. She was the kind of woman who would
grow finer with every year that passed over her head ;
who would be not a mere amiable specimen of her
sex, but a distinct and noble personality, shedding
its genial light upon every one who should come
within range of its radiance.

A few days later, Philip had an interview with Mr. Bulkley, and agreed with him upon the terms of his lease. A widowed sister of his father, a Mrs. McPherson, whose husband had been a prosperous leather dealer in the Swamp, had consented to become the nominal tenant, and let to him the third floor, where he was now already installed. Peleg, who was not the man to mix sentiment with business, held out for a rent of twenty-five hundred dollars; and although Mrs. McPherson thought this too high, Philip, by proposing to pay more for his board, persuaded her to accept.

Peleg, when he reported the interview at dinner, and rather plumed himself on having driven a hard bargain with Philip, was amazed at his daughter's lack of appreciation. "You don't mean to say, father," she said, lifting a startled gaze upon him, "that you got him to pay more than he wished?"

"Well, I should smile, daughter," he replied, leaning back in his chair with supreme satisfaction. "He thought, considering the neighborhood, that twenty-two hundred would be a fair rent; but I maintained that if twenty-six thousand was a fair price for the house, which I think it was, and four thousand for the furniture, then you ought by right to have three thousand rent, which is only ten per cent. on your investment, but we finally compromised on twenty-five hundred."

Maud ate her soup hurriedly, and, fearing to betray herself, gazed fixedly at her plate. She felt her cheeks burning, but whether with anger or embarrassment, she could not tell. She would not for the world have her mother or Sally suspect the state of her feelings for Philip.

" I must say, though," Peleg continued, as he picked up his spoon, " that he is a very decent fellow, that same Warburton—a very pleasant and likable sort of man, I reckon."

" And you showed your liking for him by—by—outwitting him," Maud could not refrain from saying. She was so mortified that she could have cried ; and yet, if she had had the least penetration, she might have known that in her father the commercial instinct would triumph over every other consideration.

" Bless my soul, Maud ! " Peleg exclaimed, staring at her with blank amazement ; " you wouldn't have me let your house for less than I could get, would you ? Why, gimme-crack-corn ! All I can say is, that in that case you've come to the wrong party, daughter."

" No, father, you misunderstand Maud," Peggy put in, anxious to come to her sister's relief; " but you know Mr. Warburton has had heavy losses recently, and much trouble. And Maud doesn't quite like to think that under such circumstances you or she has taken an advantage of him."

Maud sent a grateful glance across the table in recognition of this friendly succor.

"Well, if you had told me that, I might have let him off a hundred or two," Peleg observed, in a much lower key. "I don't believe myself in kicking a man when he is down, and as for this Warburton, I'd just as lief do him a friendly turn as not."

Peggy, who was the peace-maker of the family, saw dangerous possibilities in the continuation of this theme, and therefore made haste to introduce a new topic, at which Maud again telegraphed her gratitude in a significant glance.

On the very evening when he was threatening to arouse discord in the Bulkley family, Philip was seated peacefully in his study, on the third floor of the house that no longer belonged to him, smoking a long post-prandial pipe. There was a fire in the grate; and an air of bachelor comfort, flavored with tobacco smoke, pervaded the room. Every available inch of wall above the low book-cases was covered with old prints, engravings, and etchings, in all sorts of frames. A large and handsome writing-table, which was not in the most beautiful order, stood in the middle of the floor, and next to it a capacious leather-covered easy-chair, with a book-rest attached. A droplight with a green shade threw a clear illumination upon the book which Philip was reading—it was a recent work, called *Social Problems*—but left the rest of the room in twilight. Some athletic trophies from his college days—two crossed rapiers, and a pair of boxing-gloves, which were suspended on the wall above his head—fell, however, partly within the circle of light which was separated by a sharp boundary line from the region of the shadow.

Philip was so absorbed in his book, which from time to time he annotated in pencil, that he did not hear a knock twice repeated at the door. It was not until the door was cautiously opened, that he became aware of an alien presence. Looking up sharply, and with an air of annoyance, he saw in front of him the coffee-colored face of Mrs. McGregor. She was rubbing her hands and staring at him with a half-brazen, half-apologetic grin.

" Doan' you fret, honey! You know me—Phœbe McGregor?" was her opening remark, as she observed the frown of vexation on his brow. " I hain't got no business browsin' 'round gemmen's rooms dis time o' night. He! he! he! Doan' I know it, honey?"

Philip remembered, from previous visits, that Mrs. McGregor, probably because she doubted her welcome, had the unappreciated habit of exploring the houses of her friends unannounced, and surprising them in the deepest privacy. " Well, Mrs. McGregor, what can I do for you?" he asked, not unkindly, as he placed the book face downward upon the table.

" Do for me?" repeated his visitor, smoothing out her apron with both hands. But it was contrary to her principles to plunge headlong into any subject without a long and circuitous introduction. After a moment's embarrassment, she advanced a step nearer, laughed in a sort of vague and insinuating

manner, and then began : " Well, I jes' do declar',
Marsh Philip, you's gettin' so handsome I shouldn't
ha' known you, fo' sho' ! You know, Marsh
Philip," lowering her voice to an ingratiating whisper, "de gals—dey's jes' wild about you."

" Now, Mrs. McGregor, you surely didn't come
here to tell me such nonsense," Philip interrupted,
with a gesture of impatience.

" Did you say nonsense, Marsh Philip ? De
Lawd bress my soul, dat ain't nonsense ! Yo' s'pose
Phœbe doan' know nothin' ? You s'pose Phœbe
hain't got no eyes in her head ? Laws, honey ! hain't
I seen de gals walkin' up an' down de beach, jes'
a-spyin' fer you, and miserabler dan a coon in a trap
when dey couldn't find ye ? "

" Now, look here, Mrs. McGregor, I can't allow
you to talk such stuff to me.' I won't listen to it.
State your errand, if you have any ; if not, go. I
have no time to fool away."

But Phœbe McGregor was not easily discouraged.
She had a sly conviction that men, whatever they
might pretend to the contrary, in their heart of
hearts never objected to the kind of information
she was giving Philip ; and, after a moment's pause,
during which her face wore a rebuked and sheepish
look, she returned to her subject undaunted. " I
know a beau'ful lady, Marsh Philip. I'm a-namin'
o' no names, but she's jes' de lubliest lady I ever
seed. She's jes' daft on you, Marsh Philip. She go
up an' down on de beach, an' wring her purty hands,
case she lub you, an' she'd promised herself to 'nuther
man."

" Look here, Mrs. McGregor," Philip cried, jumping up with an angry scowl, " how many times shall I tell you that I will not listen to your silly tales? Now, I warn you that unless you stop wagging your foolish tongue, I shall be so angry that I never shall permit you to speak to me again.'

" Law, Marsh Philip," the mulatto woman replied with a meek and resigned air, " I am a-namin' o' no names. But you's right, Marsh Philip, fo' sho'. Ef people'd only keep deir mouf shet dar'd be a heap less mischief in de wurld. Dat's what I allers say to Mistah McGregor, and he bein' a bonton too. ' Mistah McGregor,' says I, ' ef you'd keep your mouf shet, when Marsh Philip scoles you fur gettin' drunk, you'd be havin' more friends now dan you's got.' But he's a goner—dat's what Mistah McGregor is, ef he doan' stop his drinkin' pow'ful soon. An' he try mighty hard too, Marsh Philip. I jes' tell you, he try all he's good fur. But it ain't no use. Dat's de fac' of de business, Marsh Philip. Ef de good Lawd can't help him, he can't help hisself. An' dat's whut I wanter speak ter you about, Marsh Philip ; Mistah McGregor he read to me in de newspapah dat dey kin cure gemmen fur drinkin' as dey cure 'em of rheumatics. Mistah McGregor he doan' speak of nuthin' else now. He's jes' crazy to go to dat doctah and git cured."

" Well," Philip remarked, gazing into Mrs. Mc-McGregor's face, which was now pathetically grave and anxious, " I should think that that would be a good plan."

" Yas, zackly, Mistah Wa'button ! " Phœbe exclaimed in high glee. "I knowed you'd say so. But six hunded dollahs, Mistah Wa'button, dat's a heap o' money. An' I hain't got no mo' dan one hunded an' twenty. I give him dat and welcome. But I kin give no mo' dan I've got."

"And you want me to pay the balance, is that it?" Philip inquired sympathetically.

"Yas, Marsh Philip, I wuz gwine ter ax you ter lòan me de balance. I pay you back, Marsh Philip, fo' sho'. I take in washin', an' I doan' spend nuthin'. In two yeahs I pay you back ebry penny."

"But, my dear Mrs. McGregor, there's one phase of this question which evidently has escaped you. You may not know that your husband has repeatedly, both in my hearing and in Mr. Fancher's, spoken of leaving you. He has intimated that he does not regard your marriage as legally binding. I am sorry to tell you this; but it is, in my opinion, only his absolute dependence upon you which makes him respect your marriage. It is neither gratitude nor love. If he were cured of his vice, don't you think he would desert you, and perhaps, if it were for his advantage, marry somebody else?"

Philip scrutinized the woman's face carefully while he spoke, and was almost disappointed at finding no trace of indignation or surprise in her features.

"Bress yer heart, honey, doan' I know dat?" she murmured in a tone of sad resignation. "Neber you spoke a truer word dan dat. But I doan' know, now, Marsh Philip; you can't blame him so monstous, he bein' a gemman an' a bonton. His paw, he's a chuke, an' his folks is awfel high nobs an' kings an'

sech like. An' I's nuthin' but a pore black niggah,
Marsh Philip; an' I hain't got no call ter hang on
ter a gemman any longer dan he wanter keep me.
Laws, Mistah Wa'button, I don't wanter be in his
way, an' keep him down, no better dan ef he was a
niggah hisself, an' him a bonton, an' kin ter chukes
an' kings an sech like."

The tears rolled down her cheeks while she spoke,
and she wiped them away with the back of her hand.
When she had finished, she dried her eyes with her
apron, heaved a big sigh, and retreated a couple of
steps towards the door.

"But, my dear Mrs. McGregor," Philip remonstrated, "you seem to forget that you are married
to Mr. McGregor. If your husband were to marry
again, without first procuring a divorce from you, he
would be put in jail for bigamy."

"Put in jail? Oh, no! I reckon not, Mistah Wa'-
button. They wouldn't do dat ter him, he bein'
kin ter chukes an' kings an' sech like."

"That wouldn't make a particle of difference in
this country."

Mrs. McGregor pondered for a moment, solemnly,
and then again drew nearer.

"It jes' break my heart, Mistah Wa'button, ter
see dat po' fellah—he bein' bawn ter be a chuke—an'
ter see him a-sittin' an' a-mopin' an' a-pinin' fer his
kind. He's all I's got, Mistah Wa'button; an' I
ain't afeerd ter tell ye dat he is a bonton an' a gemman, ebry inch ob him. Ef he kick an' beat me, an'
cut up gen'ally, when he ain't hisself, it ain't no
man's business excep' mine; an' ef I kin stan' it, it

doan' consarn nobody else. I lub him jes' de same, dat I do, Mistah Wa'button; an' I doan' mind a-tellin' you, case you nebber knowed him as I do."

Philip could not help smiling at the bewildering logic of this confession; and he would have suspected a humorous intent, if Mrs. McGregor's tearful eyes and suffering expression had not testified to the contrary. It then began to dawn upon him that this poor woman, though she loved the brute whom she styled her husband, was willing to part with him, in a spirit of self-sacrifice, because of his discontent with his lowly condition; and, knowing that his intemperate habits would be a bar to his social advancement, she had resolved to send him to the recently opened establishment in Illinois, where many were said to have been cured of the baneful appetite for alcohol. She was even willing to work and slave for years, in order to advance his ambition at her own expense. Philip was touched at the nobility of soul of this poor creature, which, through all the whimsicalities of her speech, was yet discernible. Nay, even her disrespect for the marriage tie, which to people of her race rarely presents a serious obstacle to the choice of the affections, had its sublime side. But he felt that she needed instruction on this point, and he therefore repeated his former statement that Mr. McGregor would come into collision with the courts of law if he contracted a new union.

"Why, bress yer heart, honey, dat ain't none of de cote's business!" she remonstrated in a tone of reasonable argument; "ef I kin stan' it, I reckon de cote kin. De cote hain't got no call ter stan' up

fer me ef I doan' kyeer ter stan' up fer myself.
An' den, I jes' tell you, Mistah Wa'button, a niggah pahson, he ain't no 'count nohow. Ye doan'
want fo' sho' ter have a white gemman tied fer life
by a pore no 'count cullud preachah."

There is no need of recording the little lesson in
elementary ethics by which Philip strove to impress
upon Mrs. McGregor the erroneousness of her rea-
soning. He also told her, what surely impressed her
more, that much as he would have liked to help her
with a loan, he was himself in financial straits, and
had no funds to spare. Mrs. McGregor then asked
him if he would give her a note to Miss Maud Bulkley, as she felt sure that any message from him
would be a passport to that lady's favor. Philip
frowned at this, as he fancied he began to detect
a connection between his visitor's errand and the
flatteries with which she had thought it needful to
preface her petition. Mrs. McGregor was shrewd
enough to see that it would be unsafe to press the
subject further, and she therefore took her leave
with profuse expressions of gratitude for what she
had not obtained. She fired a series of knock-down
compliments at Philip as she retired towards the
door; and even from the stairs she commented in a
spirit of appreciation upon his beauty, his goodness,
and his talents as a lady-killer. She hinted that any
young girl would helplessly succumb under the
fascination of his eyes and the charms of his manner. And to cap the climax, she remarked from
the bottom of the stairs, in her gurgling negro gut-
turals :

"I's monst'ous glad, I is, Mistah Wa'button, dat I is no mo' a young gal, an' you hangin' aroun' de premises. But you doan' know nuthin' 'bout gals, Mistah Wa'button. Ef you did, you wouldn't let the beaufullest lady in all de land be a-mopin' an' a-pinin' fer you. And you as chippah as a blue-jay, Mistah Wa'button, as ef you didn't kyeer a picayune."

XIX

DURING the week following Mrs. McGregor's visit, Philip made a discovery which brightened his outlook into the future. While rummaging among his father's papers, he found some obscure memoranda of an ancient date, which, as far as he could make out, related to the purchase of a considerable tract of land in Minnesota. After another search, he found about a dozen tax receipts and other documents, proving that the title to this property had been disputed, and that there had been a protracted litigation. After an unfavorable decision in the lower court, an appeal had been made to the Supreme Court of the State, where a decision was now pending. Philip, after having weighed his chances *pro* and *con*, made a journey to St. Paul, concluded to press the suit, and, to make a long story short, won it. It was the great value of the land which had induced some unprincipled speculators to endeavor to get possession of it, and they had exhausted the resources of the law in order to accomplish their purpose. The senior Warburton had evidently believed, after his ill luck in the lower courts, that there was no justice to be had in Minnesota for a non-resident, and this was the reason why he had not counted these disputed possessions among his assets. He had been one of those self-reliant, reticent, old-fashioned business men who carry their ledgers in their heads; and, therefore, in spite of methodical habits, leave their affairs in the most hopeless muddle.

The winter was far advanced when Philip returned from the West, and Lent was near. What rejoiced him particularly in his newly-acquired prosperity was the prospect it afforded him of taking up his work among the poor, which recently, for want of means, he had been obliged to abandon.

He had been one of six men who had guaranteed the maintenance of a lodging-house for waifs near Five Points, and nothing had hurt him more than the necessity of retiring from this obligation. It had been his habit to spend two evenings in the week at this house, telling stories to his street Arabs, usually with a pointed moral, and diverting them to the best of his ability. Sometimes he got a friend to sing for them, and play the banjo; at other times he hired a conjurer to amuse them, but usually he had to depend upon his own powers of entertainment. He had yet a vivid recollection of the first time he undertook to address them. He had then no practice in speaking, and felt a trifle embarrassed in the presence of so large an audience. During the first ten minutes he talked laboriously, with a keen sense of discomfort and restraint, feeling that he was making no impression whatever. In desperation he determined to tell them some anecdotes of his own boyhood; and, in the course of his introduction to this theme, dropped quite casually this remark:

" I may just as well confess to you, that I was not always as good a boy as I ought to have been."

This seemed suddenly to strike a small boy in the front row, and with a shrill child's voice he sang out : " You bet!"

There was something exceedingly comical to the rest in this misapplied sympathy, and they burst into laughter and applause. From that moment Philip felt that he held his audience. They knew now that he was not, as one of them expressed it, " a goody-goody Sunday-school chap ;" and when he had finished he was voted a tremendous success.

Although he had many discouraging experiences, he did not give up. He gained a personal hold upon a number of boys, and believed that he was an influence for good in their lives. He became their father confessor, who rebuked them sternly when they merited rebuke, and rewarded them generously when they deserved reward. Since his father's illness and death, which had compelled him temporarily to leave this work in other hands, he had been oppressed with a sense of aimlessness and worthlessness, to which he had formerly been a stranger ; and it was with a warm and eager courage that he returned to his congenial field of labor.

The boys gave him a right hearty welcome. He had never known until this evening how many of them were attached to him, admired him, and strove in their uncouth way to imitate him ; and he rejoiced in every evidence of their regard, because it increased his power to benefit them. Grown-up men, hardened in sin, he knew that he could not reach ;

but the children, however unfavorable their heredity and environment, were yet comparatively pliable, and whatever good there was in them might be strengthened, and the power of evil in them slowly and gradually undermined. This was, at least, his hope, which no disheartening experience had yet banished.

It was a severe struggle Philip had to endure before he arrived at the conclusion that his work and his sphere of life lay here. The image of Maud floated like a lovely vision through his mind, singing like a Loreley alluring songs, calling upon him to awake to joy and life, and renounce this gloomy asceticism. He had moments when he questioned all things; when all his cherished illusions burst like bubbles at the first touch of sceptical reason. He questioned his love for Maud in the very moment that his heart cried out for her with a wild yearning. There were times when she appeared to him as a lovely siren, tempting him away from the paths of duty. For it was inevitable that she, with her gayety and girlish light-heartedness, should seem to him, with the Puritanic strain in his blood, an embodiment of a lower view of life. She seemed made to move with a stately grace through palatial apartments, festally lighted ; while his world was in the slums, amid destitution, filth, and suffering, among the poor waifs and outcasts of humanity. What wonder if his world looked dark and forbidding to her ? What wonder if, as a condition of her love, she should call upon him to renounce it ? For Philip, especially since Mrs. McGregor's visit, had pondered much on

his relation to Maud ; and though he brushed away
the foolish woman's talk, as he would a spider-web,
a sticky strand or two would yet cling to his fingers.
Laugh as he might at its silliness, the phrase "the
beaufullest lady in all de land is a-pinin' and a-mopin'
fer ye," sang in his memory like an importunate
tune that refused to be banished.

XX

M UCH to his own surprise, Marston Fancher acted upon Maud's suggestion not to sever his connection with the Bulkley family. In the first place, he had been their social sponsor; and, as such, felt a certain responsibility for whatever fate might overtake them. He could not afford to let it be known that the Bulkleys had used him, and then, having achieved their purpose, had discarded him as of no further value. The very week after the rupture with Maud, there was a dinner party at the Van Clemmers, for which he had set all his influence in motion to secure an invitation for Miss Sally. It would not do now to scandalize his hosts and make himself ridiculous by inventing excuses. He well knew that, according to the social code, only death is a valid excuse for recalling acceptance of an invitation to dinner. And, moreover, both Mrs. Bulkley and Miss Sally took his side against Maud, and did all in their power to console him for his disappointment. They deferred to his judgment in social matters with such flattering submissiveness, showed such interest in his health, his clothes, his opinions, and petted him in so many ingenious ways, that it would have been the basest ingratitude to desert them. They soothed and smoothed him down, and applied balm to his wounded pride. They were so beautifully and delicately sympathetic, that Marston began to find a subtle joy in the very recital of his sorrows. It did not take him long to discover that they were as indispensable to him as he was to them. Accordingly, throughout the winter, he continued to appear in their company, introduced them where introductions were *en règle*, and acted as a superior major domo when they gave dinners and entertainments. And as Marston was an unquestioned authority in such matters, the success of Mrs. Bulkley's social ventures was undoubtedly due to him. He knew all the intricacies of the social machine, its screws, levers, safety valves, and wheels within wheels. He even knew the predilections and animosities of all the people worth cultivating; the exact status of everybody of whose existence society took any note. At Mrs. Bulkley's dinners he superintended eucrything, even to the minutest details, and gave directions to the butler, the florist, the caterer, with the solemnity of a general on the eve of a battle. And Mrs. Bulkley showed her appreciation of these and other services by subscribing liberally to everything which he recommended, adopting his dislikes and animosities, and relieving him of the care of some indigent relatives, which even the most aristocratic family is rarely without.

Maud, now that she was released from her promise, treated him with friendly toleration ; and Peggy, who seemed to him a most enigmatical creature, made fun of him in a good-natured way. He felt, however, an implied disrespect in her attitude towards him, and therefore could never quite like her. He confessed to Mrs. Bulkley, in the profoundest confidence, of course, that Peggy did not seem to him quite as *distinguée* as her sisters; whereto Mrs. Bulkley remarked, with a sigh, that Peggy had always resembled her father's folks. He was, indeed, on so familiar a footing with Mrs. Bulkley now, that he could venture to discuss with her such *affaires intimes*, without fear of giving offence.

The magnanimous resolve thus slowly ripened in Marston's bosom to ignore the affront which Maud had offered him in breaking their engagement, and to continue to interest himself in the social advancement of the family. To this end he brought various eligible young men to call upon the sisters, and permitted himself frequently to be seen in their box at the opera. Peleg, during his single appearance in that temple of the Muses, disgraced himself by laughing uproariously in one of the most solemn scenes, and was never again allowed to invade the sacred precincts.

Young Langley Van Horst, whom Marston never had professed to like, but who was, nevertheless, from a social point of view, a great acquisition, had, since the dinner party, been disposed to dispute with him the distinction of being the mentor and guide of these beautiful girls; and with a certain quiet persistence, that took no account of hints or rebuffs, ousted him, inch by inch, from his position as their sole keeper and custodian. It was of no use that Marston strove to assert himself in the presence of this presuming and pachydermatous young man. Langley Van Horst had such an overweening sense of his own merit, that no man, unless it were the Prince of Wales, seemed of any consequence, compared to himself. He had a very lofty manner, and patronized creation in general. He spoke in a peculiarly nervous, breathless, and jerky way, which was extremely trying, until you became accustomed to it. There was, for all that, something highly distinguished in this imperfect manner of utterance; or, at all events, it seemed so to Sally, to whom Langley addressed most of his fragmentary remarks. The severe propriety of the young Knickerbocker, and a certain pronounced race type which made you recognize in him a future dignitary, appealed to Sally's imagination. He was as far as possible removed from the good-looking clerk type, which is so distressingly common throughout the United States. Langley's heavy but regular face, his nose which was faintly aquiline, his somewhat glassy blue eyes, his handsome mouth, and the whole ponderous and premature dignity of his youthful person, had an indefinable flavor of high breeding. It was obvious that he was somebody.

You might curse his pretensions, but you could not ignore them. It made Marston, who was not himself deficient in pretensions, feel almost inferior, when he was compelled to pocket the small conversational snubs to which Langley was constantly treating him in the presence of the Bulkley sisters, and yet find no effective way of retaliating. And what was particularly annoying, the odious youth appealed with such confidence to Miss Sally, as if he could count upon her sympathy; and Sally, instead of frowning upon his presumption, actually felt flattered by it, and encouraged it.

Now Marston was, of course, well aware that Sally owed him no allegiance, and that he had no right to call her to account for her eccentric preference. But, for all that, her obvious liking for Langley Van Horst made him unhappy. He knew that Sally had the reputation of being cold, and that she was not in the habit of putting herself out to be agreeable. It was, therefore, doubly significant when she ruffled her stately plumage ever so little, or unbent from her calm and self-sufficient reserve. It was one day, while he was pondering the exact meaning of her latest remark regarding Van Horst, that a daring thought blazed up in his cranium with the suddenness of an explosion. He only marvelled that it had not occurred to him before. Was it really Langley Van Horst's attentions to Sally which made her all at once appear so desirable in his eyes? Or was it merely the stimulus of jealousy which had been needed to awaken the love which had long lain dormant in his mind? Whatever the true solution of the riddle, he was indebted to Langley for his great discovery. He began to suspect that his engagement to Maud had been a mistake, and that it was Sally who from the beginning had been his true affinity. It had never made him miserable when his friends were attentive to Maud. He had rather felt gratified at their bestowing upon her the *cachet*

which he fancied she was in need of. But in the
case of Sally, he did not seem to need the support
of the general approval ; and Langley Van Horst's
manifest concurrence in his opinion of her by turns
angered him and made him miserable.

There was not a single member of the family
who suspected the state of Marston's feelings, except Maud. She had a way of arriving at things
by inspiration, especially if they were things which
accorded with her wishes. It had long been her
ardent desire to bring about a *rapprochement* between her ex-*fiancé* and her sister. There seemed to
be such an ideal fitness in this arrangement, and she
half persuaded herself that it was a dim perception
of this which had gnawed at her heart-roots and
made her engagement to Marston so unendurable.
She was disposed to leave Langley out of her calcu-
lations, for it seemed too preposterous that such a
mere interloper should come and spoil a plot which
was so complete, and promised to work so smoothly.
In the first place, Van Horst was several years
younger than Sally ; and, in the second place, he
would, with all his distinction, be a most unpleasant
man to bring into the family.

XXI

DURING the season to which the present chronicle belongs, it was a favorite diversion in fashionable circles to make up what were called "slumming parties." Langley Van Horst, who, on general principles, upheld the superiority of all things English, had, by an unguarded remark, aroused a pugnacious spirit in Marston Fancher's breast, and a determination to prove him in the wrong. In speaking to Sally of the London fashion of "slumming," Langley had observed that, of course, we had no slums in New York to compare with those of London.; to which Marston replied, with some acrimony, that he could show him slums within twenty minutes' ride from his house-door which would make the London article pale into insignificance. And Peggy, too, whose patriotism could not brook  the imputation that anything foreign was superior to anything American, cited incontrovertible statistics to prove that there were no parts of London so densely populated as a certain part of the tenement district of New York. It was with a view to settling this controversy that Langley proposed to make up a slumming party, to which he invited all the participants in the dispute. Marston, who was about to do the very same thing, grew provoked at having his idea thus unblushingly appropriated;

and, in order to uphold his dignity, declared that the plan was preposterous, and that no lady could afford to be seen, even under the protection of the police, in the neighborhoods designated as slums. For all that, he was overridden, and Langley's invitation was accepted; whereupon Marston gracefully withdrew his objections, and concluded to join the party. Mrs. Bulkley, too, though she had not the least taste for " slumming," accepted, because she felt that the proprieties demanded a chaperon.

It was on a clear moonless night in April that Langley Van Horst called with two carriages at the Bulkley mansion on Fifth Avenue. It was one of those nights when the dusky vastness of the city makes a grand metropolitan impression. The hollow roar of the great thoroughfare, the perpetual rumble of wheels and clatter of horse-hoofs, arouses a sentiment which is semi-Parisian. You feel that you are in the midst of the mighty torrent of humanity, and that the pulse of the great world-life beats in you and about you. An endless procession of carriages with lighted lanterns kept rolling down towards Madison Square, and up towards the park ; and you caught glimpses, *en passant*, of lovely women in ravishing toilets—women who sew not, neither do they spin, but to whom you yet feel grateful for their kindness in consenting to exist.

It was with a delicious sense of adventure that the three Bulkley sisters took their seats in the comfortable landaus, and contemplated the broad backs of the two policemen who loomed up on the box next to the coachman. Langley, as Marston had anticipated, assigned himself to the carriage in which Sally and Maud were, and left his rival to rejoice in the company of Mrs. Bulkley and Peggy. Though he was filled with jealous rage as they rolled down the avenue, and cursed Langley's impudence, he was gradually sobered by the reflection that he would himself have done the same, if he had been in Langley's place. The electric blaze on Madison Square, and the magic-lantern advertisement which declared that "ladies will be delighted with the next," diverted his attention somewhat from his grievance, and made him regard Peggy's vivacious countenance opposite to him with a kindlier interest. A radiant corona of light was then suspended on a huge pole, high above the swarming tumult of the square, and, pouring its white radiance downward, silhouetted in sharpest contour the branches of maples and chestnuts on the stone pavement. The big, unlovely caravanseries, more brilliant by night than day, resounding with the turmoil of political and financial strife, exposed their ample *façades* to the electric glare, and stared out of a hundred windows at the "slummers," as they were swiftly whirled by. Peggy thought that this was certainly more beautiful than anything Europe had to show, and her American heart gave a big, patriotic throb. When they had crossed Twenty-third Street, there was for a number of blocks a sudden cessation of traffic; and the avenue spread its superb breadth, flanked with stately residences, above which here and there a colossus of masonry loomed up, in lonely magnificence. It struck Maud (though she had derived the impression, of late, that it was not good form to be proud of anything American) that there was a certain grand spaciousness, quiet richness, and palatial reserve about these mansions, which made them pleasant to look upon. They gave to the avenue a certain character of grave rectilinear severity which is thoroughly American. There is nothing fantastic, nothing flamboyant, no undue geniality or expressiveness, in these plain rectangular fronts; but neither is there any lack of dignity. We build thus, because thus we are. And down on Washington Square, which separates the respectable from the disreputable New York, what stately amplitude, suggestive of *bourgeois* comfort and copious but well-regulated expenditure, in these broad, commodious houses of brick and marble, looking out upon the noble park with its tall, interlacing elms and maples! They are, perhaps, a little too "respectable" to be really grand. There is a certain neatness and sobriety about them which is, in its origin, Dutch, and characteristic of a virtuous mercantile community. The stately ghosts of the Knickerbockers walk abroad under the shadows of these trees, and bemoan the disappearance of the New York which they knew, and the encroachments of a vast, conglomerate, alien civilization.

If our "slummers" failed to encounter any of these disgruntled phantoms hovering over their graves, hidden under the pavement, it was probably because they drove so fast from the respectable north to the disreputable south side, that no leisurely eighteenth-century ghost could have kept pace with

them. They plunged into the quarter devoted to
cabarets and *boulangeries* and *maisons garnies*, and
Gallic speech and customs, and then struck across
eastward, through some terribly ill-smelling alleys,
thronged with a dusky population, wearing ear-rings,
and gesticulating with the vehemence that was
wholly un-American. Women bare-headed, or wearing brass jewelry and gay-colored kerchiefs on their
black hair, garnished the doorsteps, chattering like
magpies, spending their lives in the midst of an alien
race in their amiable, out-of-door, Italian fashion.
Though the spring was already far advanced, there
was yet a touch of rawness in the air, but these sun-
browned children of the South ignored it, and in
their friendly gregariousness strove to counterfeit
the life which they had left behind them in Naples
and Palermo. Both Maud and Peggy craned their
necks and often rose in the carriages, standing like
breathless exclamation points, full of suppressed
amazement, while Mrs. Bulkley and Sally endeavored to hold them in check, and admonished them
to restrain their enthusiasm. They called attention to the extreme shabbiness of the streets, the
disrepair of the mottled, green-shuttered houses,
the heaps of garbage that exhaled sickening odors,
the many-colored garments that depended from the
fire-escapes, and the unclean and poverty-stricken
aspect of the men and women who crowded the
sidewalks. Their faces spoke of privations, sordid
effort, and passions easily unleashed. But to Maud,
as to Peggy, they were on that account no less interesting. They had the sensation of sitting in a

high-priced box, looking out upon a play which had been gotten up for their benefit, and pity was not their uppermost feeling. Even the children, who held out their hands to them, asking for " fiva centa," and the women, who sent volleys of sonorous but happily unintelligible observations after them, seemed to be separated from them by invisible foot-lights, and to be part of the play. It was so extremely novel to see people in this grave, silent, and Puritanical land of ours so joyous, so pictorially demonstrative, living expressive, conversational lives, full of flourish, plasticity, and happy irresponsibility. Having now, as they fancied, exhausted the interest of the East side, Mr. Van Horst's party turned westward, crossing Broadway at Prince Street.

On the west side of the great thoroughfare, as you proceed up Worth Street, there is a dingy, triangular square into which half a dozen streets and lanes converge. The east side of it is occupied by a huge iron building belonging to a well-known publishing firm, and the south side, in part, by a featureless red brick wall, which shelters a mission-house. By day and by night this neighborhood seems equally populous, and the police are continually busy punching would-be sleepers, who are curling themselves up for repose on or under the benches that adorn the square. It is not supposed to be safe for a person in respectable garb and of peaceful avocation to invade this precinct after dark, and such an invader will, if he encounters a bluecoat, be suspected of a sinister design. The only exceptions to this rule are the missionaries, soldiers of either gender wearing the uniform of the Salvation Army, and a few philanthropical cranks who run missions of their own. These are all well known to the police and to the denizens of the neighborhood, and are not frequently exposed to molestation. Here, that most noxious growth of a great city, the New York tough, flourishes; here youthful gangs of criminals have their " clubs " in the rear of saloons and dives, and plot burglaries and assaults; here vice and degradation of all kinds stalk abroad in hideous nakedness.

The occupants of the two landaus caught but brief glimpses of all this, and even that which they saw they understood but imperfectly. The front carriage, as it turned an abrupt corner, ran against a peanut and banana man who was trundling his cart homeward, and received the full blast of Italian maledictions which he fired at the coachman, until suddenly sobered by the sight of the bluecoat. The vista up the street which they now entered was one of tall brick tenements with iron balconies and fire-escapes, and in the far distance the structure of the elevated railroad, over which, every now and then, a train went clattering, and with a gust of white steam obliterated the house-fronts. Here the policeman who acted as guide ordered the coachman to stop, and in spite of his admonition to the loiterers on the sidewalk to " move on," a small crowd gathered about the carriages. It was a notorious dive, whither countrymen and strangers who want to " see life " are enticed, and whence they are

rarely permitted to depart as long as they have a
penny in their pockets. The proprietor of such
a place invariably has a political " pull," and pays a
percentage out of his ill-gotten gains to the police,
or perhaps to higher authorities, for immunity from
molestation.

Maud was seized with a chill at the sight of the
men and women who stood staring at her with a
surly ill-will which they strove in no way to disguise. They hated her and her kind ; they envied
her the comfort, the wealth, the distinction which
made her life soft and beautiful, and the absence of
which made theirs gaunt, barren, and ugly. There
was a dreadful young woman who stood leaning
against the gas-post, fixing a hard resentful glance
upon Maud, as if she would like to strike her nails
into her face, and disfigure it with hideous gashes.
Next to her stood a pallid and stunted female
creature with tousled hair and snaggled teeth, and a
ragged shawl covering half her person. She looked
wofully haggard and miserable, and there was something hunted and mutely appealing in her eyes,
which made a deep impression upon Maud. Those
keen, hungry eyes, in their dark hollows, seemed
to bore themselves into her soul and reproach
her light-hearted levity, her callous indifference, her
heedless acceptance, as a right, of all the blessings
which had been showered in her path. A young
tough, with a close-cropped bullet head and an
incredibly brutal face was edging himself up to
her, as she stepped upon the sidewalk, and, heedless of the warnings of the bystanders, he bumped,

or possibly was pushed, rudely against her. The policeman, who had for the moment been assisting Mrs. Bulkley to dismount, turned promptly about as Maud gave a little cry of distress, and only by a dexterous dodge did the young rascal escape the whack on the head that was intended for him.

This little incident somehow had a discouraging effect upon all the members of the party. They could hear, as they gathered in a group on the sidewalk, wanton yells from within, and a highly discordant noise, which seemed to proceed from some kind of instrument producing mechanical music.

"Really," said Sally, "I had no idea the slums were as bad as this. I feel as if I were inhaling typhus and smallpox and diphtheria in every breath I draw. If you will pardon me, Mr. Van Horst, I am for going home."

"I—ah—I—oh—that is to say," Langley began, with an apologetic cough, "I was—ah—really not aware that the—ah—lower classes in this—city—were —so — ah — ill-mannered — so — ah — obtrusive. In London, where I joined several slumming parties, we never had the least trouble. The rabble there, though they were probably worse off than these people, were—ah—much better behaved."

"Is there any danger of our being insulted?" asked Mrs. Bulkley of the policeman.

"That I can't say, mam," the officer replied. "It depends upon how drunk they are. Ye mustn't be fastidious, if ye want to go a-slumming."

"I say to go in, if only for a moment," ejaculated

Maud. "It would be too humiliating to go home again without having seen anything."

"The policemen will certainly protect us," Peggy observed ; " and then, you know, it would be *so* interesting!"

"Well, you may go," said Sally, decidedly ; " I shall remain here in the carriage."

" And I," Marston declared, with a grand air of protectorship, " could not think of leaving you here alone. I shall stay with you."

" Thank you ; but for protection I prefer the policeman," Sally remarked dryly.

Langley, who was torn with conflicting emotions, wishing, on the one hand, to make his slumming party a success; and being, on the other hand, reluctant to leave Fancher alone with Sally, fidgeted about from the one to the other, striving vainly to reconcile their preferences. In the meanwhile the crowd about them was growing larger, reaching now half-way into the street. They had no idea, of course, how glaringly conspicuous they were, with their rich wraps and their soft glow of health and youth and luxury, in the midst of this filthy, haggard, poverty-stricken throng. It was an effect like that of a bunch of Jacqueminot roses blooming on a dunghill. Disrespectful calls were heard, and remarks, the foulness of which made them unintelligible to all but the policeman. Faces of many types, but all bearing the stamp of misery and degradation, were thrust eagerly forward ; necks were craned ; a lot of oldish-looking boys climbed up on the carriage-steps in order to see the fun.

XXII

" For God's sake, let us get out of this!" cried Mrs. Bulkley.

She was seized with a veritable panic at an ungentle contact with a mouldy pauper who was knocked up against her by a push from behind.

" There is a mission next door," one of the policemen observed; " if you will go in there and wait for fifteen minutes, it'll be all right. If we drive along now, they will follow us and we may have trouble."

" Yes, by all means let us go to the mission. Where is it ? You lead the way."

" Oh, where is it ? " asked Sally, breathlessly; " do let us hurry."

It was high time they took their departure. For there were signs that not even the presence of the blue-coats would have sufficed much longer to restrain the crowd. As the first of the policemen took Mrs. Bulkley's arm, he had to face an unyielding wall of humanity, through which he ruthlessly broke a path with his club.

" Oh, no, don't ! The poor things !" cried Maud, who came right behind him with Langley Van Horst. The thud of the club, as it hit right and left, set her nerves tingling.

" Well, mum, you try your way, and you'll see what will become of you," the officer replied.

She was conscious of a great deal of rude horse-play behind her, as she pushed on in the wake of her guide; and she suspected, too, that the awful things she heard, the meaning of which, perhaps, vaguely dawned upon her, were but expressions of that savage rancor and hate which the step-children of Fate feel for their favored brothers and sisters. Twenty steps brought her to the door of the mission, where the whole party huddled in, while the policemen mounted guard and kept back the crowd, which was disposed to push in behind them.

It was a spacious, dark hall they entered, exhibiting on the wall opposite the doors a large canvas screen, upon which was projected a magic-lantern picture of Joseph revealing himself to his frightened brothers. The picture was greeted with a round of applause and comments uttered in a variety of languages. Maud had slipped into a seat next to the door, and her companions had filed into the same pew, thus forcing her up against the wall. The darkness was grateful to her after her agitating experience; although the hungry eyes of that pale and stunted girl, with the ragged shawl, seemed to be staring at her out of all the dusky corners. Then, all of a sudden, there came a voice out of the dark—a rich, strong voice. Maud gave a start and clutched Peggy's arm. She was thankful it was Peggy who sat next to her, for she was tremulous, unnerved, and strangely distraught; and there was such a fund of comfort and sympathy and good sense in Peggy. She let her eyes range out over the sea of heads which was dimly visible between her and the canvas screen, and she fancied she saw the strained interest in the hundreds of eager faces. The speaker, whoever he was, was relating in homely phrase, but with a vivid and dramatic realism, the scene of the meeting between the governor of Egypt and his pale and terror-stricken brothers, shivering with their consciousness of guilt, as the vision of their past iniquity rose up before them. Maud imagined she was familiar with the story of Joseph in all its details; but somehow she had never before dreamed how beautiful it was, how touching, how replete with those fine human touches that prove the world akin. She listened with a breathless interest, and when the narrator exclaimed with noble pathos: " I am your brother Joseph!" she burst into tears. Peggy gave her an admonitory nudge and began to talk nervously to Mr. Van Horst, so as to divert attention from her emotional sister. Of course, the situation had been clear to her from the moment she heard the invisible speaker's voice, which she, as well as Maud, had recognized as that of Philip Warburton. And for that very reason she interposed all the obstacles in her power to Marston, who was leaning over the intervening persons and whispering:

" I say, Maud, I'll be drawn and quartered if this isn't Phil's mission ; I am sure that's his voice."

" Why, do you really think so?" Peggy queried with brazen incredulity. " It does certainly resemble Mr. Warburton's."

Half a dozen more pictures were projected upon the screen, illustrating the return of the brothers for their father, the arrival of Jacob in Egypt, Jacob's death, etc., and the explanatory commentary was continued in the same strain. There was an obvious effort on the part of the speaker to bring the story down to the intelligence of his hearers ; and though he avoided vulgarisms, he used often startlingly homely language, and supplied a multitude of details and moral reflections of a practical kind which ranged considerably beyond his text. But what touched Maud was the breezy and yet affectionate tone in which he spoke, breathing an anxious desire to raise and benefit this herd of miserable waifs. There was nothing of sickly sweetness in it, but a warm, manly ring, waking the torpid conscience, rousing to vigilance and manly effort. It was the pouring out of a strong soul, aglow with the noblest of passions—the desire to benefit his kind. It was obvious to Maud, as she sat listening to his stirring discourse, that he had not arrived at this perfection of artless art without earnest endeavor and deep and painstaking study. There was not a particle of condescension in his manner, nor of the usual clerical, God-bless-you-my-children air ; but rather the tone of an affectionate elder brother who claimed no other authority than that which was freely accorded to his ampler experience and his sincere desire to do good.

It was well that the other members of the party were also interested in Philip's recital of Joseph's fate, for they left Maud to the luxury of long-re-restrained tears under the shelter of the grateful dusk. She did not know why she wept. Her heart was overcharged with a great dim sentiment which could find expression only in tears. It seemed, as she sat listening, that she was being slowly lifted out of her old life, with its frivolities and confusions; and something new and beautiful dawned upon her, stirred her to fresh resolutions, and filled her with a vague, anticipatory joy. She despaired no longer of the strength to put behind her all that had hitherto seemed fair and alluring. For how feeble, how flimsy, how insignificant it was in comparison with that to which she meant in future to consecrate her powers! Just as Marston Fancher and Langley Van Horst, the types of the existence she meant to renounce, paled into meanness and pusillanimity by the side of Philip, with his grand humanitarian passion. How sublime, how heroic, he seemed to her as he stood there, invisible to her eyes, but visible to her fancy, animated by generous zeal for the poor, the soul-crippled, the down-trodden! He had chosen the better part, indeed, in striving for the highest joys which come only to those capable of the greatest sacrifice. And yet she was dimly aware of doing him injustice in her very admiration. It was not for the joy of renunciation that he had entered upon this difficult path. No, it was rather, as he had more than once intimated, because of a need to do something worthy, to make his life of some account. He was too strong, too considerable a man, to find satisfaction in the petty conquests and small triumphs of society. He needed a larger field, larger obstacles, and larger results. And thus he had insensibly been drawn into the work of a social reformer.

It was while Maud sat thus, deeply absorbed in a

penitential reverie, that a disturbance arose in the hall. Angry words were heard in alien tongues, and presently the sound of the upsetting of a bench, and a body rolling upon the floor. Instantly the lights were turned up, and the discourse came to an end. Maud saw Philip quickly descend from the platform from which he had spoken, and make his way down the aisle to the scene of the disturbance. His face wore a calm and resolute expression, and there was something in the way he carried his head which made Maud thrill with admiration. The masterful masculine quality in the man shone forth with a kind of refulgence. With a quick motion he bent down and lifted up the two combatants, who had been rolling on the floor. With a tremendous thump he set them on their feet, pulled them apart, and, grabbing them by the arms, led them up to the platform. The one was a swarthy and savage-looking little Sicilian of fifteen; the other, a frowsy and ragged Pole of about the same age. As Philip opened a door behind the platform and disappeared with the culprits, a young gentleman with a banjo seated himself in front of the screen, and sang with inimitable mimicry some plantation songs in negro dialect. The audience laughed and cheered, and encored two of the songs. Marston Fancher, who knew the singer as a prominent society man and leader of Germans, was so astonished that he kept repeating: "Why, I say—that Phil—he's a trump!"

Nearly fifteen minutes elapsed before the two culprits reappeared, looking sheepish and crestfallen. They walked out of the hall, swaggering a little, perhaps, in the presence of their comrades, but yet with a deep sense of disgrace. Philip's tall form was presently seen emerging from behind the platform. He shook hands with the banjo-player, and appeared to be expressing his thanks to him for his successful entertainment. It was obvious that he was persuading him to give a few more specimens of his art, and that the banjo-player yielded. Just as he was stepping down, Philip paused an instant, and let his attentive gaze range over the audience. It was his custom to study their faces at all times with this searching glance of his, in order to ascertain how far he was succeeding in his plans to elevate and benefit them. At that very instant Maud, too, looked up, and their eyes met. A rush of color surged into her face. Her head was in a whirl. Her heart went out to him with an infinite yearning. Why did he choose to misjudge, to misapprehend her? All that was good and true and noble in her was bound up with her love for him. It seemed impossible that he could yet believe her shallow, flimsy, and frivolous. How happy she would be to tread any path, however thorny, if she could but be permitted to tread it at his side. She had that grand trust in his fundamental nobility which made her heedless of her own dignity.

These were the thoughts that confusedly whirled through her brain as she sat looking at Philip. She saw a startled recognition in his eyes, and his face suddenly flushed with a warmer animation. Then, with a restrained impetuosity, he walked down the aisle to where she was sitting, shook hands with

Mrs. Bulkley, Sally, and Peggy ; was introduced by Marston to Langley Van Horst. After having replied to their congratulations and complimentary references to his work, he finally made his way to Maud. There was a heartiness in his greeting which lifted a load from her heart. The old restraint, which had always marked his manner towards her since her engagement to Fancher, was now, for the first time, absent; and of that half-critical reserve, of which she had been uncomfortably conscious, she could now not discover a vestige.

" Well, Miss Maud," he began, under cover of the banjoist's prelude, " I am so glad to see you. It seems an age since we met."

She was on the point of answering that that was his own fault, and not hers; but somehow that seemed an ungracious thing to say, and she forbore. She therefore only smiled with a calm contentment, and gently withdrew her hand, which he still held and seemed reluctant to release.

" I wish I had come here before," she said sweetly. " I knew of your work in a general way, but I had not the courage to penetrate into this neighborhood without masculine escort. And now I can't even flatter myself that I came purposely, for it was a pure chance which drove us in here, when the crowd outside made demonstrations of hostility."

" It ought not to surprise you," Philip remarked simply. " They know and instinctively feel in what spirit you came, and they are right in resenting it. It is their honest self-respect which makes them resent it. I should despair of ever helping them, if they were meekly grateful for the crumbs of attention and pennies that fall to them from the tables of the rich."

There was, perhaps, a hint of rebuke in this; but the deep earnestness with which it was uttered made it seem half impersonal, and applicable to the class to which she belonged rather than herself. Then, too, he seemed to stand before her in a half-heroic light. The quiet warmth in his brown eyes; a certain large and rich salubriousness in his personality, of which she had never before been so keenly conscious, and, above all, a certain harmonious consonance in their thoughts and feelings seemed to have established a new relation between them which she would not allow any petty vanity to disturb. He paid her the compliment of taking for granted her interest in the things which interested him, and she would not for the world have proved herself unworthy of this confidence.

"I envy you," she said after a pause, "having found your life work, and having had the courage to seize it when you found it."

"It is not the seizing it which requires courage," he replied with grave thoughtfulness; "but the persevering in it in the face of a thousand discouragements and failures, when you have discovered just what it means."

"I thought your work, judging by what we have seen of it, was a grand success," she ejaculated with impulsive warmth. She was afraid of losing her idol, and anxious to defend him against his own deprecations.

"My dear Miss Maud," he said, looking at her with a half-compassionate tenderness, "I wish I deserved your compliment. I have gathered here about four hundred boys from among the dregs of the population of this huge city. Nine-tenths of them have inherited the ferocity, the low cunning, the savage unrestraint of the uncivilized man. You saw, a moment ago, how those two young barbarians sprang at each other like two panther cubs, simply because the one had in a teasing spirit pulled the other's hair. Such things occur almost every night. I then have to admonish and rebuke. I have to hunt for the little germ of humanity which, however hidden and trampled in the dirt, I feel sure must exist in every human soul. If they only spoke Engglish, I think perhaps I should not so often fail in my appeals to them. I have recently learned Italian, and speak it after a laborious fashion, with the sole view of finding the word that will reach an Italian heart."

He had seated himself at Maud's side and spoke in a low, confidential tone, as if he were half communing with himself, or allowing a heart that was full to overflow in speech. He seemed to think that the sentiments which animated him were normal and natural, and he was apparently not claiming the least credit to himself for entertaining them.

"Have you learned Polish too?" Maud queried, anxious to have him continue.

"No; I have tried to learn it, but have had to give it up. It took down my pride terribly, for I had fancied I could learn anything in a short time, if I gave my mind to it. I have about twenty or thirty phrases at my command, and I find they are of much use to me in trying to teach my Poles English."

"What a vast deal of good you do accomplish! It must be a great satisfaction to you to watch the results of your work."

"Only three or four times have I had that satisfaction. For every once that I succeed, I have ten or twenty failures."

"But permit me to ask you, how do you manage to support this enterprise? Are collections taken up for its benefit in the churches?"

"No, it is entirely a private affair. I have managed so far to support it largely at my own expense. It is the evening school which absorbs most money. Of the two friends who joined with me in starting it, one is dead, and the other grew discouraged and retired."

"And won't you allow another friend to take the place of the one who is dead?" asked Maud, looking up at him with a heightened color, and a smile which struck him as the sweetest thing he had ever seen. There was such a glow of generous sympathy in it.

"In such a cause I have no right to refuse," he answered simply. "I shall be much obliged to you for any aid you may be kind enough to offer."

She had half expected to be embarrassed, and to embarrass him by the suggestion of an ulterior motive; but he was too generous a man, and too much absorbed in the work itself, to be capable of such a suspicion. The animation that lighted up his face as he took her hand and shook it with hearty good-will gave her an intense sense of relief.

"I can easily spare fifteen hundred a year," she said joyously.

"Fifteen hundred! That is a good deal. Are you sure it will not inconvenience you?"

"If you knew how aimlessly I spend my money, and for what wretched frivolities, you would not ask me that. The fact is, I go about half the time full of vague benevolence which I do not expend, for want of the opportunity. I was so glad when you sent me Mrs. McGregor, for I was then simply aching for some wretched object to be good to. I needed something to bolster up my self-respect and supply me with some good reason for supporting my frivolous existence."

She spoke in a tone of airy *persiflage*, but he yet perceived an undertone of seriousness in the sympathetic quiver of her voice. Her eyes, which met his with a certain fearless trust, were good and grateful as they rested upon him, and stirred depths of tenderness in his soul.

The banjo-player had now finished his *repertoire*, and Philip rose hastily, bade his distinguished visitors good-night, and again mounted the platform. After a few announcements for the other evenings of the week, he asked his audience to join in a song, after which he declared the entertainment to be at an end. He led, himself, in the singing; and when the artless and discordant voices strayed from the tune, he jumped down and struck the chords on a piano with resounding emphasis.

Mr. Van Horst's party, not wishing to encounter this motley juvenile assembly in the street, lost no time in reaching their carriages ; and felt an acute sense of relief when they had laid the slums behind them, and found themselves once more amid the sober brown-stone respectability of the Fifth Avenue.

XXIII

IT was two months later, when Langley Van Horst for some inscrutable reason had transferred his allegiance to a far wealthier heiress, and his rival had accepted the vacated field and firmly intrenched himself in it, that society was startled by the announcement of Marston Fancher's engagement to Miss Sally Bulkley, the eldest daughter of the Honorable P. Leamington Bulkley, the well-known western millionnaire, now resident in this city. The summer was then well advanced, and the Bulkley family were once more established at Thorn Hedge, which Marston, owing to the continued absence of his mother and sisters, had concluded to let to his future father-in-law on the same terms as the previous year.

Atterbury was looking particularly lovely during those early June days, so still and radiant, so brightly prosperous and well-conditioned. The dune cottages cut their clean silhouettes against the horizon ; white sails drifted lazily upon an expanse of shining sapphire ; and the vast vault of the sky was steeped in a deep cerulean blue, which gave one a sense of purity, largeness, and glorious freedom. It seemed a luxury to breathe from the bottom of one's lungs, and feel one's being pervaded by the sweet and stainless sentiment of the day. And then all that beautiful, well-trimmed respectability of Atterbury, its aristocratic reserve, and a certain wind-swept bareness, gave a subtle distinctness of physiognomy to the place, which made it sink into its own special niche in the mind, and remain as a separate and precious memory.

It was, perhaps, to guard himself against this sentiment, which he regarded as snobbish and subtly corrupting, that Philip so rarely went to Atterbury. But for all that, Castleton, who had no patience with such scruples, persuaded him during the second week in June to pay him a brief visit. He had sat all the morning in luxurious idleness on the piazza overlooking the ocean, with Mildred at his side, and Mrs. Castleton's youngest daughter, Bertha, on his lap; and he had improvised for their entertainment, fantastic stories about mermaids, gnomes, and nixies. Mrs. Castleton, who was sitting opposite to him, engaged in some handiwork, had begged him repeatedly not to allow the children to annoy him ; but he declared with evident sincerity that he felt flattered by their liking, and that their artless demonstrations of affection warmed his chilled bachelor's soul. To have little Bertha snug up to him with such sweet trust, and take his interest in her small experiences for granted, seemed to him a most delightful thing ; and Mildred's shyer and more self-conscious admiration appealed to his gentlest emotions, and filled him with tenderness for all " little girlhood " in general.

When luncheon was over, and a cigar had been smoked, Philip excused himself, and declared that he wanted to take a tramp along the dunes. But as he was on the point of starting, the spirit moved him to make a digression towards Thorn Hedge and invite Maud to be his companion. He had seen her at least half a dozen times since their meeting at his mission, and they were on a footing of *bonne camaraderie* which made such an unceremonious request quite in order. Maud did not keep him waiting long, but reappeared in ten minutes, in a short-skirted walking costume, and with a dancing light in her eyes, and a breezy, out-of-door alertness in her look and motions which was very exhilarating. She was so friendly, so sunny-tempered and talkative, so boyishly frank and so beautifully sympathetic, and yet withal exquisitely virginal and self-respecting, full of the free and hearty confidence of a fine American girl. She was, as Philip reflected, the feminine equivalent for " a good fellow."

They walked down between neatly trimmed privet and hawthorn hedges, in full view of the whole community, talking about a new horse which Maud was trying, with a view to purchase. Marston Fancher's two huge mastiffs came running after them, with the obvious intention of sharing their walk, and had to be chased back by Maud, with a great deal of scolding and persuasion. Their fondness for her, apparently the result of intimate acquaintance, was a thorn in Philip's flesh, because it reminded him of the one episode in her life which he was trying to forget. Turk and Whiskey had evidently not been informed of the changed state of affairs, for they returned after each rebuff, and walked majestically at Maud's side, as if to protect her, in their master's interest, against any possible mischief that might be meditated by Philip, whom they regarded with undisguised suspicion. Maud finally had to sit down and reason with them, and, staring them straight in the eyes, explained that she did not want them and that they must go home. Then they looked at each other with a sort of melancholy comprehension, and, after a moment's hesitation, started homeward, shaking their heads with a deep sense of discouragement and disgrace.

Fully fifteen minutes were needed to obliterate the impression of this untoward incident, because each knew so well what was in the other's mind, that it seemed futile to ignore it. Philip had come to Atterbury this time with the definite purpose to ask Maud to become his wife, and he had hoped that the long-desired opportunity would be afforded him on this walk. But now, somehow, the dogs had spoiled his mood, by arousing the ghosts of unpleasant memories which it had cost him much trouble to banish. He had felt so near to Maud since that evening at the mission, and had felt convinced that life without her would be a joyless and dreary affair. It was only the continual embarrassment of her wealth which had restrained him from putting the fateful query. However much he reasoned about it, and in whatever light he viewed it, he could not get over the consciousness of her millions, and a sense of his own brazenness in offering his poor and undistinguished self in exchange for the tremendous advantages which she commanded. Although he knew that he was absolutely sincere in saying that he would have preferred her without her glittering frame, it seemed somehow preposterous to ask her to believe it. There was to his sensitive honor a humiliation in the very discussion of the thing. It was an obvious tax on her credulity. Any knave, trying to gain her confidence with a view to obtaining possession of her fortune, would have imposed upon her with this same pretense of disinterestedness.

These were his reflections on that memorable afternoon when he struck across the soft lawns with Maud, and climbed to the top of the dunes. All sorts of tender memories from last summer lay hidden in the sandy hollows between the grass-grown bluffs, and they started up like frightened birds as he passed the bleak, red-painted church. The ocean lay smooth as a burnished shield, except for some streaks of odd currents that broke across its surface with minute dimples and wrinkles. They waded together through the tall beach-grass which stooped from habit, though there was no wind to bend it, and slid occasionally down the sandy slope where the treacherous turf had been hollowed out by wind and waves. Having exhausted the amusement of this exercise, they continued their walk on the beach, which was hard and smooth after a recent storm, and, moreover, sheltered by the dunes from the scores of curious eyes that were hidden behind the shutters of the dune cottages. Philip's mind was still a trifle out of tune, and he had not recovered the happy audacity with which he had started out half an hour ago, resolved to settle his fate one way or another.

" How does your mission get on when you take a vacation, Mr. Warburton ?" Maud asked, after having touched upon sundry topics with slight success.

"I hire a clerical substitute," Philip answered ; " a very excellent man, who affords a pleasant variety to my boys, and gives them something which I cannot give them."

Maud looked out towards the horizon, where a big European steamer seemed to be crawling along, dragging a long trail of smoke behind it.

" Do you intend to devote your whole life to this work?" she asked at last. " Have you given up society and all thought of pleasure?"

" I never had much society to give up," he replied with grim earnestness. " I belonged only on the outskirts, at best. I once had some social ambition, which Marston did all in his power to encourage. Now I have none."

"And why did you abandon it ?"

"That is a hard question to answer. If I am to be sincere, you will think me conceited."

" No, I shall not. Nothing could persuade me that you are conceited."

" Well, then, I'll tell you. Society in New York, if you are to cut a figure in it, demands nearly your whole time. It is not compatible with a serious purpose in life ; and the satisfactions which it yields are not even remotely in proportion to the expenditure of time, money, and energy which it involves. I am no gloomy ascetic who wants to wear sackcloth and ashes ; but I claim to be a fairly rational man, capable of balancing profit and loss and counting the cost, before I engage in an enterprise."

" But the friendships which you form in society— the pleasant relations which you establish with a number of agreeable people—don't you find some satisfaction in that?"

" That is my very complaint against society—that it does not conduce to the forming of such rela- tions. The only friendships I have ever formed have been made in college and when crossing the ocean. It was on an ocean steamship I met the Castletons, who are the dearest friends I have. During those long, lazy days on shipboard we pene- trated the outer shell of conventionality which we all have to wear, and got at each other's true selves. If we had met in a New York drawing-room, we should never have discovered each other. We should have smiled to each other, perhaps, though the chances are that we should never have been in- troduced; and if by any possibility we should have engaged in conversation, we should have worn the prescribed masks of grinning amiability, and never advanced beyond the stage of a bowing acquaint- ance."

" But wouldn't that largely be your own fault?" Maud queried, with a half-anxious animation.

" I think not. I think the fault lies with the spirit of the age and the organization of society itself, which is a tremendous machine for the mu- tual advancement of its members. I am aware that there are often enormous interests, now finan- cial, now political, at stake in the apparently gay and harmless displays of society. Our convivial intercourse is modelled on that of England, and has the same objects. The French go into society as an intellectual diversion—to shine by wit and cleverness, to make themselves agreeable. We, as well as the English, go into society with the least possible expectation of amusement, because we think that in one way or another it pays to show ourselves at such and such a house, and let the world know that we have access to the very best."

"And you regard that as so very objectionable?"

" I do not regard it as morally reprehensible, but I regard it as an effectual bar to genial freedom of intercourse and the forming of enduring relations. The pervading tone is one of false and hypocritical show, of envious comment, uncharitable criticism, and vain emulation in dress, entertainment, distinction, and all sorts of foolish extravagance. The result is a tremendous overrating of the material things of life, which are not its true realities, and the wasting of life's best energy in a wild chase for vain and hollow things, which yield no lasting satisfaction. I have seen enough of it to have concluded that the game is not worth the candle, and I therefore deserve no credit whatever for having chosen to pursue my own happiness in my own way. If I had been a blue-blooded Knickerbocker and a social leader like Marston, I might, perhaps, have prided myself a little on my renunciation ; but, being essentially a plebeian, who has never been quite domesticated among the socially elect, I am entitled to no praise."

19

They paused here in their walk, and, looking back, saw the interminable trail of their foot-prints in the sand, which zigzagged and wavered in a quite unaccountable fashion. A cottage of a close-buttoned and inhospitable aspect, whose occupants had not yet arrived, stared down at them from the bluff ; and a couple of sandpipers, who had their nest in the neighborhood, flew and tripped uneasily about them, uttering their plaintive little notes, but stopping, in spite of their anxiety, to gobble up every stray sand-flea that chanced in their way. The pitiless glare of the sun on the water was getting a little trying to Maud's eyes, and she turned her parasol towards the ocean and begged Philip to walk on her other side. "I am glad," she said, with a sweet cordiality, as they wandered on at a slackened pace, "that you have told me your opinions so frankly. I—I—think I agree with you in almost everything."

"You ! You agree with me !" he exclaimed with joyous surprise ; "but I wasn't expecting you to agree with me. I fancied all the time that you regarded me as a prosy moralist, who had, somehow, gotten into the world with the wrong foot foremost, and had never been able to rectify the mistake. I was just now doing penance to you in my heart for spoiling the beautiful sunshine with my discordant talk. For you have a right to your youth, you have a right to be gay; and it is but natural that you, with your sunnier temper, should love the things which I detest simply because I was not made for them, because I have no affinity for them. It is a matter of temperament, after all, what you like and what you dislike ; and to set up one standard for all would be foolish arrogance."

He had not the least idea how his words impressed her. As he saw her in her splendid youth, he felt the grimness of his own ascetic ideal, and the cruelty of exacting conformity to it from one so manifestly born for joy and sunshine and beauty. The possibility of a compromise suggested itself to him, as a mere shadowy escape from a desperate situation. Far was he from dreaming what a passionate protest was stirring in her breast. To her he seemed bent upon stripping himself of the heroic character with which she had invested him ; and though she attributed the attempt to an excessive conscientiousness and magnanimity, she could not help regretting it. She was determined to guard her own ideal of him, and to defend it against his own assaults.

"You must take me to be a very shallow creature, Mr. Warburton," she said with sudden ardor, " if you hold me incapable of appreciating the sublimity of the work which you have undertaken. Do you really expect me to take you seriously, when you are trying to persuade me that a life of social rivalry and selfish pleasure-seeking is quite as legitimate and dignified ; that it is merely a matter of temperament which you choose, and that you deserve no more credit for choosing the one than the other?"

She would have been incapable of speaking thus a year ago. It was Philip's spirit which possessed her and spoke through her. And, wonderful to relate, a certain heaviness of heart, which was not sadness, but a mere esthetic regret, for a moment vaguely oppressed him. He felt now that he loved her so well as she was, as she had been, that the thought of converting her into something of austerer type seemed like sacrilege. No; he would surrender all for her sake, as she would surrender all for his. So it seemed to him, at least, in his exalted, lover-like mood, which only craved with an imperious yearning to touch her, to have and hold her, to call her his own for all time. Her ardor in his cause touched him with a certain exquisite tenderness. He divined, in a swift flash, all the unavowed sentiment which lay behind her words, and they filled him not with triumph, but with humility.

They had come to a boat which was pulled up on the beach, and at Maud's suggestion they seated themselves to rest in its shadow. Philip recognized it, in an instant, as the boat he had bought for the reprobate McGregor; but his mind was too full of his beautiful companion to permit even of a conjecture as to his *protégé's* fate. He had flung himself down in a careless attitude at her feet, and was gazing with undisguised devotion into her eyes. There was a glow in her cheeks which betrayed not, indeed, confusion, but a sweet consciousness of being loved. It was a happy, blushing expectancy; a beautiful, and in no wise flurried, surrender to the strong, deep, elemental joy which throbbed within her. The moment was to both so rich that they could not bear to break its charm. He noted the delicate little droop of her head as she sat idly letting the sand run through her fingers, and the tranquil smile upon her lips, so full of innocence and confidence. A couple of gulls were circling in the vast blue above their heads, and the anxious sandpipers tripped restlessly about them, and flew off with a melancholy whistle, whenever the one or the other made an unforeseen movement. But suddenly there broke through this golden calm a rich, full, guttural note, distinctly articulate, with a certain wild irrelevancy that made it almost comical :

> " Yes, you bet,
> I'm a pet,
> And my name is Olivette."

They had scarcely recovered from the shock of surprise, when, like an unsummoned Afrit in the Arabian Nights, Phœbe McGregor loomed up before them, smiling all over her coffee-colored face with an insinuating, half-sheepish brazenness, as if to ask them please not to allow her presence to embarrass them.

"I nebber should ha' knowed you wid dem clo'es on, Miss Maud," she began, with a gurgling laugh of decent embarrassment. "Law! how handsome you've growed, Miss Maud, dat's a fac'! You look jes' beau'ful! And Marsh Philip—he ain't a-gwine ter git married soon? Oh, no! Marsh Philip ain't."

Here Phœbe broke into a laugh that bent her nearly double; and looking up sideways, her black eyes dancing with roguery, she continued:

"I ain't a-namin' o' no names, Marsh Philip. Oh,

no! You doan' 'member what I say to you, Marsh Philip? Says I, 'De beaufullest lady in all de land is a-mopin' and a-pinin' fer you.'"

Philip perceiving plainly whither this was bearing, and seeing the color flare into Maud's face, wheeled himself about, and exclaimed with vehemence:

"Oh, no, Mrs. McGregor, you got that all wrong! What you said was this: 'Marsh Philip,' you said, 'you are moping and pining for the most beautiful lady in all the land.' And it was true; for I was, and I am."

Maud, scarcely daring to associate herself with this avowal, started up in jealous alarm; then, swiftly mastering her emotion, stared with an anxious bewilderment out over the ocean. Phœbe, conscious that something was wrong, noted the warning glance which Philip sent her, and dropping a courtesy made haste to retire. But to Philip's surprise Maud detained her.

"Where is Mr. McGregor now?" she asked, quickly regathering her composure.

"Mistah McGregor? Why, bress yer heart, honey, Mistah McGregor he ain't heah no mo'."

"But where is he?"

"Mistah McGregor he's so monstous pittickler, he wear seben biled shirts ebery week now. He's a bonton, he is. He send his wash ter me from New Yawk, but now he's gwine ter Newport, an' dat's too far. He eat Delmonico victuals ebery day, an' de gals dey's jess crezzy arter him. An' dey's pow'rful pittickler, dem fine ladies; but Mistah McGregor he know how ter tickle de ladies, fer he war fotch up dat way, an' kin ter chukes an' kings, an' sech like."

The tears ran down her cheeks while she gave this graphic account of her husband's condition ; but whether it was grief at his desertion of her which made her weep, or a mere emotional luxury, occasioned by his lofty estate, will always remain an open question.

She picked up her large checkered apron, selected carefully a spot which was already soiled, and applied it to her eyes. Then she dropped another courtesy and trudged back to her little hut, which was hidden by clothes-lines weighed down by many-colored garments steaming in the sun.

Philip sprang to his feet as soon as she was out of sight, and reaching both his hands to Maud he pulled her up.

" Miss Maud," he said, as they began to retrace their steps along the beach, " do you know who the most beautiful lady in the land is ? "

" No," she murmured, " how could I know ? "

" Nor do I," he answered with a warm, earnest intonation ; " but I suppose to every man the woman he loves is the most beautiful. To me you are the most beautiful woman on earth."

It seemed unnecessary to make any reply to this announcement, and Maud walked on with downcast eyes and a joyous tumult of heart. It was the blessed assurance for which she had been waiting ; and as she glanced up and saw his clear-cut, sunburnt profile, with its manly decision and rugged strength, she could with all her heart have returned the compliment.

"Maud," he resumed, after a pause, "you know what my life is.   Will you share it with me?"

"Yes," she answered, not with blushing confusion, but with a devoutness of conviction that came from the bottom of her soul. "I would share any life that was yours."

The vast publicity of the beach clearly forbade any demonstration of affection.   But, strange to say, Philip did not feel it as a deprivation.   The sentiment which bound him to Maud was primarily a sense of her preciousness—a sense of noble comradeship and a deep congeniality of soul.   Such a relation, though it disdains not a caress at the proper moment, does not crave it with the amorous yearning of a mere passionate attachment.   Philip rejoiced, as he walked at Maud's side, in her stately womanhood and the beautiful simplicity of her bearing, so far removed from the shrillness, the nervous distortions, the shallow little affectations of common American girlhood.   A glow of tenderness shot through his veins, and he seemed conscious even to the tips of his fingers of her divine loveliness.   His pulses thrilled with joy at being loved by this glorious woman, and the future spread out in wide, shining vistas before him.

A grateful breeze had sprung up and swept across the sea, breaking the smooth, bright mirror into minute undulations.   The European steamer was visible as a remote black speck on the horizon, and its trail of smoke as a mere shadowy suggestion.

St. Paul-on-the-Dunes lay bare and bleak amid the waving beach-grass, and through its opened door came the rich strains of the organ, mingled with voices practising a sacred chorus. Moved by a common impulse, Philip and Maud went in and seated themselves in the remotest corner, where a friendly wooden pillar shielded them from observation. A seraphic solo of an exquisite purity and tender devoutness kept repeating in varying strains the passage:

" Thou wilt show me the path of life. In thy presence is fulness of joy."

They sat for perhaps half an hour listening, in an acutely sympathetic mood; and when they perceived by the gathering volume and quickened *tempo* of the organ that the oratorio was nearing its end, they quietly slipped out. They walked along in silence across the smooth lawns, and all the while the solo strain rang in their ears.

It was about five o'clock when they arrived at Thorn Hedge. They met Peleg in the hall, wearing a black alpaca coat and smoking his short pipe.

" Well, daughter," he began cheerfully, " you look a bit flustered. I reckon you've walked too far."

" No, father," Maud answered, stepping up to him and affectionately clasping his arm; " but I have something I want to tell you. I am engaged to Mr. Warburton."

She made the important announcement with the impressive solemnity which the occasion demanded, and the forced levity of her father's response therefore jarred cruelly upon her exalted mood.

" Jimmie-crack-corn ! " Peleg exclaimed in his high-pitched voice. Then after a vacuous pause, during which he seemed keenly conscious of being unequal to the situation, he added : " Well, I reckon you might have gone farther and fared worse."

He then, with a vague sense of embarrassment, shook hands with Philip and hurried into the library, as if he feared that he might be called upon to officiate at more " paternal functions."

Maud, just because she knew that her father liked Philip and must be deeply gratified at her engagement, felt so mortified that she could scarcely restrain her tears. She begged Philip to stay to dinner, and was just gently pushing him into the parlor, when Peggy ran vehemently against her and flung her arms about her neck, whispering with tearful ecstasy :

" Oh, Maud, I am so happy ! I am so happy !"

Peleg, with an acute sense of his shortcomings, had in the meanwhile invaded the drawing-room, in the hope of correcting the unfavorable impression he must have made upon his future son-in-law. Peggy's unexpected demonstrativeness somehow conveyed an implication of reproach to him. Suddenly pulling himself together, he walked up to Philip, grasped his hand cordially, and said :

" You know I ain't much of a hand at speech-making. But—but—all the same—I'm mighty glad you two—have come to an—an understanding."

It was a heroic effort, and Peleg was dimly aware that at last he had acquitted himself creditably. He was still holding Philip's hand and blinking uneasily towards his daughter, as if waiting for some token of her approval. To Maud there was something almost touching in this dumb appeal. As soon as she had extricated herself from her sister's embrace, she went towards him, kissed him with unwonted tenderness, and murmured:

"You dear old father!"

BRIEF LIST OF BOOKS OF FICTION PUBLISHED BY CHARLES SCRIBNER'S SONS, 743-745 BROADWAY, NEW YORK.

William Waldorf Astor.

VALENTINO: An Historical Romance. (12mo, $1.00).—SFORZA: A Story of Milan. (12mo, $1.50.)

" The story is full of clear-cut little tableaux of mediæval Italian manners, customs, and observances. The movement throughout is spirited, the reproduction of bygone times realistic. Mr. Astor has written a romance which will heighten the reputation he made by 'Valentino.'"—*The New York Tribune.*

Arlo Bates.

A WHEEL OF FIRE. (12mo, paper, 50 cts.; cloth, $1.00.)

" The novel deals with character rather than incident, and is evolved from one of the most terrible of moral problems with a subtlety not unlike that of Hawthorne. One cannot enumerate all the fine points of artistic skill which make this study so wonderful in its insight, so rare in its combination of dramatic power and tenderness."—*The Critic.*

Hjalmar H. Boyesen.

FALCONBERG. Illustrated (12mo, $1.50)—GUNNAR. (Sq. 12mo, paper, 50 cts.; cloth, $1.25)—TALES FROM TWO HEMISPHERES. (Sq. 12mo, $1.00)—ILKA ON THE HILL TOP, and Other Stories. (Sq. 12mo, $1.00) —QUEEN TITANIA (Sq. 12mo, $1.00).

" Mr. Boyesen's stories possess a sweetness, a tenderness, and a drollery that are fascinating, and yet they are no more attractive than they are strong."—*The Home Journal.*

H. C. Bunner.

THE STORY OF A NEW YORK HOUSE. Illustrated by A. B. Frost. (12mo, $1.25)—THE MIDGE. (12mo, paper, 50 cts.; cloth, $1.00)—ZADOC PINE, and Other Stories. (12mo, paper, 50 cts.; cloth, $1.00.)

" It is Mr. Bunner's delicacy of touch and appreciation of what is literary art that give his writings distinctive quality. Everything Mr. Bunner paints shows the happy appreciation of an author who has not alone mental discernment, but the artistic appreciation. The author and the artist both supplement one another in this excellent 'Story of a New York House.'"—*The New York Times.*

Frances Hodgson Burnett.

THAT LASS O' LOWRIE'S. Illustrated (paper, 50 cts. ; cloth, $1.25)—HAWORTH'S. Illustrated (12mo, $1.25)—THROUGH ONE ADMINISTRA-TION. (12mo, $1.50)—LOUISIANA. (12mo, $1.25)—A FAIR BARBARIAN. (12mo, paper, 50 cts. ; cloth, $1.25)—VAGABONDIA. A Love Story. (12mo, paper, 50 cts. ; cloth, $1.25)—SURLY TIM, and Other Stories. (12mo, $1.25) EARLIER STORIES—First Series, EARLIER STORIES—Second Series (12mo, each, paper, 50 cts.; cloth, $1.25).

THE PRETTY SISTER OF JOSÉ. Illustrated by C. S. Rheinhart (12mo, $1.00).

LITTLE LORD FAUNTLEROY. (Sq. 8vo, $2.00)—SARA CREWE; or, What Happened at Miss Minchin's. (Sq. 8vo, $1.00)—LITTLE SAINT ELIZABETH, and Other Stories. (12mo, $1.50.) Illustrated by R. B. Birch.

"Mrs. Burnett discovers gracious secrets in rough and forbidding natures—the sweetness that often underlies their bitterness—the soul of goodness in things evil. She seems to have an intuitive perception of character. If we apprehend her personages, and I think we do clearly, it is not because she describes them to us, but because they reveal themselves in their actions. Mrs. Burnett's characters are as veritable as Thackeray's."—RICHARD HENRY STODDARD.

William Allen Butler.

DOMESTICUS. A Tale of the Imperial City. (12mo, $1.25.)

"Under a veil made intentionally transparent, the author maintains a running fire of good-natured hits at contemporary social follies. There is a delicate love story running through the book. The author's style is highly finished. One might term it old-fashioned in its exquisite choiceness and precision."—*The New York Journal of Commerce.*

George W. Cable.

THE GRANDISSIMES. (12mo, paper, 50 cts. ; cloth, $1.25)—OLD CREOLE DAYS. (12mo, cloth, $1.25; also in two parts, 16mo, cloth, each, 75 cts.; paper, each, 30 cts.)—DR. SEVIER. (12mo, paper, 50 cts.; cloth, $1.25)—BONAVENTURE. A Prose Pastoral of Arcadian Louisiana. (12mo, paper, 50 cts. ; $1.25.)

The set, 4 vols., $5.00.

"There are few living American writers who can reproduce for us more perfectly than Mr. Cable does, in his best moments, the speech, the manners, the whole social atmosphere of a remote time and a peculiar people. A delicious flavor of humor penetrates his stories."—*The New York Tribune.*

Richard Harding Davis.

GALLEGHER, and Other Stories. (12mo, paper, 50 cts.; cloth, $1.00.)

The ten stories comprising this volume attest the appearance of a new and strong individuality in the field of American fiction. They are of a wide range and deal with very varied types of metropolitan character and situation ; but each proves that Mr. Davis knows his New York as well as Dickens did his London.

Edward Eggleston.

ROXY—THE CIRCUIT RIDER. Illustrated (each 12mo, $1.50).

"Dr. Eggleston's fresh and vivid portraiture of a phase of life and manners, hitherto almost unrepresented in literature ; its boldly contrasted characters, and its unconventional, hearty, religious spirit, took hold of the public imagination."—*The Christian Union.*

Erckmann-Chatrian.

THE CONSCRIPT. Illustrated—WATERLOO. Illustrated. (Sequel to The Conscript.)—MADAME THÉRÉSE—THE BLOCKADE OF PHALSBURG. Illustrated — THE INVASION OF FRANCE IN 1814. Illustrated — A MILLER'S STORY OF THE WAR. Illustrated.

The National Novels, each, $1.25 ; the set 6 vols., $7.50.

FRIEND FRITZ. (12mo, paper, 50 cts. ; cloth, $1.25.)

Eugene Field.

A LITTLE BOOK OF PROFITABLE TALES. (16mo, $1.25.)

"This pretty little volume promises to perpetuate examples of a wit, humor, and pathos quaint and rare in their kind. Genial and sympathetic, Mr. Field has already made a mark in the literature of the day, which will not quickly wear out."—*New York Tribune.*

Harold Frederic.

SETH'S BROTHER'S WIFE. (12mo, $1 25)—THE LAWTON GIRL. (12mo, $1.25; paper, 50 cts.)—IN THE VALLEY. Illustrated (12mo, $1.50).

"Mr. Frederic's new tale takes a wide range, includes many characters, and embraces a field of action full of dramatic climaxes. It is almost reasonable to assert that there has not been since Cooper's day a better American novel dealing with a purely historical theme than ' In the Valley.' "—*Boston Beacon.*

Octave Thanet.

EXPIATION. Illustrated by A. B. Frost. (12mo, paper, 50 cts. ; cloth, $1.00.)

"This remarkable novel shows an extraordinary grasp of dramatic possibilities as well as an exquisite delicacy of character drawing. Miss French has with this work taken her place among the very foremost of American writers of fiction."—*Boston Beacon.*

James Anthony Froude.

THE TWO CHIEFS OF DUNBOY. An Irish Romance of the Last Century. (12mo, paper, 50 cts.; cloth, $1.50.)

"The narrative is full of vigor, spirit, and dramatic power. It will unquestionably be widely read, for it presents a vivid and life-like study of character with romantic color and adventurous incident for the background."—*The New York Tribune.*

Robert Grant.

FACE TO FACE. (12mo, paper, 50 cents; cloth, $1.25)—THE REFLECTIONS OF A MARRIED MAN. (12mo, paper, 50 cents; cloth, $1.00.)

A delicious vein of humor runs through this new book by the author of "The Confessions of a Frivolous Girl," who takes the reader into his confidence and gives a picture of married life that is as bright and entertaining as it is amusing.

Edward Everett Hale.

PHILIP NOLAN'S FRIENDS. Illustrated (12mo, Paper, 50 cents; Cloth, $1.75.)

"There is no question, we think, that this is Mr. Hale's completest and best novel. The characters are for the most part well drawn, and several of them are admirable."—*The Atlantic Monthly.*

Marion Harland.

JUDITH: A Chronicle of Old Virginia. (12mo, paper, 50 cts.; cloth, $1.00) —HANDICAPPED.   (12mo, $1.50).—WITH THE BEST INTENTIONS. A Midsummer Episode. (12mo, Cloth, $1.25; Paper, 50 cents.)

"Fiction has afforded no more charming glimpses of old Virginia life than are found in this delightful story, with its quaint pictures, its admirably drawn characters, its wit, and its frankness."—*The Brooklyn Daily Times.*

Joel Chandler Harris.

FREE JOE, and Other Georgian Sketches. (12mo, paper, 50 cts., cloth, $1.00.]

"The author's skill as a story writer has never been more felicitously illustrated than in this volume. The title story is meagre almost to baldness in incident, but its quaint humor, its simple but broadly outlined characters, and, above all, its touching pathos, combine to make it a masterpiece of its kind."—*The New York Sun.*

Augustus Allen Hayes.

THE JESUIT'S RING. A Romance of Mount Desert (12mo, paper, 50 cts.; cloth, $1.00).

"The conception of the story is excellent."—*The Boston Traveller*

George A. Hibbard.

THE GOVERNOR, and Other Stories. (12mo, cloth, $1.00; paper, 50 cents.)

Six of the best of Mr. Hibbard's magazine stories are included in this volume. Mr. Howells, in *Harper's*, refers to Mr. Hibbard's work as having a "certain felicity of execution and a certain ideal of performance which are not common. The wish to deal with poetic material in the region of physical conjecture is curiously blended with the desire of portraying the life of the society world."

E. T. W. Hoffmann.

WEIRD TALES. With Portrait. (12mo, 2 vols., $3.00.)

"All those who are in search of a genuine literary sensation, or who care for the marvelous and supernatural, will find these two volumes fascinating reading."—*The Christian Union.*

Dr. J. G. Holland.

SEVENOAKS—THE BAY PATH—ARTHUR BONNICASTLE—MISS GIL-BERT'S CAREER—NICHOLAS MINTURN.

Each, 12mo, $1.25; the set, $6.25; Sevenoaks, paper, 50 cents.

"Dr. Holland will always find a congenial audience in the homes of culture and refinement. He does not affect the play of the darker and fiercer passions, but delights in the sweet images that cluster around the domestic hearth. He cherishes a strong fellow-feeling with the pure and tranquil life in the modest social circles of the American people, and has thus won his way to the companionship of many friendly hearts."—*The New York Tribune.*

Thomas A. Janvier.

COLOR STUDIES, AND A MEXICAN CAMPAIGN. (12mo, paper, 50 cts.; cloth, $1.00.)

"Piquant, novel, and ingenious, these little stories, with all their simplicity, have excited a wide interest. The best of them, 'Jaune D'Antimoine,' is a little wonder in its dramatic effect, its ingenious construction."—*The Critic.*

Virginia W. Johnson.

THE FAINALLS OF TIPTON. (12mo, $1.25.)

"The plot is good, and in its working-out original. Character-drawing is Miss Johnson's recognized *forte*, and her pen-sketches are quite up to her best work."—*The Boston Commonwealth.*

Lieut. J. D. J. Kelley.

A DESPERATE CHANCE. (12mo, paper, 50 cts.; cloth, $1.00.)

The King's Men:

A TALE OF TO-MORROW. By Robert Grant, John Boyle O'Reilly, J. S., of Dale, and John T. Weelwright. (12mo, $1.25.)

Andrew Lang.

THE MARK OF CAIN. (12mo, papor, 25 cts.)

" No one can deny that it is crammed as full of incident as it will hold, or that the elaborate plot is worked out with most ingenious perspicuity."—*The Saturday Review.*

George P. Lathrop.

NEWPORT. (12mo, paper, 50 cts; cloth, $1.25)—**AN ECHO OF PASSION.** (12mo, paper, 50 cts.; cloth, $1.00)—**IN THE DISTANCE.** (12mo, paper, 50 cts; cloth, $1.00.)

" His novels have the refinement of motive which characterize the analytical school, but his manner is far more direct and dramatic."—*The Christian Union.*

Brander Matthews.

THE SECRET OF THE SEA and Other Stories. (12mo, paper, 50 cts.; cloth, $1.00)—**THE LAST MEETING.** (12mo, cloth, $1.00.)

" Mr. Matthews is a man of wide observation and of much familiarity with the world. His literary style is bright and crisp, with a peculiar sparkle about it—wit and humor judiciously mingled —which renders his pages more than ordinarily interesting."—*The Rochester Post-Express.*

George Moore.

VAIN FORTUNE. (12mo, $1.00.)

In this novel Mr. Moore has presented a subtle and powerful study of character and temperament. An English girl, impulsive, passionate, jealous, is the heroine of the story, which portrays very vividly and with extraordinary truth to human nature her emotions and experiences. No less masterly is the author's study of the young playwright and of the other personages in this drama in real life.

Fitz-James O'Brien.

THE DIAMOND LENS, with Other Stories. (12mo, paper, 50 cts.)

" These stories are the only things in literature to be compared with Poe's work, and if they do not equal it in workmanship, they certainly do not yield to it in originality."—*The Philadelphia Record.*

Duffield Osborne.

THE SPELL OF ASHTAROTH. (12mo, $1.00.)

Bliss Perry.

THE BROUGHTON HOUSE. (12mo, $1.25)

An artistic and vivid picture of New England village life

Thomas Nelson Page.

IN OLE VIRGINIA—Marse Chan and Other Stories. (12mo, $1.25)—ON NEWFOUND RIVER. (12mo, $1.00)—ELSKET, and Other Stories. (12mo, $1.00.)

" In 'On Newfound River,' the rich promise of Mr. Page's rarely beautiful short stories has been fulfilled."—*Richmond Despatch.*

Saxe Holm's Stories.

FIRST SERIES.—Draxy Miller's Dowry—The Elder's Wife—Whose Wife Was She?—The One-Legged Dancers—How One Woman Kept Her Husband —Esther Wynn's Love Letters.

SECOND SERIES.—Four-Leaved Clover—Farmer Bassett's Romance—My Tourmalene—Joe Hale's Red Stocking—Susan Lawton's Escape.

Each, 12mo, paper, 50 cts.; cloth, $1.00.

"Saxe Holm's' characters are strongly drawn, and she goes right to the heart of human experience as one who knows the way. We heartily commend them as vigorous, wholesome, and sufficiently exciting stories."—*The Advance.*

Robert Louis Stevenson.

STRANGE CASE OF DR. JEKYLL AND MR. HYDE. (12mo, paper, 25 cts.; cloth, $1.00)—KIDNAPPED. (12mo, paper, 50 cts.; cloth, $1.00, illustrated, $1.25)—THE MERRY MEN, and Other Tales and Fables. (12mo, paper, 35 cts.; cloth, $1.00)—NEW ARABIAN NIGHTS. (12mo, paper, 30 cts.; cloth, $1.00)—THE DYNAMITER. With Mrs. Stevenson (12mo, paper, 30 cts.; cloth, $1.00)—THE BLACK ARROW. Illustrated (12mo, paper, 50 cts.; cloth, $1.00)—THE WRONG BOX. With Lloyd Osbourne (12mo, paper, 50 cts.; cloth, $1.00)—THE MASTER OF BALLANTRAE. A Winter's Tale. (12mo, paper, 50 cts.; cloth, illustrated, $1.25)—THE WRECKER. With Lloyd Osbourne. (12mo, paper, 50 cts.; cloth, illustrated. *In Press.*)

"Stevenson belongs to the romantic school of fiction writers. He is original in style, charming, fascinating, and delicious, with a marvelous command of words, and with a manner ever delightful and magnetic."—*Boston Transcript.*

T. R. Sullivan.

DAY AND NIGHT STORIES. (12mo, cloth, $1.00; paper, 50 cts.)—ROSES OF SHADOW. (12mo, $1.00.)

" Mr. Sullivan's style is at once easy and refined, conveying most happily that atmosphere of good breeding and polite society which is indispensable to the novel of manners, but which so many of them lamentably fail of."—*The Nation.*

Frederick J. Stimson (J. S., of Dale.)

GUERNDALE. (12mo, paper, 50 cts.; cloth, $1.25)—THE CRIME OF HENRY VANE. (12mo, paper, 50 cts.; cloth, $1.00)—THE SENTIMENTAL CALEN-DAR. Head Pieces by F. G. Attwood (12mo, $2.00)—FIRST HARVESTS. An Episode in the Career of Mrs. Levison Gower, a Satire without a Moral (12mo, $1.25)—THE RESIDUARY LEGATEE; or, The Posthumous Jest of the Late John Austin. (12mo, paper, 35 cts.; cloth, $1.00.)

"No young novelist in this country seems better equipped than Mr. Stimson is. He shows unusual gifts in this and in his other stories."—*The Philadelphia Bulletin.*

Frank R. Stockton.

RUDDER GRANGE. (12mo, paper, 60 cts.; cloth, $1.25; illustrated by A. B. Frost, Sq. 12mo, $2.00) — THE LATE MRS. NULL. (12mo, paper, 50 cts.; cloth, $1.25)—THE LADY, OR THE TIGER? and Other Stories. (12mo, paper, 50 cts.; cloth, $1.25)—THE CHRISTMAS WRECK, and Other Stories. (12mo, paper, 50 cts.; cloth, $1.25)—THE BEE-MAN OF ORN, and Other Fanciful Tales. (12mo, cloth, $1.25)—AMOS KILBRIGHT, with Other Stories. (12mo, paper, 50 cts.; cloth, $1.25)—THE RUDDER GRANG-ERS ABROAD, and Other Stories. (12mo, paper, 50 cts.; cloth, $1.25.)

"Of Mr. Stockton's stories what is there to say, but that they are an unmixed blessing and delight? He is surely one of the most inventive of talents, discovering not only a new kind in humor and fancy, but accumulating an inexhaustible wealth of details in each fresh achievement, the least of which would be riches from another hand."—W. D. HOWELLS, *in Harper's Magazine.*

Stories by American Authors.

Cloth, 16mo, 50c. each; set, 10 vols., $5.00; cabinet ed., in sets only, $7.50.

"The public ought to appreciate the value of this series, which is preserving permanently in American literature short stories that have contributed to its advancement. American writers lead all others in this form of fiction, and their best work appears in these volumes."—*The Boston Globe.*

John T. Wheelwright.

A CHILD OF THE CENTURY. (12mo, paper, 50 cts.; cloth, $1.00.)

"A typical story of political and social life, free from cynicism or morbid realism, and brimming over with good-natured fun, which is never vulgar."—*The Christian at Work.*